THE LAST TABOO . . .

He was totally still, serene. Then he moved close to me, and took my face in his silver hands, and bowed his auburn head and kissed me with his silver mouth.

I tell myself it's the electric current running through the clockwork mechanisms that I felt, as if a singing tide washed through me. His skin is poreless, therefore not human. Cooler than human. His hair is like grass. He has no scent, being without glands or hormones or blood. Yet there was a scent, male, heady and indefinable. Something incorporated, perhaps, to "please." And there was only him. Everything else became a backdrop, and then it went away altogether. And he went away, and nothing came back to replace him.

He's a machine, and I'm in love with him.

He's been packed up in a crate, and I'm in love with him.

I'm in love with a robot.

THE SILVER METAL LOVER

Tanith Lee

BANTAM BOOKS

New York Toronto London

Sydney Auckland

THE SILVER METAL LOVER

A Bantam Spectra Book

DAW Books, Inc. edition published 1981
Bantam Spectra edition / May 1999

ISBN 0-553-58127-9

Published simultaneously in the United States and Canada

Bantam Books are published by Bantam Books, a division of Random House, Inc. Its trademark, consisting of the words "Bantam Books" and the portrayal of a rooster, is Registered in U.S. Patent and Trademark Office and in other countries. Marca Registrada. Bantam Books, 1540 Broadway, New York, New York 10036.

PRINTED IN THE UNITED STATES OF AMERICA

OPM 10 9 8 7 6 5 4 3 2 1

To Chelsea Quinn Yarbro,
Between picnics.

THE SILVER METAL LOVER

CHAPTER ONE

Mother, I am in love with a robot.

No. She isn't going to like that.

Mother, I am in love.

Are you, darling?

Oh, yes, mother, yes I am. His hair is auburn, and his eyes are very large. Like amber. And his skin is silver.

Silence.

Mother. I'm in love.

With whom, dear?

His name is Silver.

How metallic.

Yes. It stands for Silver Ionized Locomotive Verisimulated Electronic Robot.

Silence. Silence. Silence.

Mother . . .

1

I grew up with my mother in Chez Stratos, my mother's house in the clouds. It's a beautiful house, but I never knew it was beautiful until people told me so. "How beautiful!" They cried. So I learned it was. To me, it was just home. It's terrible being rich. One has awful false values, which one can generally only replace with other, falser, values. For example, the name of the house, which is, apparently, very vulgar, is a deliberate show of indifference to vulgarity on my mother's part. This tells you something about my mother. So perhaps I should tell you some more.

My mother is five feet seven inches tall. She has very blond hair, and very green eyes. She is sixty-three, but looks about thirty-seven, because she takes regular courses of Rejuvinex. She decided to have a child rather late, but the Rejuvinex made that perfectly all right. She selected me, and had herself artificially inseminated with me, and bore me five months later by means of the Precipta method, which only takes three or four hours. I was breast-fed, because it would be good for me, and after that, my mother took me everywhere with her, sometimes all round the world, through swamps and ruins and over broad surging seas, but I don't remember very much of this, because when I was about six she got tired of it, and we went to Chez Stratos, and more or less stayed here ever since. The city is only twenty miles away, and on clear days you can see it quite easily from the balcony-balloons of the house. I've always liked the city, particularly the look of it at night with all the distant lights glittering like strings and heaps of jewels. My mother, hearing this description once, said it was an uninspired analogy. But that's just what the city at night looks like to me, so I don't know what else to say. It's going to be very difficult, actually, putting all this down, if my analogies turn out badly every time. Maybe I just won't use analogies.

Which brings me to me.

I am sixteen years old and five feet four inches tall, but mother says I may grow a little more. When I was seven, my mother had a Phy-Excellence chart done for me, to see what was the ideal weight and muscle tone aesthetically for my frame, and I take six-monthly capsules so I stay at this weight and tone, which means I'm a little plump, as apparently my frame is Venus Media, which is essentially voluptuous. My mother also had a coloressence chart made up to see what hair color would be best for my skin and eyes. So I have a sort of pale bronze color done by molecular restructuring once a month. I can't remember what my hair was originally, but I think it was a kind of brown. My eyes are green, but not as green as my mother's.

My mother's name, by the way, is Demeta. Mine's Jane. But normally I call her "Mother" and she calls me "Dear" or "Darling." My mother says the art of verbal affection is dying out. She has a lot of opinions, which is restful, as that way I don't have to have many of my own.

However, this makes everything much more difficult, now.

I've written bits of things down before. Or embarrassing poetry. But how to do this. Perhaps it's idiotic to try. No, I have to, I think. I suppose I should begin at the beginning. Or just before the beginning. I have always fallen in love very easily, but usually with characters in visuals, or books, or with actors in drama. I have six friends, of roughly my own age—six is a balanced number, according to the statistics—and three of these have fathers as well as mothers. Clovis, who has a father, said I fell in love easily—but only with unreal men—because I didn't have a father. I pointed out that the actors I fell in love with *were* real. "That's a matter for debate," said Clovis. "But let me explain. What you fall for is the invention they're playing. If you met them, you'd detest them." One morning, to prove his theory, Clovis introduced me to an actor I'd seen in a drama and fallen in love with the previous night, but I was so shy I couldn't look at the actor. And then I found out he and Clovis were lovers, and I was brokenhearted, and stopped being shy and scowled, and Clovis said: "I told you so." Which was hardly fair. Secretly, I used to wish I were Clovis and not me. Clovis is tall and slim, with dark curly hair, and being M-B, doesn't have to take contraception shots, so tells everyone else who does they're dangerous.

I don't really like my other five friends. Davideed is at the equator right now, studying silting—which may indicate the sort of thing about him that I have no rapport with. Egyptia is very demanding, and takes over everything, though she's lovely to look at. She's highly emotional, and sometimes she embarrasses me. Chloe is nice, but not very exciting. Jason and Medea, who are brother and sister, and have a father too, are untrustworthy. Once they were in the house and they stole something, a little blue rock that came from the Asteroid. They pretended they hadn't, but I knew they had. When my mother asked where the blue rock was, I felt I had to tell her what I thought, but she said I should have pretended I had broken the rock so as not to implicate Jason and Medea, who were my friends. Loyalty. I see it was rather unsubtle of me to betray them, but I didn't know any better. Being unsubtle is one of my worst faults. I have a lot.

Anyway, I'll start when Egyptia called me on the video, and she cried and cried. Egyptia is unhappy because she knows she has greatness in her, and so far she can't find out what to do with it. She's just over eighteen, and she gets terribly afraid that life is moving too fast for her. Though most people live to be a hundred and fifty, or more, Egyptia is frightened a comet will crash on the earth at any moment and destroy us all, and her, before she can do something really wonderful. Egyptia has horrible dreams about this a lot. One can't comfort her, one merely has to sit and watch and listen.

Egyptia never had a coloressence chart or a Phy-Excellence chart done. Recently, her dark hair was tinted dark blue, and she's very thin because she's been dieting—another of her fears is that the world would run out of food because of earthquake activity, so she practices starvation for days on end. At last she stopped crying and told me she was crying because she had a dramatic interview that afternoon. Then she began to cry again. She knew, when she sent the voice and phy-tape to the drama people that she had to do it, as her greatness might occur in the form of acting. But now she knew she'd judged wrong and it wouldn't. The place where the interview was being held was the Theatra Concordacis, which had been advertising for trainees for weeks. It was a very little drama, with a very little paying membership. The actors had to pay to be in it, too, but Egyptia's mother, who was at the bottom of an ocean exploring a pre-Columbian trench, had left a lot of money to look after Egyptia instead.

"Oh, Jane," said Egyptia, blue-tinted tears running through her blue mascara. "Oh Jane! My heart's beating in huge thuds. I think I'm dying. I shall die before I can do the interview."

My eyes were already wet. Now my heart started instantly to bang in huge painful thuds, too. I am very hyperchondriacal, and tend to catch the symptoms of whatever disease is being described to me. My mother says this is a sign of imagination.

"Oh, Egyptia," I said.

"Oh, Jane," said Egyptia.

We each clung to our end of the video, gasping.

"What shall I do?" gasped Egyptia.

"I don't know."

"I must do the interview."

"I think so, too."

"I'm so afraid. There may be an earth tremor. Do you remember the tremors when we trapped the Asteroid?"

"No—"

Neither of us had been born then, but Egyptia had dreamed about it frequently, and got confused. I wondered if I felt Chez Stratos rocking in an incipient quake, but it's supposed to be invulnerably stabilized, and anyway does sometimes rock, very gently, when there's a strong wind.

"Jane," said Egyptia, "you have to come with me. You have to be with me. You have to see me do the interview."

"What are you dramatizing?"

"Death," said Egyptia. She rolled her gorgeous eyes.

My mother likes me to spend time with Egyptia, who she thinks is insane. This will be stimulating for me, and will teach me responsibility toward others. Egyptia is, of course, afraid of my mother.

The Baxter Empire was out with Mother, it's too extravagant anyway, and besides, I can't drive or fly. So I walked over the Canyon and waited for the public flyer.

The air lines glistened beautifully overhead in the sunshine, and the dust rose from the Canyon like soft steam. As I waited for the flyer to come, I looked up at Chez Stratos, or up where I knew it was, a vague blue ghost. All you can really see from the ground are the steel supports.

Just before a flyer comes the air lines whistle. Not everyone knows this, since in the city it's mostly too noisy to hear. I pressed the signal in the platform. The flyer came up and stopped like a big glass pumpkin.

Inside it was empty, but some of the seats had been slashed, presumably that morning, otherwise the overnight repair systems would have seen to it.

We sailed over the Canyon's lip, into space as it were, and toward the city I could no longer see now that I was lower down than the house. I had to wait for the city now to put up its big grey-blue cones and stacked flashing window-glass and pillars on the skyline.

But something else had absorbed me. There was something odd about the robot machine which was driving the flyer. Normally, of course, it was just the box with driving digits and a slot for coins. Today, the flyer box had a head on. It was the head of a man about forty years of age, who hadn't taken Rejuvinex (or a man of about seventy, who had), so there were some character lines. The eyes and the hair were colorless, and the face of the head was a sort of coppery color. When I put my coin in the slot, the head disoriented me by saying to me: "Welcome aboard."

I sat down on a seat which hadn't been slashed, and looked at the head. I had, of course, seen lots of robots, as we all do, since almost everything mechanical is run by robots in the city. And even Mother has three robots who are domestic in Chez Stratos, but they're of shiny blue metal with polarized screens instead of faces. They look like spacemen to me, or like the suits men wear on the moon, or the Asteroid, and I always called our robots, therefore, the "spacemen." In the city, they're even more featureless, as you know, boxes on runners or panels set into walls.

Eventually I said to the flyer driver: "Why have you got a head today?"

I didn't think it could answer, but it might. It did.

"I am an experimental format. I am put here to make you feel at home with me."

"I see."

"Do you think I am an improvement?"

"I'm not sure," I said nervously.

"I am manufactured by Electronic Metals Ltd., 2½ East Arbor."

"Oh."

"If you wish to receive a catalog of our products, press the button by my left ear."

"I'll ask my mother."

Demeta would say: "You should make the decision yourself, darling."

But I gazed at the back of the colorless hair, which looked real but peculiar, and I thought it was silly. And at the same time it was human enough so that I didn't want to be rude to it.

Just then the outline of the city came in sight.

"You may see," announced the head, "several and various experimental formats in the city today. It will also be possible to see nine Sophisticated Formats. These are operating on 23rd Avenue, the forecourt of the Delux Hyperia Building, on the third floor of Casa Bianca, on Star Street—" I lost track until it said "—the Grand Stairway leading to Theatra Concordacis." Then I visualized Egyptia going into hysterics. "You may approach any of these formats and request information. The Sophisticated Formats do not dispense catalogs. Should you wish to purchase any format for your home, request the number of the model and the alphabetical registration. Each of the Sophisticated Formats has a specialized registration to enable the customer to memorize more clearly. These Formats do not have numbers. There is also . . ."

I lost interest altogether here, for the flyer was coming in across Les Anges Bridge. Below was all that glorious girderwork like spiderweb, and underneath, the Old River, polluted with chemicals and fantastically glowing purple with a top sheen of soft amber. I'm fascinated always by the strange mutated plants that grow out of the water, and the weird fish in armor that go leaping after the riverboats, clashing their jaws. A great tourist feature, the Old River. Beyond it, the city, where the poor people work at the jobs the machinery has left them to do, atrocious jobs like cleaning the ancient sewers—too narrow and eroded for the robot equipment to negotiate safely. Or elegant jobs in the department stores, particularly the more opulent second owner shops, which boasted: "Here you will be served only by *human* assistants." It's curious to be rich and miss all this. My mother considered sending me to live for a year in the city without money, but with a job, so I'd learn how the poor try to survive. "They are the ones with backbone and character, dear," she said to me. Sociologically she is highly aware. But in the end she realized my unfair advantages would have molded my outlook, so that even if I succeeded among the poor, it would be for the wrong reasons, and so would not count.

I got out of the flyer at the platform on the roof of Jagged's, and went down in the lift to the subway. There was a gang fight going on in one of the corridors and I could hear the scream of robot sirens, but I didn't see anything, which was a disappointment and a relief. I did once see a man stabbed at an outdoor visual. It didn't upset me at the time. They rushed him away and replaced the parts of him that had been spoiled, though he would have had to pay for that on the installment plan—clearly he hadn't been rich—which would probably mean he'd end up bankrupt. But later on, I suddenly remembered how he had fallen down, and the blood, and I began to get a terrible pain in my side where I pictured the knife going into him. My mother organized hypnotherapy for me until it went away.

Egyptia was standing at the foot of the Grand Stairway that leads up to the Theatra Concordacis. She was wearing gilt makeup, and a blue velvet mantle lined with lemon silk, and people were looking at her. A topaz hung in the center of her forehead. She made a wild gesture at me.

"Jane! Jane!"

"Hallo."

"Oh, Jane."

"Yes?"

"Oh, Jane. Oh, Jane."

"Shall we go up?"

She flung up her arm, and I blushed. She made me feel insignificant, superior and uneasy. As I was analyzing this, I saw someone hurrying over, a man, who grasped Egyptia's raised arm excitedly.

"All right," he said. "Tell me your number."

Egyptia and I stared at him. His eyes were popping.

"Go away," Egyptia said. Her own eyes filled with tears. She couldn't bear the stupid things life did to her.

"No. I can pay. I've never seen anything like it. I heard it was lifelike, but Jesus. You. I'll take you. Just give me your registration number—wait—you don't have one, do you, that's the other type. Okay, it's alphabetical, isn't it? Somebody said it's to do with the metal. You'd be gold, wouldn't you? G.O.L.D.? Am I right?"

Egyptia lifted her eyes to the tall building tops, like Jehane at the stake. Suddenly I knew what was happening.

"You've made a mistake," I said to the man.

"You can't have it," he said. "What do you want it for? Mirror-Biased, are you? Well, you go and find a real girl. Young bit of stuff like you shouldn't have any trouble."

"She isn't," I insisted.

"She? It's an it."

"*No.*" I felt on fire. "She's my friend. She isn't a Sophisticated Format robot."

"Yes it is. They said. Operating on the Grand Stairway."

"No."

"Oh, God!" cried Egyptia. Unlike the rest of us, He didn't answer.

"It's all right, Egyptia. Please, please," I said to the man, "she isn't a robot. Go away, or I'll press my code for the police."

I wished at once I hadn't said it. He, like Egyptia and me, was rich, and would have his own code round his neck or on his wrist or built into a button. I felt I'd been very discourteous and rash, but I couldn't think of anything else to do.

"Well," he said. "I'll write to Electronic Metals and complain. A piece of my mind."

(I saw this as some sort of surgical operation, the relevant slice delivered in a box.)

But Egyptia spun to him abruptly. She fixed him with her eyes which matched the topaz, and screeched wordlessly like a mad bird of prey. The man who thought she was a robot backed sideways along the steps. Egyptia seemed to close her soul to us both. She flung her mantle round herself and stalked away up the stairs.

I watched her go, not really wanting to follow. Mother would say I should, in order to observe and be responsible.

It was a beautiful day in autumn, a sort of toasted day. The sides of the buildings were warm, the glass mellow, and the sky was wonderful, very high and far off, while in the house it looks near. I didn't want to think about the man or about Egyptia. I wanted to think about something that was part of the day, and of me. Without warning, I felt a kind of pang, somewhere between my ribs and my spine. It might have been indigestion, but it was like a key turning. It seemed as if I knew something very important, and only had to wait a moment and I would recall what it was. But though I stood there for about five minutes, I didn't, and the feeling faded with a dim, sweet ache. It was like being in love, the moment when, just before the visual ends, I knew I must walk away into the night or morning without him. Awful. Yet marvelous. Marvelous to be able to feel. I put this down because it may have a psychological bearing on what comes next.

I began to imagine Egyptia acting death in the Theatra, and dying. So finally I went up the Grand Stairway.

At the top is a terrace with a fountain. The fountain

pours over an arch of glass, and you can stand under the glass with the fountain pouring, and not get wet. Across from the fountain is the scruffy peeling facade of the once splendid Theatra. A ticking clockwork lion was pacing about by the door. I hadn't seen anything quite like it, and wondered if this was the Sophisticated Format. Then something caught my eye.

It was the sun gleaming rich and rare on auburn.

I looked, and bathed my eyes in the color. I know red shouldn't be soothing to the eyes, but it was.

Then I saw what the red was. It was the long hair of a young man who was standing with his back to me, talking to a group of five or six people.

Then he began to sing. The voice was so unexpected. I went hot again, with embarrassment again, because someone was singing at the top of his lungs in a crowded busy place. At the same moment, I was delighted. It was a beautiful voice, like a minstrel's, but futuristic, as if time were playing in a circle inside the notes. If only I could sing, I vaguely thought as I heard him. How wonderful to have such sounds pour effortlessly from your throat.

There were bits of mirror on his jacket, glinting, and I wondered if he was there for an interview, like Egyptia, and warming up outside. Then he stopped singing, and turned around and I thought: Suppose he's ugly? And he went on turning, and I saw his profile and he wasn't ugly. And then, pointing something out to the small gathering about him, he turned fully toward me, not seeing me. He was handsome, and his eyes were like two russet stars. Yes, they were exactly like stars. And his skin seemed only pale, as if there were an actor's makeup on it, and then I saw it was silver—face, throat, the V of chest inside the open-necked shirt, the hands that came from the dripping lace at his cuffs. Silver that flushed into almost natural shadings and colors against the bones, the lips, the nails. But silver. Silver.

It was very silly. I started to cry. It was awful. I didn't know what to do. My mother would have been pleased, as it meant my basic emotions—whatever they were—were being allowed full and free reign. But she'd also have expected me to control myself. And I couldn't.

So I walked under the fountain and stared at it till the tears stopped in envy. And then I was puzzled as to why I'd cried at all.

When I came out, the crowd, about twenty now, was dispersing. They would all have taken his registration, or whatever, but most of them couldn't afford him.

I stood and gazed at him, curious to see if he'd just switch himself off when the crowd went away. But he didn't. He began to stroll up and down. He had a guitar slung over his shoulder I hadn't noticed, and he started to caress melodies out of it. It was crazy.

Then, quite abruptly and inevitably, he registered that someone else was watching after all, and he came toward *me.*

I was frightened. He was a robot and he seemed just like a man, and he scared me in a way I couldn't explain. I would have run away like a child, but I was too frightened to run.

He came within three feet of me, and he smiled at me. Total coordination. All the muscles, even those of his face. He seemed perfectly human, utterly natural, except he was too beautiful to be either.

"Hallo," he said.

"Are you—" I said.

"Am I?"

"Are you—the—are you a robot?"

"Yes. Registration Silver. That is S.I.L.V.E.R. which

stands for Silver Ionized Locomotive Verisimulated Electronic Robot. Neat, isn't it?"

"No," I said. "No." Again without warning, I began once more to cry.

His smile faded. He looked concerned, his eyes were like pools of fulvous lead. His reactions were superb. I hated him. I wished he were a box on wheels, or I wished he were human.

"What's the matter?" he said eventually, and very gently, making it much worse. "The idea is for me to amuse you. I seem to be failing. Am I intruding on some sort of personal grief?"

"You horrible thing," I whispered. "How dare you stand there and talk to me?"

The reactions were astounding. His eyes went flat and wicked. He gave me the coldest smile I ever saw, and bowed to me. He really did turn on his heel, and he walked directly away from me.

I wished the concrete would open and swallow me. I truly wished it. I wanted to be ten years old and run home to my mother, who might comfort or lecture me, but who would be omnipotent. Or I wanted to be a hundred and twenty, and wise, and not care.

Anyway, I raced off the terrace, and to Clovis.

Clovis's apartment overlooks a stretch of the New River, which is clean and sparkling. People who live along the banks can open their windows on it, unlike the people who live along the banks of the polluted Old River, who have to use the filtered air-conditioning even in winter. Every apartment there has a warning notice cut into the window frame, which says: The Surgeon General has established that to open this window for more than ten minutes every day can seriously damage your health. Clovis has friends on the Old River who leave their windows open all the time. "Will you look at the muck on the buildings," they say. "Why don't the Godawful Surgeon General and the Goddamn City Marshal clean up the air and the traffic fumes before going dippy over the Godball river?" Clovis also asserts that he never opens his own windows as the view of the New River is too hygienic and bores him. But so far he hasn't moved.

When I arrived on the fifteenth gallery and spoke to Clovis's door, it wouldn't let me in for a long time. When it did, I found Clovis was in the process of trying to get rid of a live-in lover by holding a seance.

Clovis doesn't like relationships, except sometimes with women, and they are non-sexual. He once shared his apartment with Chloe for ten months, but his boyfriends come and go like days of the week. Actually, the term Mirror-Biased really applies to Clovis. He doesn't just sleep with his own sex, his lovers always look like him. This one was no exception. Tall and slim, with dark curly hair, the young man lay on the couch among the jet black cushions, eyeing me solemnly.

"This is Austin," said Clovis.

"Hallo," said Austin.

I remembered the robot saying "Hallo" to me in his smiling, musical voice. I wished I hadn't come here.

"And this is Jane," said Clovis to Austin. "Jane is really a boy in drag. Awfully effective, isn't it?"

Austin blinked. He looked rather slow-witted, and I felt sorry for him, trying to cope with Clovis.

Clovis finished arranging the plastic cards with letters, basic punctuation and numbers one to ten around the seance table.

"Get up and come and sit down, Austin. And Jane, since you're there, come here."

This playful phraseology showed Clovis was in a deadly mood. He seated himself cross-legged on the rug before the table.

"Oh, Clo," said Austin in a whine, "what ever do you think you can pick up in a modern building like this?"

"You'd be surprised what I've picked up here," said Clovis.

Austin didn't get this. But he slunk over to the table.

"But the apartment is so *new,*" whined Austin.

"Siddown," barked Clovis.

"Oh all right. If you're going to go all brutal. I'll sit down. But it's infantile."

He folded himself on the rug like a rope. I went over and sat on the other side. A cut-glass goblet, that had been chipped a year ago when one of Clovis's lovers had thrown it at him, rested in the table's center. We each put a finger on it.

"This is so childish," said Austin. "If it *does* move, it's just pressure. Your hand trembling."

"My hand doesn't tremble," said Clovis.

"Oh, I *know,* dear," said Austin.

I felt very alone, and I began to cry again, but neither of them noticed me. By lowering my head, I could let the tears just fall straight out of my eyes onto my lap, where they made a strange abstract pattern of dark polka dots. It became quite interesting, wondering where the next tear would land.

"Oh, dear," said Austin. "This is dull."

"I do it all the time," said Clovis.

"How dull of you."

"I am dull."

"I just hate dull men."

The glass began quite suddenly to move. It glided across the table and back again, and started a liquid circling motion around the fringe of letters and numbers.

"Ooh," said Austin. "*You're* doing it."

Clovis took his finger off the glass. The glass, with Austin and me still adhering, went on.

"*She's* doing it," sneered Austin. "I might have known."

"Take your finger off the glass, Jane," said Clovis.

I did. The glass went on twirling with Austin still attached.

"Ah!" screamed Austin. He let go as if it had bitten him. Undeterred, the glass swirled about the table.

"Oh God," said Austin.

"I don't think it's actually God. You could ask."

"I'm not speaking to it."

"Everyone," said Clovis, as if addressing a crowd of thirty people, "put your fingers back on. First Jane, then Austin. Then I will."

I did as Clovis said, and Austin anxiously followed suit, yelping as he touched the glass. Clovis put his finger on the glass and Austin said, "Has someone died in this room?"

"Not yet," said Clovis.

"Then how can it get anything?"

"People have died everywhere. And don't forget, twenty years before this block went up, there was a condominium on the site. It fell down with a massive loss of life. And we are sitting, as it were, on the rubble and the bones."

"You do have a horrible turn of phrase. Why did it fall down anyway?"

"Did you not," said Clovis patiently, "ever hear of the earthquakes, tsunamis and geological collapses that occurred when we captured the Haemeroid?" (The Haemeroid is Clovis's name for the Asteroid.) "When a third of Eastern Europe sank and North America gained seventy-two Pacific islands it hadn't had before. Little, easily overlooked things like that."

"Oh," said Austin. "Is this a history lesson?"

The glass jumped up from the table and came down again with a noisy crack.

I thought of all the people dying in the earthquakes,

and swept away, shrieking, in the seas, and tried not to sob aloud. I had seen lots of ruins, lots of swamps, but I had been too young and didn't remember them. I saw Chez Stratos falling out of the sky. I saw the city tilt into the purple river and the clean river, and Silver lying trapped under the water, not dead because water couldn't kill him, but rusting away, and my tears joined together in the lap of my dress, making the map of a weird new continent.

"What do we do now?" said Austin, as the glass made bullfrog leaps all over the table.

"Ask it something."

"Um. Is there anyone there?"

"Obviously there isn't," said Clovis.

"Oh. Er, well. Who are you?"

The glass rushed to the letter N, and then to the letter O.

"In other words," said Clovis sternly, "mind your own damn business. Do you have," Clovis demanded of the energetic glass, "a message for someone here?"

The glass flew to the letter A, letter U, letter S, letter T—

"Ooh!"

"Sit down, Austin."

"But it's—"

"Yes, Austin. Austin would like to know what the message is."

"No," cried Austin, alarmed. "I don't want to know."

"Too late," said Clovis with great satisfaction.

Swiftly the glass spelled out, Clovis reading off the letters and then the words: *There is a negative influence about you. You must take a risk. Excitement is waiting for you, but not here. Be warned.*

"Well, *thanks,*" said Clovis.

The glass shuddered to a halt.

"You've frightened it off," complained Austin.

"Well, you saw what it said. I'm supposed to be a negative influence. Bloody thing. Comes into my home and insults me. Where are you going?"

Austin had risen and sauntered to the apartment door.

"I need some cigarines," said Austin.

"I thought you gave them up."

"Oh, that was yesterday."

The door let him out, the closet handing him his three-tone jacket as he passed. The door buzzed shut, and presently we heard the lift.

"If only it could be so quick," mourned Clovis, clearing the seance table. "But he'll come back. He'll come back and he'll brood for at least another day before he takes the message to heart and goes."

The table is rigged. Jason, who's very clever with electrical stuff, did it for Clovis, and put the electronic magnet, the size of a pinhead, in the glass—you can just see it, if you know. Clovis memorized the sequence of letters and the message is always nearly the same. Clovis is really very cruel. He prefers to play with his lovers and watch them react to just telling them to get out. Of course, this probably works better, in the long run.

"Hallo, Jane," said Clovis, after the sound of the lift had faded. "If you were trying to water the plants, your aim is a little out."

"I didn't think you saw me."

"Weeping so bitterly? Since when have I been blind?"

I stopped crying, and Clovis brought me a glass of applewine. His comfort is limited to words and gestures at a distance. I don't think he's ever touched me, and I never saw him touch one of his lovers, though they constantly touch him. To be hugged by Clovis would, now, be embarrassing.

I told him about S.I.L.V.E.R., rather fast, not really

explaining it properly, partly because I didn't understand myself, and partly in case Austin came back quickly.

Clovis listened, detached and elegant, and beyond the window, the New River quivered in the late afternoon sunlight.

"What a nasty idea," Clovis said when I stopped. "A metal man. Sounds like a comic strip. Decidedly kinky."

"No, no, it wasn't like that—he—he was—"

"He was beautiful. Well, he sounds beautiful."

"It's simply that—how can he be a robot *and* a—"

"He can't. He isn't. He's just a bit of metal. Worked metal that can move fluidly, like a sort of skin. They've been easing up to it for years, you know. Someone had to make one. Clockwork and machinery designed to look like musculature from the outside. A wonderful sort of super male doll. Take off the skin and you find cogs and wheels—what's the matter? Oh, Jane, you're not going to throw up on my rug, are you?"

"N-no. I'm all right."

"If he—it—has this effect on everyone else, Electronic Metals Ltd. are going to regret their advertising campaign."

"Everyone else was fascinated."

"And you were allergic."

"I was—" My eyes spilled water again.

"Poor Jane," said Clovis. "What a gargantuan emotional reaction. I wonder if," said Clovis, "he'd go with the furnishings? I could buy a model and install it in the wardrobe. Then, when I wanted to get rid of an Austin, I'd just trundle out the robot. They're fully equipped, I suppose."

"What?"

"Jane, your innocence can only be assumed."

"Oh. I suppose they are."

"I do believe you've missed the point of the Sophisticated Formats altogether. They're sex toys. Nine models, the flyer robot said? Nine *Sophisticated* Formats—"

"No, Clovis."

"Yes."

"But he sang. He was playing a guitar."

"All extras built in. A robot can do anything. Pretty soulless music, I'd say."

"No, it was—"

"And pretty soulless in bed. Still, buggers can't be choosers."

When Clovis says things like that he is disturbed in some way. Perhaps my own disturbance was affecting him. Most of the time I forget that he's only a year older than I am. Much of the time, he seems a great deal older, twenty, maybe. The robot had looked about twenty.

"And," elaborated Clovis, "he could march out and play Austin a tune—you *are* going to be sick."

"Yes."

"You know where the bathrooms are."

"Yes—"

I ran into the green bathroom and banged the door. I hung over the pale green lavatory basin, which I matched, but I wasn't sick at all. Eventually I lay down full length on the marble tiles, not knowing what was wrong with me, or where I wanted to be, or who I wanted to be with. As I lay there, I heard the lift, and the apartment door, and Clovis saying with irritation: "Don't blow that foul corner-store marijuana over me."

When I came sheepishly out, Austin had put on a rhythm tape and was gyrating before the window, perhaps hoping someone with powerful binoculars on the other side of the river would see him.

"Shall I call you a taxi?" said Clovis. "There's a new line running from Jagged's with human drivers. A gimmick. It won't last."

"I'll take the flyer. There's one due at the corner of Racine at five P.M."

"Racine is a rough stop. I shouldn't like your little blond face to get carved up."

"I've got my policode."

"Ever called the cops with it? I once did, and it was two whole minutes before they arrived to rescue me, by which time I could have been structurally redesigned."

Austin giggled, waving his hips wildly.

Everything was normal again. I would be normal. I had already recollected Egyptia, and wondered if I should try to find her, at the Theatra, or her apartment block on The Island, or the Gardens of Babylon where she sometimes sat drinking among the flowery vines. Or I could go off alone, there were a hundred places I could go to. Or I could call Chloe, or Medea. But I knew I wouldn't do any of those things. I knew I'd go home, just as Clovis anticipated.

Chez Stratos was my security. Whenever anything went wrong, I felt shaky until I got back there. I would go home, and I'd tell my mother what had happened to me—Clovis had merely been a way of putting it off. Already I felt safer, just thinking of telling her, though probably it would turn out that my reactions were suspect.

Anyway, Clovis wanted me to go. He doodled on a pad on the coffee table, drawings of a beautiful young man with long hair and a key protruding from his back.

"Don't look so stricken, Jane," he said. "You have it out of proportion. As usual. Go home and relax."

Austin ran his hands down his body and blew me a kiss.

I didn't like Clovis then, and I turned on my heel just like the robot and went to the door and out.

It must be odd to live on Social Subsistence. Odd to have to palm print every month and get a sub. check in the mail every week. There are all sorts of training schemes, aren't there, but mostly they're dead ends. The colossal boom in robot circuitry, essential after the Asteroid threw everything into confusion, has left all these gaping holes with human beings in them, frantically swimming and trying not to go down. Mother says the creative arts are the safest, there are jobs there. But if robots can start to make music beautifully and expertly, and sing like angels, what then?

And if they can even make love—

I'd been very silly to get sick over that. Was it so revolting? After all, if they could make love, then they must feel of skin and flesh to the touch, feel human, too, in . . . every way. Only it wasn't revulsion, somehow. Somehow, it was worse. I sat in the cab I had, after all, dialed from a kiosk, sticking my nails in my hands to stop my recurring nausea from getting a grip.

I'm not very good at being alive. Sometimes I despair of ever mastering it, getting it right. When I'm old, perhaps, when I'm thirty—

The cab drove fast on the highway, and the dust spooned up on either side, glowing a lovely gold in the westering sun, that calmed me. The robot driver was just a panel and slot for coins and notes. The flyer costs much less and is much nicer, because it travels a hundred feet above the ground.

The Baxter Empire travels in the air too, one of those old vertical lift-offs. Mother used it in the jungle, its blades smashing the forest roof out of the way as it went up, and portions of severed monkeys falling past the windows. Although I've forgotten all the important parts of my early travels, that's one part I do remember, and I remember I cried. Mother then told me nothing dies ever, animal or human. A psychic force inside us survives physical death, and continues on both in the spiritual, and in other bodies. At the time I thought rebelliously for five minutes she was just making an excuse for killing the monkeys, as if killing them didn't matter, because they weren't really dead. But even so, I guessed she was right. It was easier to believe it anyway.

It was peculiar thinking of the monkeys now, over ten years later. What was the connection between them and the red-haired robot outside the Theatra? I wanted to stop thinking about him. But I wouldn't be able to until I'd told mother. That was peculiar, too. Even when I hadn't wanted to bother her with things, with my problems, or events which had unnerved me, I never could deal with them until I'd discussed them with her. Or rather, till I'd told her and she'd told me what to do. Doing what my mother says makes life, which I find so confusing, much simpler. Like adopting her opinions, and so thinking on a sort of permanent tangent that's probably wrong so doesn't matter. My living is like that, too. I do what she says, and follow her advice, but somehow my life—my true response to life—goes on quite differently and somewhere else. How strange. Until I wrote it here, I'd never thought about it before.

After about twelve minutes, the slim steel supports of the house appeared. But not even a ghost was visible of the house now, in the thickening light. I paid the cab the balance, and got out and walked up the white concrete approach between the conifer trees. The house lift is in the nearest support, and when I speak to it it always says: "Hallo, Jane." When I was a little girl, all the mechanisms in the house would speak to me. I was, am, very used to intelligent mechanical things, totally at home with them.

Until today.

The lift went up, smooth as silk, and gaining terrific momentum until its gradual slowing near the top of the support, neither of which processes can be felt at all. I'd thought perhaps my mother wouldn't be home yet. She'd been addressing a meeting somewhere, or giving a talk. But there had been a faint scent of pear-oil gasoline vaguely noticeable on the approach, the gas the Baxter burns. And the conifers had the slightly sulky back-combed look they get from the down-gale of a VLO. Even so, I might be mistaken. Once when I was eleven and very upset, and had rushed home, I smelled the Baxter's gas though my mother had been away. I tore into the house, and found she still was; it had been a psychosomatic wish-fulfillment odor. My olfactory nerves had made it up to kid me she was there when I needed her, and she wasn't, and didn't come back for hours.

When the lift stopped and the door slid away, however, I also caught a faint, faint whiff of her perfume: *La Verte.*

When I was a child, the scent of *La Verte* could make me laugh with pure happiness. Then one morning, I poured it all over the carpets and the cushions and the drapes, so the whole house would smell like my mother. She sat with me, and explained my psychology to me, very carefully, and meanwhile everything was de-odorized. My mother never hit me, never smacked me, or ever shouted at me. She said this would be a sign of failure. Children must have everything explained. Then they could function just as concisely as adults.

The funny thing is, I think I was more mature as a child than I am now.

The lift opens on the foyer, which is, apparently, imposing. ("How imposing!") Egyptia said that when she first saw it, it seemed to be made of frozen white ice cream, which would devour her. But really it's white marble with tawny veins. Pencil-thin pillars rise in groups to discs which give a soft light at nighttime. But during the day, the light comes in from round high portholes. They're too high, actually, to see much out of, just a glimpse now of the goldening sky—probably I shouldn't make up adjectives, but it was. In the middle of the foyer is the openwork lift to the next floors. Mother had it designed like something she saw in an old visual once. Leading from the foyer is a bathroom suite, and door to the robot and mechanical storage hatches under the house, a kitchen and servicery, and the wine cellar. There are also two guest apartments with two more bathrooms in an annex to the east. When you get in the house lift and go up, you pass a mezzanine floor with more things like guest rooms, and a tape-store which locks itself and which only the spacemen can open. The tapes are house accounts or business records, or else very precious and ancient documentation. Only mother goes in there. There's also a book library, with a priceless globe of the world as it used to be before the Asteroid altered it. One of the balcony-balloons runs off from the library, and sometimes I sit there to read, but I never do, because the sky stops me from concentrating.

The top floor has mother's suite and study and studio on the north, all together, and these are soundproofed, and also locked. The rest of the floor is the Vista, a wonderful semicircle running almost all round the outside of the house, and blossoming into huge balcony-balloons like great crystal bubbles with the sky held in them. When you come in, the sky fills the room. One is in the sky, and not in a room at all. To make sure of the effect, the furniture is very simple, and either of glass or pale white reflective materials, which take on the colors of the upper troposphere outside. We're not really up into the stratosphere, of course, that would be dangerous. Even up where we are, the house is pressurized and oxygenized. We can't open our windows either. Nor do we ever close the drapes.

This evening, when I came into the Vista, the room was gold. Gold carpets, gold chairs, a dining table in a balloon-bubble seeming made of palest amontillado sherry. The chemical candelabra in the ceiling were unlit, but had gold fires on them from the sky. The sky was like yellow plum wine. I walked into one of the western bubbles, dazed, and watched the sunset happen there. It seemed to take weeks, as it always does so high, but as soon as the sky began to cool I crossed over into an eastern bubble and watched the Asteroid appear. It looks like a colossal blue-green star, but it pulls the winds with it, and the sea tides answer it in huge heaves and buffetings. It should have hit the Earth, but some of it burned off as it fell, and then the moon's gravity also attracted it; it shifted, and then it stabilized. I think I have that right, don't I? Men have walked on the Asteroid. Jason and Medea stole the bit of blue rock we had that came from it. It's beautiful, but it killed a third of all the people in the world. That's a statistic.

At the southern curve of the room is another little annex, and a small stair that goes up to my suite. The suite is done in green and bronze and white to match my physical color scheme. It has everything a contemporary girl could want, visual set, tape deck and player, hairdresser unit, closets full of clothes, exotic furnishings, games, books. But, though there are windows, they aren't balcony-balloons, so I tend to stay in the Vista.

I was just wandering over to the piano, which was turning lavender-grey now, with the sky, when my mother came into the room.

She was wearing the peacock dress, which has a high collar that rises over her head and is the simulated erect fan of a male peacock, with staring blue and yellow eyes like gas flames. She was obviously going out again.

"Come here, darling," said my mother. I went to her and she took me in her arms. The gorgeous perfume of *La Verte* enfolded me, and I felt safe. Then she eased me away and held me, smiling at me. She looked beautiful, and her eyes were green as gooseberries. "Did you look after Egyptia, darling?"

"I tried, Mother. Mother, I have to tell you about something, ask your advice."

"I have to go out, dear, and I'm already late. I waited in the hope of seeing you before I left. Can you tell me quickly?"

"No—I don't—I don't think so."

"Then you must tell me tomorrow, Jane."

"Oh, Mother," I wailed, starting to cry again.

"Now, darling. I've told you what you can do if I'm not able to be with you, and you've done it before. Get one of the blank tapes and record what happened to you, imagining to yourself that I'm sitting here, holding your hand. And then tomorrow, about noon, or maybe one P.M., I can play it through, and we'll discuss the problem."

"Mother—"

"Darling," she said, shaking me gently, "I really must go."

"Go where?" I listlessly inquired.

"To the dinner I told you about yesterday."

"I don't remember."

"That's because you don't want to. Come along, Jane. Let go of my sleeves. You're intelligent and bright, and I've encouraged you to think for yourself."

"And to talk to you."

"And we will talk. Tomorrow."

Although as a baby she had taken me everywhere, as a child, she had sometimes had to leave me, because my mother is a very busy woman, who writes and researches, is an expert perfumier and gem specialist, a theologian, a rhetorician—and can lecture and entertain on many levels. And when she used to leave me, I never could hold back the tears. But now I was crying anyway.

"Come along, Jane," said my mother, kissing my forehead. "Why don't you go to your room and bathe and dress and makeup. Call Jason or Davideed and go out to dinner yourself."

"Davideed's at the equator."

"Dear me. Well I hope they warned him it was hot there."

"Up to his eyes in silt," I said, following her from the room and back toward the lift. "Mother, I think I'll just go to bed."

"That sounds rather negative." My mother looked at me, her long turquoise nail on the lift button. "Darling, I do hope, since you haven't yet found a lover, that you're masturbating regularly, as I suggested."

I blushed. Of course, I knew it was idiotic to blush, so I didn't lower my eyes.

"Oh. Yes."

"Your physical type indicates you're highly sexed. But the body has to learn about itself. You do understand, darling, don't you?"

"Oh. Yes."

"Good-bye, darling," said my mother, as the lift, a birdcage with a peacock in it, sank away.

"Good-bye, Mother."

In the ethereal silence and stillness of the house, I just caught the thrum of the white Chevrolet as it was driven out of the second support pillar. And I could just see the tiny dazzle of its lights as it ran away into the darkness. I strained my eyes until I could see the dazzle no more.

3

I fell asleep in my sunken bath, and my bathroom video telephone woke me. I turned off the video and answered it. It was Egyptia.

"Jane, Jane. They accepted me."

In the background were noises like a party.

"Who?" I sleepily asked.

"Don't be stupid. The Theatra Concordacis drama group. They responded to the interview. It was as if we'd known each other always. I've paid my subscription. I'm giving a party in the Gardens of Babylon. It's a wonderful party. Champagne is flowing, simply gushing, down the terraces."

I recalled my mother's advice.

"Can I come to the party?"

"Oh," Egyptia's voice was more distant.

I didn't want to go anyway. The bath was cold, I was depressed. But my mother had thought it was best for me to go out.

"It isn't really the sort of party you'd like," said Egyptia.

Normally, I would retreat at that. I had before, quite often. Why was it that Egyptia always wanted me to herself? She wasn't M-B. Was it that she was ashamed of me? Something made me say: "I'm unhappy. I can't bear to be alone."

Sometimes, by sounding like Egyptia, I could evoke a reaction. I realized I'd done this intuitively before, not knowing I did it, but now it was calculated. I didn't want to go to the party, but I didn't want to be alone.

"So unhappy, Egyptia. When that man upset you on the Grand Stairway, I was so shocked. I couldn't bear to go with you. I was afraid for you."

"Yes," she breathed. I could imagine her eyes swimming, reliving it all.

And I was lying. I shouldn't be lying like this, not consciously, not for something I didn't even want.

"Egyptia, I want to come to the party to see you. To see you're all right. To see you happy."

"It's on the third tier, under one of the canopies. . . ."

Probably she was paying for the party. Of course she was, and the whole horrid Theatra group battening on her misguided euphoria. Why did I want to go?

But the most extraordinary thing was happening. I was hurrying. Out of the bath, into the wardrobe. I was even singing, too, until I recalled how awful my singing is, and stopped. I stopped again, briefly, when I had put on green lingerie and a green dress, to look at my wide hips. I don't really like being a Venus Media type. Once, when Clovis was drunk, he told me I had a boyish look. "But I'm a

Venus Media." Clovis had shrugged. It's possibly my face, which is almost oval, but has a pointed chin with an infinitesimal cleft—like that of a tom-cat?

I tried to put up my hair myself, but despaired, and combed it down again. I made up, using all the creams and powders and shadows and heightenings and mascaras and rouges and glosses. Until I looked much older and more confident. Sometimes I've been told I'm pretty or attractive, but I'm never sure. I wish I were someone else really.

I got the automatic on the phone to fetch another cab, and at nine P.M. I drove back into the city, which I think is amazing by night. The buildings seem made of thousands of little cubes of light that go up and up into the darkness. In the distance, they look like sticks of diamanté. But I expect that's a bad analogy. The jewelry traffic goes by on the roads, and clatters past overhead, punching out rosy fumes. I felt excited. I was glad I'd come back.

I felt at least twenty-five as I paid off the cab, and stepped on the moving stair that flows into Babylon, among the hanging mosses and garlands lit to liquid emeralds by the neons under the foliage.

The autumn night was soft. The lights in the bushes melted in the softness, and were only hard where they streamed out from under the canopies with the hard music of orchestras and stereophonics. Under the Theatra-Egyptia canopy, the light was hardest of all, but that may only have been the hard, beautiful makeup everyone was wearing.

I stood at the brink of the light and saw Egyptia in sequins dancing the snake dance with a thin handsome man among other couples doing the same. People and bottles were strewn thickly on the grass and currents of blue smoke went through the air. It was the sort of party

Clovis liked a lot, because he could be so terribly, cuttingly rude about it.

Someone came up to me, a man about twenty-one, and said, "Well who are you?"

"My name is Jane. I'm a friend of Egyptia's."

"I didn't know she had any friends. Why not be *my* friend instead, then you can come in."

"Thank you."

"Oh, don't thank me." He looked at my dress, which is pre-Asteroid Asian silk. There isn't a thing in my wardrobe I can put on which isn't expensive and doesn't look it. "Sweet little rich girl," said the young man, who was good-looking and nasty. "Would you like an interview for the drama, too?"

"I can't act."

"Everyone can act. We spend our lives acting."

"Not on a stage."

"Theatra Concordacis can't afford a stage. We put tables together."

He was probably joking, and I didn't know what to say. I'm a failure as a wit, too.

He led me by the hand—his hand was dry but limp—under the canopy, and told me his name was Lord. He poured a glass of fizzy greenish wine and gave it to me and kissed me on the lips as he did so. If I say that to be kissed by men, even passionately with the mouth open, bores me, it sounds like a silly attempt to be blasé. But it's true. I've tried to get interested, but I never can. Nothing happens, except sometimes a faraway sensation that I always hope will become pleasant but is really only like a vague itch somewhere under my skin. So I shrank back from the young man called Lord, and he said, "How fascinating. You're shy." And I blushed, and I was glad that my makeup hid it. But I didn't feel twenty-five anymore. I felt about eleven, and already I wanted to leave.

Then the snake dance ended as there was an interval on the rhythm tape. I wondered if Egyptia would see me and come over, or pretend she hadn't seen me and not come over. But she seemed very interested in her partner, and truly didn't see me. She looked so exotic. I sipped my icy wine and wished very much that she'd be a wonderful success at the Theatra. Her eyes shone. She had forgotten about comets crashing on the earth.

"Oh, no more rhythm, per-leez," someone called. "I've been waiting all evening to hear these songs. Do they exist? Am I at the wrong party?"

Other voices joined in, with various clever, existentialist comments.

I tensed for a song tape to be put on, probably raucous. But a lot of people were surging across the open space where the dancers had been, waving glasses.

"Improvisation!" somebody else yelled. Mostly they were rather high. I was envious. *Another* failure. I find it difficult to smoke, the vapor refusing to sink below my throat into my lungs. It's very awkward. I have to pretend to be high, usually, when I'm not. (We spend our lives acting.)

Then another rhythm tape, or the same one, came on. Then, after four beats, the song came. Of course, rhythm has no melody, just the percussion and the beat, for dancing. I've heard people improvise tunes or songs over it before; Clovis is quite good at this, but the songs are always obscene. This song was savage, the words like fireworks—but they dashed away from me, while the chords of a guitar came up from the ground, resonating, and hung in the hollows of my bones, trapped there. Almost everybody was quiet so they could listen. But Lord-who-had-kissed-me said, "It sounds pretty good, doesn't it? Better than I'd have thought. Have you seen it yet? It's awfully effective. Come on, I'll show you."

I was thinking, Who is singing like that? But I said to Lord: "No, I don't want to."

So I knew.

My feet were stumbling over the grass as Lord led me, with his limp hand on my waist, toward the savage music. And the guitar played up through my feet and my legs and my stomach and my heart, and filled my skull. All my blood seemed to have run into the ground in exchange. I dropped the glass of green wine. I couldn't breathe. I thought I would die.

My guide went on telling me things. I heard, but didn't hear, how Egyptia had informed the Theatra group, in scorn and despair, how the man had mistaken her for a robot. Three of her new friends had gone to look for the original. Egyptia flashed her money like a sequined scarf, flaunting it, drunk on the prospect of being generous to those who loved her and could give her the means to explore her own genius. They took the real robot's registration, called Electronic Metals Ltd., and hired him for the party. Hired him as they had hired the canopy, the tapes, the machinery that kept the bottles coming up onto the lawn in little crates.

We were on the periphery of the crowd. He sang. The robot sang. He sang into my veins where my blood had been and where instead the notes and throbbing of the guitar now flowed. I could feel his song vibrating in my throat, as if I sang it too. I couldn't see him. If the crowd parted and I saw him, I would die.

Why had I come here? Why had I hurried here, almost as if I had known? But if I had known, I should never have come.

Someone moved, and I saw a white muslin shirt sleeve with a silver pattern sewn on it, and a silver hand and flecks of light on steely strings. I shut my eyes, and I began to push my way viciously through the crowd toward him. I was cursed and shoved, but they moved away for me. I only told from the feeling of space across the front of my body that I had come through the crowd. Only he was in front of me now.

The earth shook with the beat of the rhythm and the race of the guitar following it. Sheer runs of notes. It was very clever but not facile. It didn't sound like a robot, though it was too brilliant for a human musician. No man could play as quickly and clearly. Yet, it had the depth, the color-tones—as if he felt, *expressed* what he played. There had been a brief interlude, without voice, but then he sang again. I could hear all the words. They didn't make sense, but I wanted to keep them, and only a phrase was left here and there, snagged on the edges of me as the song flung past—fire-snow, scarlet horses, a winged merry-go-round, windshields spattered with city lights, a car in flight and worlds flying like birds—

I opened my eyes and bit my tongue so I couldn't scream.

His head was bowed. His hair fell over his face and his broad shoulders and the muslin shirt sewn with silver. Clovis has a pair of jeans like that, the color of a storm cloud, and Clovis might like the boots the color of dragon's blood, or he might not. The robot's hair looked like somber red velvet, like a sort of plush. His eyebrows and eyelashes were dark cinnamon. There were hairs on his chest, too, a fine rain of auburn hair on the silver skin. This frightened me. All the blood that had run away came crashing back, like a tsunami, against my heart so I nearly choked.

"Shut up," someone said to Lord, who I suppose was still talking or trying to talk to me. I hadn't heard him at all anymore.

The song ended, and the rhythm section ended. Of course, he would be able, computerlike, to judge where the section would end, and so end the song at the right place to coordinate. No human could do that, unless he knew the section backwards.

Someone switched the tape right off. Then there was silence, and then a detonation of applause that tailed off in self-conscious swearing and giggling. Did one applaud a performing machine?

He looked up then. S.I.L.V.E.R. looked up. He looked at them, smiling. The smile was friendly; it was kind. He had wanted to give them pleasure, to carry them with him, and if he had carried them and pleased them, he was glad, so glad.

I was afraid his eyes would meet mine, and my whole face began to flinch. But they didn't. What did it matter anyway? If he saw me with his clockwork amber eyes.

Egyptia and her partner came through the crowd. Egyptia dropped like a swath of silk at the robot's feet. She offered him a glass of champagne.

"Can you drink?"

"If you want me to, I can," he said. He conveyed amusement and gentleness.

"Then," said Egyptia, "drink!"

The robot drank the champagne. He drank it like someone who has no interest in drink, yet is willing to be gracious and is gracious, and as though it were lemonade.

"Oh God what a waste," someone said loudly.

"I'm afraid it is," said Silver, grinning at them. The grin was gorgeous, and his teeth were white, just as he had whites to his eyes. There was that faint hint of mortal color, too, in his mouth and in his nails.

"You are so beautiful," said Egyptia to the robot.

"Thank you."

People laughed. Egyptia took the robot's hand.

"Sing me a love song."

"Let go of my hand and I will."

"Kiss me first."

The robot bowed his head and kissed her. It was a long, long kiss, as long a kiss as Egyptia indicated she wanted, presumably. People began to clap and cheer. I felt sick again. Then they drew apart and Egyptia stared at the robot in deliberate theatrical amazement. Then she looked at the crowd, her hired crowd, and she said: "I have news for you. Men could become redundant."

"Oh, come on," muttered Lord, "there are female formats, too, you know."

Egyptia sat at the robot's feet and told him again to sing her a love song. He touched the guitar, and then he sang. The song was about five centuries old, and he was changing the words, but it was "Greensleeves."

"Alas, my love, you do me wrong, to cast me off discourteously. If passion's limit is a song, the lack will work hell with my circuitry."

Laughter burst out again. Egyptia laughed too.

"Greensleeves is my delight, in her dress like summer leaves. Greensleeves, truly, I never bite—unless so requested, my Greensleeves."

This produced mild uproar. Egyptia smiled and pouted in her sleeveless gown. Then he struck the last chord and looked straight at me. And I remembered the color of my dress.

I think I was petrified. I couldn't move, even to flinch, but my cheeks and my eyes burned. Nor could I immediately look away. His eyes on me had no expression. None of the coldness, the potential cruelty I had seen before—or had I imagined it? Was a robot permitted to be cruel to a human?—and no kindness, and no smile.

In desperation, frantic, my eyes slid away to Egyptia.

Pretending to see me for the first time, acting friendship now where she had acted Cleopatra-in-lust a second before, she rose and swam toward me.

(We spend our lives acting.)

"Darling Jane. You came after all."

She threw her arms around me. I felt comforted in the midst of fear, and I clutched her, being careful not to spoil her clothes, a trick I sort of mastered with my mother. Over her shoulder, the silver robot looked away and began to tune the guitar. People were sitting down by him, asking him things, and he was answering, making them laugh over and over. I hadn't seen him before because he was surrounded by people. Built-in wit. If only I had some.

"Jane, you look adorable. Have some champagne."

I had some champagne.

I kept hoping the leaden feeling would go away, or the other feeling of burning up inside would go, but neither did. Later he played again, and I sat alone, far away amid the bushes, forcing back the stupid uncontrollable tears. In the end, the nasty Lord took me to a grove in the gardens, and seated under the vines there, which were heavy with grapes, he fondled me and kissed me and I let him, but I kept thinking: I can't bear this. How can I make him stop?

About one in the morning, as he was telling me to come along, we'd go to his apartment, I thought of a way.

"I—I haven't had my contraception shot this month. I'm overdue for it."

"Well, I've had mine. And I'll be careful."

"No, I'm a Venus Media, very fertile. I can't risk it."

"Why didn't you bloody well tell me before?"

Acutely self-conscious and ashamed, I stared at the grapes. If I cried again, my mascara would run and he would hate me and go. So of course, I couldn't cry. I thought of the robot. I thought of the robot kissing Egyptia, and all the women who would ask to be kissed. If I asked, he would kiss me. Or bite me. Or—do anything I said, providing someone paid Electronic Metals Ltd.

"I feel sick," I said to Lord. "Nauseous. I'm sorry."

"Don't vomit over *me,*" he said, got up, and fled.

There was some wine left, so I sat in the grove and drank it, though it had no taste. I tried to make believe I was in Italy, long ago, the grapes around me, the heavy autumn night pressed close as a lover to the city. But I heard gusts of a band somewhere, or a rhythm tape elsewhere.

Catching the lights in the leaves, his silver skin glowed, though his hair only fired up when he was ten feet from me. I thought he was coming toward me and my heart stopped. Then I realized I was close to the non-moving stair going down to the street, and he was simply leaving the gardens, the guitar on its cord over one shoulder, and a blood-red cloak from the old Italy I'd been trying to go back to slung over the other.

He went by me and down the steps. He ran down them lightly. A eucalyptus tree screened him and he was gone.

My heart restarted with a bang that shook me to my feet.

Holding up my long skirt, I ran down the steps after him.

There were bright lights, and quite a few people out on the sidewalk, and cars hurtling by. All the shops and theatres and bars which stayed open flared their signs and their windows. And he passed through the lights and the neons and the people and the fumes of the traffic, now a slim dark silhouette, now a crimson and white one. He walked with a beautiful swagger. When a flyer went over like a prism, he put back his head to look at it. He *was* human, only his skin gave him away—and the skin might be makeup. He moved like an actor, why not paint himself like one? People on the street looked at him, looked after him. How many guessed? If they hadn't heard Electronic Metals' advertising, *no one.*

I followed him. Where was he going? I supposed he was pre-programmed to go back to—to what? A store? A factory? A warehouse? Did they put him away in a box? Turn off his eyes. Turn out the smile and the music.

A man snatched my arm. I snarled at him, surprising him, and myself. I broke into a run in my high-heeled shoes.

I caught up with the robot at the corner of Pane and Beech.

"I'm sorry," I said. I was out of breath, but not from running or balancing on my high heels. "I'm sorry."

He stopped, looking ahead of him. Then he turned slowly, and looked down at me.

"I'm sorry," I repeated quickly, blinded by the nearness of him, of his face. "I was rude to you. I shouldn't have said what I did."

"What," he asked me, "did you say?"

"You know what I said."

"Am I supposed to remember you?"

A verbal slap in the face. I should be clever and scornful. I couldn't be.

"You sang that song to embarrass me."

"Which song?"

"Greensleeves."

"No," he said, "I simply sang it."

"You stared at me."

"I apologize. I wasn't aware of you. I was concentrating on the last chord, which required complicated fingering."

"I don't believe you."

"I can't lie," he said.

Something jerked inside me, like a piece of machinery disengaging. My eyes refused to blink, had set in my face, felt huge, as if they had *swallowed* my face. *I* couldn't swallow at all.

"You—" I said. "You can't be allowed to act this way. I

was scared and I said something awful to you. And you froze me out and you walked away, and now—"

He watched me gravely. When I broke off, he waited, and then he said, "I think I must explain an aspect of myself to you. When something occurs that is sufficiently unlike what I'm programmed to expect, my thought process switches over. I may then, for a moment, appear blank, or distant. If you did something unusual, then that was what happened. It's nothing personal."

"I said," I said, my hands clenched together, "you're horrible. How dare you talk to me?"

"Yes," he said. His gaze unfocused, re-focused. "I remember you now. I didn't before. You started to cry."

"You're trying to upset me. You resent what I said. I don't blame you, but I'm sorry—"

"Please," he said quietly, "you don't seem to understand. You're attributing human reactions to me."

I backed a step away from him and my heel caught in a crack in the pavement. I seemed to unbalance very slowly, and in the middle of it, his hand took my elbow and steadied me. And having steadied me, the hand slipped down my arm, moving over my own hand before it left me. It was a caress, a tactful, unpushy, friendly caress. Preprogrammed. And the hand was cool and strong, but not cold, not metallic. Not unhuman, and not human, either.

He was correct. Not playing cruelly with me, as Clovis might have done. I had misunderstood everything. I had thought of him as a man. But he didn't care what I thought or did. It was impossible to insult or hurt him. He was a toy.

The heat in my face was white now. I stared at the ground.

"Excuse me," he said, "but I have to be at The Island by two A.M."

"Egyptia—" I faltered.

"I'll be staying with her tonight," he said. And now he smiled, openly, sweetly.

"You and she will go to bed," I got out.

"Yes."

He was a robot. He did what he was hired to do, or bought for. How could Eygptia—

"How can *you?*" I blurted.

I would never have said that to a man, for Egyptia's lovely. It would be obvious. But he, with him it was a task. And yet—

"My function," he said, "is to amuse, to make happy, to give pleasure." There was compassion in his face for me. He could see me struggling. I, too, a potential customer, must be pleased, amused, left laughing.

"I suppose you're a wonderful lover," I shocked myself by saying.

"Yes," he answered simply. A fact.

"I suppose you can—make love—as often as—as whoever hires you—wants."

"Of course."

"And sing songs while you're doing it."

He himself laughed. When he did, his whole person radiated a kind of joy.

"That's an idea."

Irony of the gentlest sort. And he hadn't remembered me. The wicked flatness of his eyes had been a readjustment of his thought cells. Of course. Who else had been averse to him?

I raised my head and my eyes looked into his, and there was no need to shy away from him because he was only a machine.

"I was at the party you were hired for. You're still hired, aren't you, until tomorrow? So." The last words didn't come out bravely, but in a whisper. "Kiss me."

He regarded me. He was totally still, serene. Then he

moved close to me, and took my face in his silver hands, and bowed his auburn head and kissed me with his silver mouth. It was a mannered kiss, not intimate. Calm, unhurried, but not long. All he owed me as Egyptia's guest. Then he stepped away, took up my hand and kissed that too, a bonus. And then he walked toward the subway, and left me trembling there. And so I knew what had been wrong all day.

I tell myself it's the electric current running through the clockwork mechanisms that I felt, as if a singing tide washed through me. His skin is poreless, therefore not human. Cooler than human, too. His hair is like grass. He has no scent, being without glands or hormones or blood. Yet there was a scent, male, heady and indefinable. Something incorporated, perhaps, to "please." And there was only him. Everything else became a backdrop, and then it went away altogether. And he went away, and nothing came back to replace him.

I've written this down on paper, because I just couldn't say it aloud to the tape. Tomorrow, my mother will ask what I wanted to discuss with her. But this isn't for my mother. It's for some stranger—for you, whoever you are—someone who'll never read it. Because that's the only way I could say any of it. I can't tell Demeta, can I?

He's a machine, and I'm in love with him.

He's with Egyptia, and I'm in love with him.

He's been packed up in a crate, and I'm in love with him.

Mother, I'm in love with a robot. . . .

CHAPTER TWO

Spoiled little rich girl. Always someone to do things for you. Always someone to rescue you. Your mother. Clovis. And always a castle in the clouds to run back to.

And now?

1

It's so dark, I can hardly see to write this, and I'm not certain why I'm writing it. Superstitiously, I think I believe I made everything happen by writing the first part of it down. And so, if I write another part of it, another part will come after. But things may only get worse. As if they could. But no, they could.

And then, somewhere inside myself, I don't care. I don't care about anything, because the thing I need is something else than what I've lost. And then again, I go on thinking, beyond this grimy darkness and the shadows like purple rust flaking on the page. I think about tomorrow and the next day, and I wonder what will become of me.

• • •

In the morning, at seven A.M., because I couldn't sleep, I got up and made a short tape for my mother. I said: "My problem was about Clovis and the callous way he treats his boyfriends, and about how M-Bs behave to each other anyway. But I'm over it now. I was just being silly."

It was not exactly the first time I'd lied to my mother. But it was the first time I knew I'd have to stick to the lie. I couldn't break down. I couldn't tell her. I couldn't decide if I was desperate, or only desperately ashamed. But I'd tried to cry myself out in the night, and by six A.M. the pillows were so wet I'd thrown them on the floor.

I knew there was no solution.

At eleven-thirty A.M., the video phone rang in the Vista. I knew who it was so I didn't answer. At noon, it rang again. Somehow it sounded louder. Soon my mother would emerge from her suite, and then I'd have to answer it, so I answered it.

Egyptia reclined in the video in a white kimono.

"Jane. You look terrible."

"I didn't sleep well."

"Neither did I. Oh Jane—"

She told me about Silver. She told me in enormous detail. I tried not to listen, but I listened. Beauty, acrobatics, tenderness, humor, prowess.

"Of course, the stamina, the knowledge, the artistry are built in. But I believed he was human. Oh, he's magic, Jane. It's ruined me for a man for weeks. But I nearly fainted this morning. So much ecstasy is destructive. I think I have a migraine attack. This awful pain in my temple. Oh, he should carry a government health warning, like the windows by the Old River."

A wire was stretching tighter and tighter in my spine, and the end of the wire was in my head. She hadn't said which temple had the migraine, so both my temples beat as narrow spikes ran through and through them. The room clouded. When the wire snapped in the middle I would scream.

"I checked my account to see if I could buy one, but I've overdrawn for this month. And then there's the Theatra. Oh, Jane. He's taught me so much about myself. He found such sensual nuances in me—I was a woman with him. That's so strange. He's a robot, but he made me feel more like a woman, more conscious of my desires, my needs, than any man ever did. But I had to beg him to stop—"

One of the spacemen entered with a breakfast tray for my mother, and I said, "My mother's just coming, Egyptia."

"Oh. All right. Call me back."

"Yes."

I turned off the phone and started to fall, but I landed on my knees in an attitude of prayer as my mother walked through the doors.

Even when she gets up, my mother is beautiful, her face empty of makeup and full of green eyes, her hair loose on her shoulders.

If only I could tell her—

"Hallo, darling."

"Hallo, Mother."

"Did you drop something under the couch, darling?"

"Oh—I—" I stood up. "I was speaking to Egyptia," I added, for this might well explain any strange behavior.

"In half an hour," said my mother, "you can tell me what it was you wanted to talk to me about."

"I—"

I must tell her, I must.

No, no, no.

"I left a tape. But it doesn't seem important now. Mother, I'm so tired. I have to go back to bed."

Shut in my suite, I wept all over again. How I needed,

how I wanted to tell her what had happened to me. She'd be able to rationalize it all. She would show me why I felt as I did, and how to get over it.

Thank God Egyptia couldn't buy him this month.

How horrible, to sleep with—

I shut my eyes and knew his kiss again on my mouth, that silver metal kiss.

I fell asleep lying on the wet pillows on the floor, and I dreamed of all kinds of things, but not of Silver.

At two P.M., my mother called my suite on the internal phone, and asked me to have lunch with her in the Vista. My mother was very concerned about my having privacy, and the feeling that I could be alone when I wished; she never simply knocked on the door. But I felt I had to go down, so I went down and we ate lunch.

"You're very quiet, darling. Has anything else happened that you want to tell me about?"

"Nothing, really. Was the dinner interesting?"

My mother told me about the dinner, and I tried to hear what she said. Sometimes what she said was very funny and I laughed. I kept beginning to say to her, "I've fallen in love," and preventing myself. I imagined saying: "I'd like to buy a special format robot." Would my mother let me? Generally, I pay for things I want with a credit card that links into my mother's own account, but there was a monthly one thousand I.M.U. limit on the card. This was just so I'd appreciate about not overspending, because my mother always made it quite clear that what was hers was mine. But she wanted me to be sensible. A verisimulated robot would cost thousands. The ionized silver alone would cost thousands. A purchase like that wouldn't seem sensible at all.

In any case, if Egyptia hadn't bought him, someone else had. He belonged to *them.* To an Egyptia, or an Austin. Did he enjoy giving joy? What happened to *him* when he made love?

After lunch, my mother switched on the news channel of the Vista visual, and took notes. She's a political and sociological essayist and historian, too, but mainly as a hobby. There had been another bad subsidence in the Balkans. Social collapse seemed likely again in Eastern Europe, but reports were garbled. An earthquake had rocked the top off a mountain somewhere. There were subsistence riots in five Western cities. My mother didn't switch to the local news channel, which might have carried something about the Sophisticated Format robots, but when she switched the visual off my throat had closed together with nerves.

Then I realized she'd made a sacrifice to be with me, since generally she watches the visual in her study. She must guess something was wrong, and I didn't really know how long I could hold out. What would she say if I told her? "Darling, this would be quite all right if you were sexually experienced. But you're a virgin. And to make love, initially, with a nonhuman device, is by no means a good idea. For all sorts of complicated reasons. Firstly, your own psychological needs. . . ." I could just distinguish her voice in my head. And she'd be right. How could I ever hope to have a proper relationship with a man if I began by going to bed with a robot? (He *is* a man. No, fool, he isn't. He *is*.)

I went down to the library and took a book, and sat in the balcony-balloon watching the sky drifting out from the house and fathoming away in a luminous nothingness below me. And eventually I seemed to be hanging by a string over the nothingness, and I had to move from the balcony, and go back to my suite and lie down on the bed. It was the only time I'd ever had vertigo in Chez Stratos, though Clovis won't visit us, saying all the while he's in the house he can feel his groin falling farther and farther away below him.

Finally I called Clovis, not knowing what to say.

"Hallo?" said Austin invisibly. Clovis has never incorporated a video.

"Oh. Hallo. This is Jane."

"James?"

"Jane. Can I speak to—"

"No. He's in the shower."

Austin sounded like a fixture, despite the seance, if a not very happy one.

"Is that a *woman?*" Austin demanded.

"It's Jane."

"I thought you said James. Well, look, Jayven, why don't you call later. Like next year?" And he switched off.

As a matter of course, then, I dialed Chloe, but she didn't answer. I looked at Jason and Medea's number, but didn't dial it.

My mother called me on the internal phone.

"I've run your tape, Jane. It's rather vague. What did Clovis do?"

"He had another seance."

"And this disturbed you."

"Only because he plays with people like a cat."

"Cats don't play with people. Cats play with mice. The seance table is rigged, I seem to recall."

"Yes, Mother."

"The spirit world can be reached, under the correct circumstances," said my mother.

"Oh, you mean ghosts."

"I mean the psychic principle. A soul, Jane. You mustn't be afraid to use the correct terminology. A released soul, unattached to the physical state, and which has lived through many lives and a diversity of bodies, may sometimes wish to communicate with the world.

There was a great incidence of this at the turn of the century, for example, prior to the Asteroid Disasters. A theologian notes a connection. Clovis shouldn't be meddling with table-tappings."

"No, Mother."

"I've left you some vitamins in the dispenser. Robot three will give them to you when you come down."

"Thank you."

"And now, I must get ready."

Having avoided her for hours in terror of giving away my awful secret, I was now stricken with horror.

"Are you going out?"

"Yes, Jane. You know I am. I'm going upstate for three days. The Phy-Amalgamated Conference."

"I'd—I'd forgotten—Mother—I really must speak to you after all."

"Darling, you've had all day to speak to me."

"Only four hours."

"I really can't stop now."

"It's urgent."

"Then tell me quickly."

"But I can't!"

"Then you should have spoken earlier."

"Oh Mother!" I burst into tears. Where did so many tears come from? A lot of the human body is water. Did I have any left?

"Jane, I'm going to make an appointment for you with your private doctor."

"I'm not ill. I'm—"

"Jane. I will take half an hour away from my schedule. I will come up to your suite now, and we'll talk this through. Do you agree?"

Panic. Panic.

The door opened, and my mother, already burnished, pomaded, glittering, stepped through. An abyss gaped before me. And behind me. I could no longer think. I'd always, always leaned on my mother. Was anything so perverse, so precarious, so precious I couldn't share it with her, especially now she'd wrecked her schedule for me?

"As precisely as you can, dear," said Demeta, beckoning me into her arms, into *La Verte*, into bliss and anchorage. "Now, does this have anything to do with Clovis?"

"Mother, I'm in love!" I tumbled against her, but not too hard. I could tell her. I *could*. "Mother, I'm in love." No, I couldn't. "Mother, I'm in love with Clovis," I shrieked.

"Good Lord," said my mother.

2

It was almost six P.M. when I did what, of course, I had been bound to do virtually from the start. My mother had at last gone, and I had plunged deep in my lagoon of guilt because I'd lied to her this terribly, and—much worse—made her late. She really is so concerned to do the best for me. It's her grail, or one of them. Luckily, I was able to plaster over my lie very swiftly. "I know Clovis is M-B and will never return my feelings," I'd said, again and again. "It's just a silly crush. I've done what you taught me, and gone through my own psychological motivations. I'm almost over it. But I had to let you know. I always feel better when I tell you things." Oh, how could I cheat her of the facts like that? Why should I have felt so sure I mustn't reveal the truth? Eventually she mixed me a sedative and she left me. The sedative was whipped-strawberry flavor, and I was tempted to drink it, but I didn't. Quite suddenly, about ten minutes after I heard the Baxter rumble up out of the roof-hatch, and the Vista had stopped vibrating, what I had said about loving Clovis abruptly struck me as hilarious, and I howled with laughter, rolling all over the couch. It was, possibly, the stupidest thing I could have come up with, even in sheer desperation. One day I might tell him, and Clovis would howl, too.

When I stopped laughing, I keyed the alcohol dispenser and got it to pour me one of the martinis my mother likes. I had another bath, and put on a black dress, and plugged in the hairdresser unit and let it put rollers in my hair. My face in the mirror was white, and my eyes, too dark to be properly green, were almost black. I don't like makeup, actually. It feels sticky on my skin, and sometimes I forget I'm wearing it and rub my hands over my cheeks and smear my rouge. But there was a lot of mascara left on I hadn't taken off last night or cried off this morning. It's supposed to be runproof, and it partly is. I tidied it and added some more, and crayoned my mouth Autumn Beech Leaf. I drank the salty martini, pretending I liked it, and the hairdresser took out the rollers and brushed my hair, and I painted my nails black. All of which, in a way, tells you what I was about to do.

When I dialed the robot operator, my hands and my voice were shaking.

"What number do you require?"

"The number of Electronic Metals Ltd."

"At your service."

The video shook with me, in little lines of light, then cleared. There was a small blank area with a man projected like a cutout on it, in one of those four-piece suits, jacket, pants, waistcoat and shirt of a matching pale grey silky material, and tinted glasses on a classic nose. He looked cheerfully at me, his manicured hands holding on tight to each other. A small sign lit up in front of him, which said: SWOHNSON.

"Swohnson of Electronic Metals. How can I help you?"

And he beamed and licked his lips. He was eager. For a sale?

"This is just an inquiry," I said. I pitched my voice over its own cracks and tremors. "You *are* the firm that sent those robots out into the city yesterday?"

"Er, yes. Yes. Electronic Metals. That's us."

"The special and the Sophisticated formats?"

"The specials. Twenty-four models. Metal and reinforced plastic. Sophisticated Format line. All-metal. Nine models. What was your inquiry?"

My white face flamed, but perhaps he couldn't see it.

"I'm interested in the cost of hire."

"Hire not sale. Er. We're thinking of cutting back on that."

"I happen to know one of the Sophisticated line was hired last night."

"Oh, yes. They all were. But that was part of the, ah, the advertising campaign. A one day, one night venture. These robots are really for exhibition only. At the present."

"Not for sale."

"Ah. Sale might be a different matter. Did you have purchase in mind?"

I wouldn't let him upstage me. For some reason, he was as nervous as I was.

"No. I had hire in mind. Let me speak to the Director."

"Ah—just wait a moment—I'm not trying to give a bad impression here." Human employee, a good job, worried about losing it. I felt mean. "Ah. We have a few problems at this end."

"With the robots."

"With, er, transportation."

"Your robots are locomotive. They were walking all over the city like people yesterday. If I hire one, why can't it just walk out of the door with me?"

"Um. Between ourselves, not everyone likes the idea of what these magnificent robots can do. A further threat to the last bastions of human employment potential. You know the sort of thing. Bit of a crowd. Bit of trouble."

"Trouble?"

"The, ah, the police have arrived. But it's a peaceful demonstration, so far. Until any violence breaks out, the crowd probably can't be moved. And if it does break out—well, we'd rather none of our merchandise was in the thick of it—Ah!" He glanced downward, and his eyes behind the tinted spectacles bulged. A white glow was playing over his chin and through the sign with his name. I realized a message panel must have lit up out of sight on his desk console. The message didn't look as if it was very comforting. "Um," he said. "I, er, think I said more than I ought. Ha, ha. Look, madam, I'll patch you through to our contact department on relay. Leave your code and number and E.M. can call you tomorrow to discuss your wishes. Just hold, if you will, and I'll put you through."

The video fluttered, and I hit the switch wildly.

And why did I do that? Maybe only because tomorrow was a hundred years away, and would be too late.

And what now?

I walked along the Vista, past all the bubbles of sky, and back again. It was a red dog-end of a sunset tonight. Claret-colored, like Silver's cloak. Like Silver's hair.

I thought about the subsistence riots on the news channel. They say no one can really live on a sub. check. Sometimes robot circuits were vandalized by the frenzied unemployed, though usually the built-in alarms and defense electric-shock mechanisms deter vandals. But the news channel had reported a machinery warehouse had burned down in one riot. That was thousands of miles away. But suppose the peaceful crowd outside Electronic Metals got out of hand? Not water, but fire. His face, like a wax angel's, dissolving—

I ran to the phone and called Clovis again.

"This is Clovis's answering tape. Right now Clovis is committing sodomy. Call back in an hour, when I regret you may still receive the same answer."

(Clovis, actually, leaves this message even if he's gone out to a restaurant, or to the beach for a week. Davideed, who once got the message over and over for two days, rushed to the New River apartment and shouted at the door, which was locked. And when one of Clovis's discarded, left-behind, just-packing-to-leave lovers opened it, Davideed hit him.)

The sunset turned to hot ashes, and then to cold ones. The night would gather in the city and the lights would flower. The crowd waiting outside Electronic Metals would begin to understand how pretty buildings look when they burn in the dark.

I switched on the local news channel. They talked about a new subway to be built, about a gang fight near the Old River, about a rise in cigarine prices due to the heavy crop losses in one of the more earthquake-active zones. Then I heard and saw the crowd, which had gathered in East Arbor around the gates of Electronic Metals Ltd., and they were growing restless. People shouted before the shabby glass facade. The newscaster told me about robots, how they're important, and why workers hate them. The news didn't seem to have grasped that E.M.'s robots were different. Or perhaps they were just trying not to advertise. The crowd went on shouting. There only appeared to be a couple of hundred people. Enough to start a fire. But I would be safe. The policode I wore would protect me, with its guaranty that it takes exact body-readings of anyone who assaults the wearer, while instantly summoning the police. There were police anyway, watching the crowd. I could see their little planes going over and back against the deepening sky of dusk in the screen, and sometimes their lights played on the building and the people.

But if I were there, what would I do? What difference could I make? It was pointless to go, to be there. If I negotiated the mob, who would open E.M.'s door to me with all that outside? I might be a ringleader determined to force an entry.

I left the news channel on as I walked up and down the Vista. Then someone threw a bottle. The camera followed it. It hit the facade of Electronic Metals and shattered.

Outside, across the Canyon, the seven P.M. flyer would be floating like a moth toward the platform. In fifteen minutes I could be over the Old River, in twenty I could be getting off at South Arbor, running the three blocks to East. The Arbors are a rough area, a big trash can of derelict offices and subsided stories not yet rebuilt after the Asteroid tremors, with, here and there, a nightclub perched like a vulture deliberately on the ruins, or some struggling enterprise starting up in a renovated warehouse, with a frontage of sprayed-on glass.

If I let the flyer go, there wouldn't be another one until nine P.M. If I dialed a cab, I might have to wait for half an hour.

The police would stop anything from happening, and I could do nothing, and here was my unfinished martini, and there my strawberry sedative, and here my purse with my credit card with the thousand I.M.U. a month limit on it, which meant I could not afford a robot. It would be much better if I stayed at home. Much better if I forgot about everything. Starting with the first sight of his hair and the mirror fragments on his jacket, ending with the kiss which had meant nothing to him because he couldn't feel emotion, except, perhaps, the delight of giving, for which he was randomly pre-programmed.

I almost missed the flyer. There were twenty or so other travelers on it, some in gaudy evening clothes going to the city for a night out, some with grey harried faces, night workers going in to work at some job a robot couldn't do. But the mechanical driver was without a head.

I don't recall seeing the city appear in its constellations, or even getting off at the South Arbor platform. I think there were some docile men drinking on a corner as I ran. And then the sky over my head was full of little robot planes, a swarm of them with their lights blinking and their sirens hooting, and buzzing away into the city center.

Almost instantly I met with a stream of people jeering and swearing and arguing. A board trailed on the ground. By means of stray street lamps I read: SCREW THE MACHINES. The surge broke around me to let me through, or else pushed me aside out of its way, and was gone. Bits of glass, scraps of paper, were left in its wake. It seemed the demonstration had lost heat, or been compulsorily broken up before real violence erupted. A solitary police cab cruised up the uneven concrete, showered me over with its spots, registering my code, and nosed on after the crowd, leaving me in the long shadows between the erratic lamp poles.

When I came to it, the gate of Electronic Metals, illumined now in rainbow neon, stood open. Another police car lurked on the forecourt. A knot of human beings huddled in a corner, lost in debate, sometimes caught by a winking light on the police machine that constantly circled them.

It was a strange scene, one I'd often looked at on a

visual, or in a side street, but never been part of. But I walked through the gate and across the forecourt. No one paid any attention to me. I touched the visitor's panel in the door. A luminous dot appeared. It said softly: "This building is now closed." Since most display warehouses in the city are mechanically staffed and stay open all night, eager for custom, I wondered if E.M. had closed itself for good in dismay.

"I called earlier," I said to the door panel. "I'm interested—in buying one of your Sophisticated Format robots."

"Please visit, or telephone, tomorrow."

"I've come twenty miles," I said, as if that meant anything.

"Due to unforeseen circumstances," said the door, "this building is now closed. Please visit, or telephone, tomorrow."

Quite without warning, my legs changed to air, to nothing: I had no legs. I slid down the door and sat in the dirty shadows of the portico, in my black dress. I might have been a robot with my power switched off. I, too, might have been closed for the night.

Presently the people and the police went away. I went on sitting on the ground, like a lost child who doesn't know the way home. I knew I ought to get up and go and find a taxi. If I stayed here, another police patrol might pick me up, thinking I was ill.

Beyond the gate, I could see the Asteroid burning like a green-blue flaw in the darkness. The skeleton of a tremor-smashed apartment block teetered on a slope, stripped of lives like a winter tree of leaves. I saw it this way, knowing the insecurity of life as I never had before. How smug, how complacent I'd been. Egyptia was right to be afraid.

If I went home, I'd get into bed in my suite in Chez

Stratos, I'd pull the green sheets over my head, and I'd never have the courage to come back here. For all I knew, they'd dismantled him. An exhibition robot. Perhaps there was a fault somewhere, the man on the video—Swohnson—had sounded so unsure. Was it more than the unemployment demo? There were always demonstrations. Perhaps the City Senate had approached Electronic Metals and vetoed this omen of ultimate redundancy, men who excelled men in every way.

Finally, I got up, and dusted off my dress carefully, though I couldn't see properly, even in the neon from the open gate.

What happened next was odd, because it was almost as if I made it happen, somehow. I suddenly concluded that the open gate was a mistake the mechanism left unattended in the confusion, for if the building was shut, so should the gate be. And then I judged how somebody would have to come back and shut it. And about one second after that, a lean black picard drove through onto the forecourt, pulled up, and a man got out. Two lightnings streaked over his upper face—the neon shining in his spectacle lenses. He almost walked into me, and grunted with surprise. He fumbled at his jacket.

"I'm coded," he said. "Don't try anything."

It was Swohnson.

"Are you going," he said, "or do I, ah, signal the police?"

It would have been nice to say something razor-sharp and succinct. Clovis would have. But it was my mouth, not my wit, that was dry.

"I called you. You spoke to me on the video, earlier."

"Threats won't do you any good."

In a moment he would press his silly code button.

I blurted rapidly: "I decided I'd buy one of the formats."

"Uh—oh," said Swohnson. "Oh," he said, shifting so he could see the candy neon on my face. "Madam, I do apologize. But I never thought you'd come here, after the operator cut us off."

His indiscretion with me before had caused a row, perhaps, and now he might redeem himself with a sale. Or was he just feeling unorthodox?

"I came back to lock up," said Swohnson. "Dogsbody, that's me." He palmed the door panel. He had been drinking. "Director's daughter's lover," he said, "that's me, too. My qualifications. How I got the job. Liaison, public relations, locker-up of doors. But I mustn't put all this onto you, madam." The door recognized him and opened with a sullen hiss. "Please walk inside."

He thought I was a rich eccentric. The rich part was easy. It's awful, the way we have this look to us, of being rich. Eccentric because I waited in doorways in East Arbor, alone, on the off chance people like Swohnson would come by to shut the gate.

In the foyer, which was also glass-sprayed and dismal, he hit some switches and saw to the gate, and summoned a lift. Then he took me up to the shop floor.

The place we came into was a tepid office in leather, and by now my bluff was already turning cold inside me, congealing. I told myself I could back out, so long as I didn't handprint or sign anything, or as long as I didn't record my assent verbally on tape. He'd need my permission for any of those. Or, if I did, maybe Demeta would have to honor the transaction? Maybe it would be clever to do just that. But basically I hate lying, big lies. It's so complicated.

He sat in a chair and a drinks tray came out of the wall. We had a drink. His hands trembled, and my hands trembled. But both our hands still trembled on our second drinks, his around the rye whisky, mine around the lemon juice. I guess we had both, in our different ways, had a rough day. He told me all about Electronic Metals, but I don't remember what he said. I had to pretend I was alert, or thought I did, the prospective buyer making sure everything was in order, and all my concentration went into that. I think I heard one word in twenty. I still couldn't quite believe I'd gotten into the building.

"There's an exhibition formula we have here," he said, and I heard that because instinctively I knew it was a prelude to the display of E.M.'s wares. "I dreamed it up myself, actually, to show off the three types to full advantage. If you'll step through?" He drained his glass, took another, and held my arm as one of the walls folded back. "Excuse me, madam, but you're ver-ry young."

"I'm eighteen." Should I have tried for twenty?

"Gorgeous age, eighteen. Can just remember it, I think." (It occurs to me now, writing it out, that he may have been making a halfhearted pass at me. He was attractive in a stereotyped way, and knew he was attractive and not that he was stereotyped, merely in the mode. And he'd made it with a rich girl before. Perhaps he thought I'd be useful, somehow, if I fell for him and poured cash over him. How embarrassing. I never even thought of this at the time.) "Actually, um, I think I know which of the Formats you'll choose. It's proficient in pre-Ast. oriental dance—one of the female Golder range. But wait till you see."

He knew I wasn't even eighteen. He thought me an innocent, even if he made a pass, unless he thought I was M-B. How would I be able to tell him now, past the barriers in my throat and soul, that my chosen robot was masculine?

Riven with my shyness, I moved away from his guiding hand, and into the area beyond the reception office. It was a large room we entered, windowless, with a soft suffused light all over the ceiling. The floor was polished.

"Don't step beyond the red line," said Swohnson. "Let's just sit here and see what happens." Proud of his innovation in the boss's workshop, he waved us into tubular chairs. Obviously that activated a control somewhere. A slot opened in the far wall, and a woman came through.

She was tall and slender and beautiful. Hair blond as cereal haloed her head and shoulders. Her tawny-yellow cat's eyes fastened on mine and she smiled. She was pleased to see me, you could tell. A dress like a tulip flame swathed her, and she held a purple rose. Her skin was a pale creamy copper.

"Hallo," she said. "I'm one of Electronic Metals' experimental range. My registration is Copper. That is C.O.P.P.E.R.: Copper Optimum Pre-Programmed Electronic Robot." She half closed her eyes. A stillness seemed to enfold her. The music of her voice grew hushed, hypnotic. "Gallop apace," she said, "you fiery footed steeds, to Phoebus' lodging. . . ." She spoke Juliet's lines in a way I never heard before. The air scintillated, my eyes filled with tears. She spoke of love, knew love, *was* love. ". . . If he should die, take him and cut him out in little stars, and he will make the face of heaven so fine that all the world will be in love with night—" Two men stepped through the wall. They were Copper's brothers. One wore a jacket of yellow velvet with medieval sleeves, and white denim jeans. The other wore damson jeans, a sauterne-colored shirt, and a magenta sash from the Arabian Nights. Each smiled at me. Each told me he, too, was registration Copper. They acted a scene together from a drama I'd sat through the month before. It far outshone the original performance. The three copper robots linked arms, bowed smiling to me, and went back through the wall, which closed.

The left hand wall opened.

A man strode through. Hair like smooth black ink, splashing over his head to his shoulders. Black silk eyes. Skin like molten gold. He wore black, his cloak lined with the green of sour apples. His registration, he told me, was Golder: G.O.L.D.E.R.: Gold Optimum Locomotive Dermatized Electronic Robot. His eyes smoldered at me, burning through to my deepest awareness. He flung himself suddenly into an aerial cartwheel that flowed and sliced, and landed in strange graceful menacing ripplings and contortions of his frame. It was a dance, but a dance capable of dealing death.

"Based on Japanese martial arts," Swohnson muttered to me. "Not only elegant, but will make an excellent bodyguard for someone who likes that kind of show. And particularly good skinlinings in this type." Having started to talk, Swohnson didn't stop. As the golden midnight figure swirled and leapt, Swohnson said, "the Copper line are the actors, the Silvers the musicians, the Golds are dancers." He went on, and I forgot to listen. Two women, the golden robot's sisters, came into the room, their hands lightly connected, and repeated who they were. Their long fingers had long nails, one set jade green, one set jade white. Their trousers were Asian, cream silk, green silk. Above the trousers one wore a bolero and gold-embroidered shirt. The other a waistcoat of emerald spangles, fastened with three malachite butterflies. The dance was slow, incredible, balletic, impossible. Human muscles would have evaporated and human bones dislocated. Their black hair mopped the floor and furled over the ceiling. "Jetté, lift measured at seven feet from the ground. But they make good teachers. Charming teachers. Wonderful exercise for the human body, even if you can never be as good. My God, they *are* good, aren't they?" Swohnson drank his rye and sighed. His attitude to the

Golder female robots was not innocent, as mine was expected to be.

They went away, and my heart burst, disintegrated, as it had begun to do when the Coppers went out. I was waiting for the third door to open. This time, it would have to be—

It opened. Silver's sister came through. Her auburn hair was dressed with blue carnations. She wore snow fringed with blood. A keyboard glided after her on runners. She stood before it, and played something I didn't know, like a shower of sparks shooting from a volcano. Then she looked at me, smiling. I knew what she'd say. "I'm Silver. . . ."

A man walked through the opening, and I stopped breathing. Because it wasn't him. Alike, but not like. The same hair, but different. The same amber eyes; different, different. The movements, the voice, the same, the same, yet different. Different, different. Utterly, wholly different. Not like at all. I forget what he wore. I couldn't seem to see him properly.

"I'm Silver. S.I.L. . . ."

The features of the face weren't even similar. I was so glad, I could have wept. The silver woman played Vivaldi on the electric piano and the silver man sang a futuristic melody against it, in a beautiful, unrecognized voice. The words were about a star, a girl in love with the star, and the star saying to the girl, "I am too old for you."

"Dammit," said Swohnson. "Where's the other one?"

My eyes blurred. The silver robots were walking into the wall.

"There's another of the bloody things. I beg your pardon, er, madam. It's been a helluva day. These exhibition models are in blocks of three. There's a third one with the silvers. A guy. Damn. Wrecks the whole display. He's supposed to come in with a guitar. God. You spend days and nights dreaming up these gimmicks, and then the relay screws it. Excuse me." He went to a wall phone and hit buttons unsteadily. He'd forgotten I would want the Golder format. He was angry because his artistic interpretation had been spoiled.

My eyes were filming over. The lemon juice had a smoky taste. Where is the third silver robot? Where? Where? Oh, he's in bits, taken apart. Piece of wiring fouled, cog busted. Have to scrap it. Put it in the dustbin. Melt it down. Make it into objets d'art for rich bitches like this fourteen-year-old I've got in here right now.

Don't be stupid. Why are you so obsessed with the idea that he has been . . . taken to bits.

How could I have—

Swohnson was spluttering at the phone.

"What? Why wasn't I told? When? Um. Um? I didn't see it."

Then he came back from the phone. He looked at me.

"Well, you can judge anyway, bright, er, lady like you. You don't need to see that other one. He's just like the other male silver. Of course, some customers would want to see the full physique. Stripped. But really, madam—do I have to keep calling you that?—I don't think that's your problem. Is it?"

I gripped the tube arms of the chair, and refused to think about what he'd just said.

"The other robot," I said.

"Oh, some damn machine left me a memo. Never got it. Something they're checking for. Er—nothing wrong with the model, you understand." Even drunk, he recalled his valuable-employee's lines just in time. "It's a routine check E.M. runs when we put any display mechanism out. We're very thorough. The slightest thing—we've been testing, perfecting these models for years. How else could we let them roam the city without escort? (Which, actually, I thought was taking a bit of a risk, but, ah, who the hell listens to me around here?) Still. Looks good. Then, um, of course, one comes back and doesn't check out."

"What—" I said. I didn't know what to say. How do you ask after a robot's health? I was shaking, shaking. I tried to be my mother. "What's wrong with this one?"

"Nothing. Nothing the E.M. computer can pin down. Just some of the readings are altered. Nothing that affects any of the other, er, models, I can assure you, ah, of that. You know computers. An eyelash out of place . . . I don't understand a word of that side of it. Jargon. Nothing for *you* to worry about. There's a makeshift check they'll run here. Then tomorrow it'll go down to the production center."

"Where?"

"The production center? The basement. Curious little thing, aren't you, madam? Can't take you there, I'm afraid. Big hush-hush. Lose me my wonderful enviable job as doorman."

"The robot," I said, "this one, the one that doesn't check out, is the—one I wanted to buy." Oh God, how did I ever get it out? His eyes goggled. I swallowed. I couldn't tell if I was red or white, but cold heat was all over my face, my body. I tried to be self-assured in the middle of the raging of the cold heat and the shaking, and in my breathless, stilted voice: "He was recommended to me by a friend. He's the one I wanted. The only one." And then, while Swohnson went on standing there gaping, "If the format is still up here, I'd like to see him. It. I'd like to see it now."

"Ah," said Swohnson. Suddenly he smiled, remembering about whisky, and drinking some. And getting some more. "Er, how old did you say you were?"

"Eighteen. Almost nineteen."

"You see why I'm asking? To buy an item of goods like

this, not just a servant but a companion, a performer . . . in all sorts of ways, you have to be over eighteen. Or we need your mother's signature. What's your name?"

"My name isn't any of your business," I said, amazing myself. "Not until I agree to buy. And I haven't, because the one robot I want you can't give me."

"Didn't say that, did I?"

"Then let me see him."

"Keep calling it 'him,' don't you. Must make a note of that. Most of the callers we've had do. Him, her. Really got you all fooled, ain't we. Good old E.M. Good old my lover's daddy."

I shrank, but somehow I kept hold.

"Are you going to let me see him?"

"Visiting the sick," said Swohnson, viciously hitting on the exact horrid sensation I had, and hadn't been able to explain to myself. "Okay. Come on. Madam. Let's go and see the patient."

Rye in hand, he led me, no longer opening doors for me which were not automatic, so they almost banged in my face each time. I couldn't go back now and find the way—I didn't see it. We came into a corridor with unlit cubicles. Then into a cubicle that made a humming noise, and, as Swohnson's white suede shoes went over the threshold, switched a light on. A cold light, very stark and pale, like in a hospital theatre in a visual.

There was a thing like a closed upright coffin, with wires coming out of holes and into a box that was ticking and whirring to itself.

"There you are," said Swohnson. "Just press that knob there, and you can see it. In all its glory."

I was afraid to, and I didn't move for a long time.

Then I walked over and touched the knob, and the machine stopped making a noise, and the front of the coffin slid slowly up. There's no point in dragging this out, though I don't like putting it down on paper, no I don't. The figure in the checking coffin was swathed in a sort of flaccid opaque plastic bag, to which the wires were attached. Only the head was visible at the top of the bag. And it was Silver's head, clouded round by auburn hair, but under the long dark cinnamon eyebrows were two sockets with little slim silver wheels going round and round in them, truly just like the inside of a clock.

"You can see a bit more, if you like," said Swohnson, spitefully. He went to the bag and split a seam somewhere, and so I saw the shoulder and the arm of a silver skeleton, and more of the little wheels turning, but no hand. That had been removed. Swohnson painstakingly pointed this out.

"Special check on the fingers. Important in a musician model. Wonder what else has gone?" He peered into the bag.

I remembered Silver as he played the guitar and sang the songs that were like fires, the fiery chords. I remembered how he kissed Egyptia, and ran lightly down the stair in the gardens with the claret velvet cloak swinging, and how he sauntered along the street, and put back his head to watch the flyer go over, and how he rested his mouth on mine.

"Not very glamorous now, is it?" said Swohnson.

Something odd was happening to me. I felt it uncertainly in my confusion, and got to know it, and was dully, stonily, relieved. I'd been cured of my crush. Of course. Who wouldn't be?

"No," I said to Swohnson. "It's a mess."

And I turned and walked out of the room.

I waited in the corridor, no longer shaking, until—disappointed—he slunk out and guided me back to the office, where I told him I'd think about it, and when he protested, I said: "I'll have to ask my mother."

"Goddamn. I *knew* you were a minor. Wasting my time—"

"Let me out," I said.

"You little—"

"Let me out, or I'll use my policode."

"Just looking for kicks. I'd *like* to kick you. Rich kid. Never needed to do a day's work in your, ah, life."

"My mother," I said, "knows E.M.'s Director, intimately."

Swohnson stared at me. He didn't believe me, but nevertheless he dimly began to try to recollect everything he'd said about the Director, father of his girlfriend, and E.M., and what he thought of them. And as he did so, he absentmindedly got the lift for me.

I went down, coolly. Self-possessed. I went into the forecourt and the gate opened for me. Not wavering, I walked out. The gate didn't close behind me, and I smiled a superior smile because he'd forgotten to auto-lock it, again.

3

I felt twenty-five. I felt sophisticated. I was free of my silliness, my adolescent dreams. I could do anything I wanted now. What a fool I'd been. I was proud of myself, for coming through, for growing old and wise, and for liberating myself. My mother's training was at last paying off, and I was a whole person. I *understood* myself.

I thought about Silver, and was faintly sorry for it, not that it had any emotions. But all in bits like that, though they would put him, it, together again, skin-spray over the joints to keep the smoothness of the muscles and complexion. Re-articulate. I wondered for half a second what it must be like for him, it, in a bag, a coffin—then realized it didn't know anything about it, having been shut off like a lamp. Tomorrow they'd put it in the basement and take it *all* to bits, and maybe not reassemble it.

I rode the escalator up on to Patience Maidel Bridge, and walked over the Old River in the oxygenated glass tunnel, sometimes stopping to watch the lights of apartment blocks reflecting downward into the poisoned water, or the gleaming river boats with their glass tops and wakes of foam and snarling mutated fish. There were three or four people busking on the bridge, as there often are. They were all quite good. One was juggling in time to music a girl played on a mandolin. One had a marvelous voice. Not, of course, as good as the robot's voice.

Off the bridge, there had been a break-in at Staria's Second Owner Emporium, and another at Finn Darl's Food-o-Mart, a soup of police and flashing lights and hospital wagons. A giant can of baked fruit had rolled into the road and was being flung away from each rushing car, into the path of another.

I was blasé. I knew the violence of the city, and the uneven quality of its life. I took a bus to Jagged's and went into the restaurant for iced coffine, and as I drew the first sip through the chocolate-flavored straw, someone pinched my arm.

"You're out late," said Medea, seating herself opposite me.

"Does your mother know?" said Jason, seating himself next to her.

They both watched me with their narrow eyes.

I hadn't choked at the ferocious pinch, I had been through too much to let a pinch bother me, was too collected, or perhaps anesthetized.

"My mother's upstate."

"Ooh," said Medea. "Naughty goings-on at Chez Stratos."

Like Egyptia, Medea had had her hair toned dark blue,

but unlike Egyptia's long silken rope, Medea's hair had been crimped and crinkled. Jason's hair was coloressence charted, a sort of beige, and he had a deep tan from surfing at Cape Angel. But Medea just lies under a black sunshade and never tans. I never know why they're my friends, because they're not.

"Did you go to see the anti-robot demo?" I asked. I knew they hadn't, and I said it deliberately, to bask in my uninvolvement.

"What demo?" said Medea.

"Oh, those robots that are supposed to look like people," said Jason. "Some morons making a fuss. How long is your mother away?" Jason asked me.

"Not long."

"Why not have a party before she comes back?"

"She's *much* too good to do that," said Medea.

"Are you?" Jason demanded.

"Yes," I said.

"You're getting very fat," said Medea. "Why don't you come off those capsules? I'm supposed to be a Eunice Ultima—terribly thin. But I just put the pills in the disposal."

I was twenty-five and clever. For once, I knew I was only a little plump.

"Why don't you try red hair for a change?" Jason said to me.

That was odd. My stomach turned over. Had Jason heard about my silliness? I hoped not. Jason liked to gain an advantage. When I was a child, he took care of me once when I was frightened. He was my age, but he was very kind, or seemed to be. But he liked the power. Later the same day he tried to frighten me again, just so he could reassure me. He'd do that sort of thing a lot. He used to have several little pets, and they were always getting sick so he had to care for them. But then they would get sick again, and one day Jason's father—Jason and Medea have a father—stopped Jason from having pets. Since then he's played with electric gadgets instead.

"She won't do anything Mother doesn't want," said Medea.

She got up again, and Jason got up too, as if he were attached to her by a string. She's sixteen and a half, and he is sixteen. They were born by the Precipta Split-Tempo method, and are really twins.

"Good-bye, Jane," said Jason politely.

"Good-bye, Jane," said Medea.

They went out, and the robot waiter came over on its tripod of wheels and charged me with Jason and Medea's bill, which they'd told it I'd be paying. Not that they couldn't pay it, it was just a joke. So I joked too, and refused, and gave the waiter their address. Their father would be furious (again), and normally I wouldn't have done such a thing, just paid for them. But tonight. Oh, tonight, I had wings.

Worlds flying like birds; my car's in flight. The city lights are spattered on my windshield like the fragments of the night. And I'm in flight. The sky's a wheel, a merry-go-round of wings and snow and steel, and fire. We'll tread the sky, we'll ride the scarlet horses—

What was *that?* A song—what—what—Silver's song.

I left the waiter robot and my unfinished coffine. I went into a booth and dialed Clovis.

"Infirmary," said Clovis, cautiously.

"Hallo," I said.

"Thank God. I thought it was Austin ringing back."

"Clovis," I said.

"Yes, Jane," said Clovis.

"Clovis," I said. "Clovis. Clovis."

A pause.

"What's the matter?" he asked me so gently his voice was, for a second, like the voice, the voice—

"Clovis, you see—Clovis—Clovis—"

"Where's your mother?"

"She's—away. Clovis—"

"Yes, I'm Clovis. Where are you?"

"I can't remember. Yes. I'm in Jagged's. I'm in the restaurant."

"I'm not coming to get you, do you understand? Go down to the taxi-park. Get a cab and come here. If you're not here in ten minutes I'll worry. Jane?"

"Yes?"

"Can you do it?"

"*Clovis!* Oh, Clovis, black water's coming out of my eyes!"

"Your mascara is running."

"Oh—yes. I forgot I had any on." I laughed.

"Pull yourself together and get a taxi," he said.

I was quite calm and rather amused. I walked into the ladies room and washed my face, and then went down to the taxi-park. I looked at the wonderful star-fields of the city below, above and alongside. The city lights are spattered on my windshield—I'm in flight—we'll tread the sky—

"Block 21, New River Road," I said to the driver, who was an astoundingly humanlike robot. "Good Lord," I said, waving my black nails at him, "you're almost as realistic as the special E.M. formats."

"Which?" he asked.

"Electronic Metals. Copper, Golder and Silver."

"Never heard of 'em."

"Have you ever been dismantled?"

"Not so you'd notice."

"I wonder what it's like. He looked so—he looked—"

"Could you please," he said, "not cry like that when you get *out* of the cab? It might be bad for business."

He was human of course, I'd forgotten about Jagged's gimmick line of real drivers.

He'd been more forbearing than Egyptia.

Lights hit the windshield. We flew.

I managed to stop crying. The worst thing was not knowing why I was.

When I got up to the fifteenth gallery of Clovis's block, his door rushed open before I even spoke to it, set for sight. Clovis stood in the middle of the rug, barefoot, in a shower robe, frowning.

"He's dying," I said. "They're going to kill him."

The sedative Clovis gave me wasn't flavored. It had a bitter taste. I slept in the spare bedroom, which has black satin sheets, alternating with green or oyster satin sheets. The satin is a deliberate gesture, for you slide all night from one end of the bed to the other. Clovis usually makes his guests uncomfortable, in the hopes they'll soon go away. Drugged, I slept. When I woke up, he gave me China tea and an apple.

"If you can find anything to eat in the servicery, you can eat it."

Sleepwalking, drug-dazed, I found some instant toasts. Clovis stood in the doorway.

"I think I gave you too much Serenol. Do you remember what you told me last night? You were in very dramatic shock."

I watched the instant toast rising from the hot plate, and I saw two silver eye-sockets with wheels turning.

"No, I didn't give you enough Serenol," said Clovis, as I wept.

I had told him everything, sitting on his couch, giving a performance Egyptia might have envied.

"I'm surprised you went as far as you did," Clovis now said, handing me a large box of tissues, and removing the jumping toast from the floor. "Timid little Jane, confronting the might of Electronic Metals Ltd. What was the name of that prat?"

"Sw-Sw-Sw—"

"Swohnson, that's right. I'm quite looking forward to meeting him."

"What?"

"What?" Clovis copied my astonishment.

"Clovis, I can't go back. I can't do anything. I told him I was under eighteen. I haven't enough money. And my mother wouldn't—"

"It's too boring to explain twice. Follow me."

Clovis walked back across the main living area and dialed a number on the videoless phone, turning up the sound reception as he did so.

I stood where he had in the servicery doorway, and presently I heard Egyptia's sultry, seductive, sleepy voice.

"Good morning, Egyptia."

"Oh God. Do you know what time it is. Oh, I can't bear it. Only an idiot would call at this hour."

"An idiot would be unable to use the telephone. I take it you were asleep."

"I never sleep." She yawned voluptuously. "I can't sleep. Oh Clovis, I'm terrified. Too terrified ever to sleep. I have a part. Theatra Concordacis are doing *Ask the Peacock For My Brother's Dust.* They said only one person could play Antektra. Only I could play her. Only I had the resonance, the scope—But, Clovis, I'm not ready for it. I can't. Clovis, what shall I—"

"I'm going to buy you a lovely, lovely present," said Clovis.

"What?" she demanded.

"Jane tells me you're hooked on a robot."

"Oh! Oh, Clovis, would you? But, no. I can't. I have to concentrate on this part. I have to be celibate. Antektra was a virgin."

"I'm happy to reveal I don't know the play."

"And Silver—he's called Silver—he is the most wonderful lover. He can—"

"Please don't tell me," said Clovis. "I shall feel inadequate."

"*You'd* love him."

"Everybody, apparently, loves him. I wouldn't be surprised if he ran for Mayor next year. Meantime, they're dismantling him at E.M. Ltd. in a hellish basement that also produces a sideline of meat pies."

"Clovis, I can't follow you."

"It seems you did something to the metal-man. His clockwork has ganged agley. He's for the chop. Or the pie."

"I didn't do anything. Do they expect me to pay for it?"

"I'm paying. For possession. In your eighteen-year-old name. At a reduction, if I play my cards right. Faulty goods."

"Clovis you *are* wonderful, but I really can't let myself accept."

"Then you can loan him to Jane until you're free. Just to keep his hand in, if you'll excuse the expression."

"Jane wouldn't know one end of a man—"

"I think she might. Might you not, Jane?"

Egyptia fell silent. I had turned to glass, immovable, easily broken.

"One hour," said Clovis. "The Arbor side of the bridge."

"I'm not going to the Arbors. I'll be mugged and raped."

"Of course you will, Egyptia. Wish on a star."

Clovis killed the line. He dialed.

"Electronic Metals? No, I don't want the contact department. I want somebody by the avian name of Swohnson."

He waited. I said, "Clovis, they won't," and stopped because Swohnson's voice came on the line and my whole body withered like an autumn leaf. I sat on the floor and put my head on the wall, and the Serenol swam over me.

Out of the haze I heard Swohnson start to wither too.

"How do you *know* one of the Silver Formats is faulty?"

"My spies," said Clovis, "are everywhere."

"What? Er. Look here—"

"I don't happen to use a video."

"It's that—ah—that darn girl. Isn't it? And you're another rich kid—"

"I am another very rich kid. And I advise you to calm down, my feathered friend."

"*What?* Who the—"

"Swan," said Clovis clearly, "son."

"It's spelled S.W.O.H.," exclaimed Swohnson.

"I don't care if it's spelled S.H.I.T.," said Clovis. "I'm calling on behalf of the lady who hired your ballsed-up, badly-made substandard rubbish the night before last."

I got up and went into the green bathroom, and ran a tub. I couldn't bear to listen anymore.

About fifteen minutes after, as I lay there in the water, Clovis knocked on the door and said,

"You're a rotten audience, Jane. Are you all right? If you've slashed your wrists, could you hold them down in the bath and try not to mark the wall covering? Blood is very difficult to clean off."

"I'm all right. Thank you for trying."

"Trying? Son of the Swohn is pure cast-iron jello. I'm assuming, by the way, you'll pay me back in hard cash as soon as you can wring Demeta's blessing from her. Then we can edge Egyptia out of the picture, too."

"They won't let you," I said. Tears ran in the water. I was a bath tap, which nobody could turn off.

"Why am I doing this?" Clovis asked someone. "Moving heaven and Earth to get her some run-down heap of nuts and bolts that will probably permanently seize up as it walks through the door? Or at some other, more poignant, crucial moment. Oh, more! More! Sorry, honey, my spring's bust."

He went away and I heard the shower sizzle alive in the mahogany bathroom.

A timeless gap later, I heard him go out of the apartment, whistling. It isn't true what they say about male M-Bs. At least, Clovis can certainly whistle.

I lay in the tub, letting the vital oils be washed from my skin, as my mother had always told me not to. ("You can put skin elements back from a jar. But nature should never be wasted, darling.")

Clovis couldn't mean what he said. If he did, Electronic Metals would never let a faulty robot go. Or the demonstrators would have come back. Or Egyptia, if she signed, would assert her legal claim, and keep him. Or he would already be a pile of cooling clinker.

Yet even as I wept, the tempo of my tears had abruptly changed. I was now weeping quickly, and I was hurrying suddenly to get out of the bath. Hurrying as I had on the night I went to Egyptia's party. Because somehow I already knew.

When I heard the lift again, another lift went down through my insides. When the door asked me to let someone in I didn't stop to reason. I flung the door open. And there was Austin.

"Where's Clo?" said Austin.

I stared at Austin. I had expected anything but him.

"Well, I know I'm beautiful," he said.

"I thought you had a key," I stammered.

"Threw it back in his face," said Austin. "All that crap about a seance. Did you know that table's *rigged?* Bet you did, you girl."

"Clovis isn't here," I said.

"Then I'll wait."

"He's gone to the beach." Another lie. Austin believed it.

"Hope someone kicks sand in his face."

He turned, flowed straight down the corridor and banged the button for the lift to come back. I felt guilty and glad, and the lift swallowed him and he was gone.

It was one P.M., according to Clovis's talking clock when I switched it on. I had combed my hair for the thirtieth time. I sat in my black frock and black nails and white strained face, and gazed at the New River through the window. There were bruised-looking clouds. It might rain. *I* had stopped raining; my tears were dry. I made some real coffee, of which Clovis has accumulated a whole cupboard. But I couldn't drink it. There was dust on the coffee table. Obviously the block's automatic cleaner had remained unsummoned for days.

What was I waiting for? For Clovis to call and say he'd failed? For the door to open and Clovis to come through, shrug and say—what surprisingly he hadn't last night—you'd better forget it, Jane. After all, it's this fear of men thing again, isn't it, due to your lack of a physically present father?

Last night, I had known where I was, for all of one hour. I'd known that women don't love robots. That a doll with its clockwork showing meant nothing to me. But I hadn't been able to hang on to that truth. For me—he was alive. A man, Clovis. Real.

I heard the lift.

Wasn't there another small apartment in an annex at the end of this gallery? It might be the people from there.

The door seemed to tremble, ripple, as if underwater, and opened. Clovis and Silver walked through it.

Silver wore blue clothes, mulberry boots. I couldn't stop looking at them. Then I looked at Clovis's face. Clovis was surprised. He had been surprised, one could tell, for quite a while. He came over to me and said, "Jane, Jane, Jane." Then he handed me a plastic folder. "Papers," said Clovis briskly. "Duplicates of reassembly order, possession rights and receipt for cash transfer with bank stamp. Two-year guaranty, with a bar sinister on it due to incomplete check being waived by customer. And Egyptia's signed confirmation that you have right of loan. For six months it may say, or years, or something. Egyptia is vaguely aware, by the way, of having been cheated of something, so I'm taking her to lunch, and buying her a steel-grey fur cloak. For which you'll also owe me the money."

"I may not be able to repay you," I said. I was numb. Silver was standing near the door, standing at the edge of my vision, blue fire burning the rest of the room to cinders.

"See you in court, then," said Clovis.

Inanely I said, "Austin came up. I said you were at the beach."

"I think I am," said Clovis. "Certainly there is a distinct notion of sand underfoot. Shifting, I surmise." His face was still surprised. He turned from me and walked back to Silver, glanced at him, walked by him, and reached the door. "You know where everything is," Clovis said to me. "And if you don't, now is the time to find out.

Jesus screamed and ran," added Clovis. The apartment door slammed behind him, jarring its mechanisms. And I was alone. Alone with Egyptia's robot.

I had to force myself to look at him. From the boots to the long legs, and across—one hand, two hands, loosely at rest by his sides. Arms. Torso. Shoulders with the hair glowing against the blue shirt. Throat. Face. Intact. Whole. Tiger's eyes. In repose. And yet, what was it? Was I inventing it? The ghost of something, some disorientation, the look on the face of someone who has been sick and is convalescing. . . . No, imagination.

Did he know the legal position, who owned him, who was borrowing him? Did I have to tell him?

His amber eyes went into a long, slow blink. Thank God they worked. Thank God they were as beautiful as when I'd first seen them. He smiled at me. "Hallo," he said.

"Hallo," I said. I was so tense I scarcely felt it. "Do you remember me?"

"Yes."

"I don't know what to say to you," I said.

"Say whatever you want."

"I mean, do I say: Please sit down, won't you? Will you have some tea?"

He laughed. I loved his laugh. Always loved it. But it broke my heart. I was so sad, so sad now he was here with me. Sadder than I'd been at any time, a sadness beyond all tears.

"I'm quite relaxed," he said. "I'm always relaxed. You don't have to work at that one."

I was thrown, but now I expected to be thrown. I had to say something to him, which I kept biting back. He saw my hesitation. He raised one eyebrow at me.

"What?" he said. Human. *Human.*

"Do you know what happened? What they did to you?"

"They?"

"Electronic Metals."

"Yes," he said. No change.

"I saw you then," I said. It came out raw and harsh.

"I'm sorry," he said. "That can't have been very nice for you."

"But *you,"* I said. *"You."*

"What about me?"

"Were you unconscious?" I said.

"Unconscious isn't really a term you can apply to me," he said. "Switched off, if you mean that, then partially. To perform the check, at least half of my brain had to be functioning."

My stomach knotted together.

"You mean you were aware?"

"In a way."

"Did it—was it painful?"

"No. I don't feel pain. My nerve centers react by a method of alarm reflex rather than a pain reflex. Pain isn't necessary to my body as a warning signal, as it would be in a human. Therefore, no pain."

"You heard what he said. What I said."

"I think so."

"Are you incapable of dislike?"

"Yes."

"Of hate?"

"Yes."

"Of fear?"

"Maybe not," he said. "I don't analyze myself the way a human does. My preoccupations are outward."

"You're *owned,"* I said. "You belong to Egyptia. You've been *lent* to me."

"So?"

"So, are you angry?"

"Do I look angry?"

"You use the ego-mode: 'I' you say."

"Yes. Rather ridiculous if I spoke any other way, not to mention confusing."

"Do I irritate you?"

"No," he laughed again, very softly. "Ask whatever you want."

"Do you like me?" I said.

"I don't know you."

"But you think, as a robot, you can still get to know me?"

"Better than most of the humans you spend time with, if you'll let me."

"Do you want to?"

"Of course."

"Do you want to make love to me?" I cried, my heart a hurt, myself angry and in pain and in sorrow, and in fear—all those things he was spared.

"I want to do whatever you need me to do," he said.

"Without any feeling."

"With a feeling of great pleasure, if you're happy."

"You're beautiful," I said. "Do you know you're beautiful?"

"Yes. Obviously."

"And you draw people like a magnet. You know that, too?"

"You mean metaphorically? Yes, I know."

"What's it like?" I said. I meant to sound cynical. I sounded like a child asking about the sun. "What's it *like*, Silver?"

"You know," he said, "the easiest way to react to me is just to accept me, as I am. You can't become what I am, any more than I can become what you are."

"You wish you were human."

"No."

I went to the window, and looked at the New River, and

at the faint sapphire and silver reflection of him on the glass.

I said to it, forming the words, not even whispering them: I love you. I love you.

Aloud, I said: "You're much older than me."

"I doubt it," he said. "I'm only three years old."

I turned and stared at him. It was probably true. He grinned at me.

"All right," he said. "I'm supposed to appear between twenty and twenty-three. But counting time from when I was activated, I'm just a kid."

"This is Clovis's apartment," I found myself saying then. "What did you say to him to startle him like that?"

"Like you, he had trouble remembering I'm a robot."

"Did he . . . want to make love to you?"

"Yes. He suppressed the idea because it revolted him."

"Does it revolt you?"

"Here we go again. You asked that already, in another form, and I answered you."

"You're bi-sexual."

"I can adapt to whoever I'm with."

"In order to please them?"

"Yes."

"It gives you pleasure to please."

"Yes."

"You're pre-programmed to be pleased that way."

"So are humans, actually, to a certain extent."

I came back into the room.

I said, "What do you want me to call you?"

"You intend to rename me?"

"Silver—that's the registration. Not a name."

"What's in a name?" he said.

"A rose by any other name," I said.

"But don't, I think," he said, "call me Rose."

I laughed. It caught me by surprise, like Clovis's surprise, but unlike.

"That's nice," he said. "I like your laugh. I never heard it before."

Like a sword going through me. How could I feel so much, when he felt nothing. No, when he felt so differently, so indifferently.

"Please call me," I said, "Jane."

"Jane," he said. "Jane, a pane of crystal, the sound of rain falling on the silken grain of marble, a slender, pale chain of a name."

"Don't," I said.

"Why not?"

"It doesn't mean anything. It's too easy for you. Nobody ever made a poem out of my name, and you can do it with anything. It's a very ordinary name."

"But the sound," he said, "the sheer phonetic *sound*, is clean and clear and beautiful. Think about it. You never have until now."

Amazed, I lifted my head.

"Jane," I said, tasting my name, hearing my name. "Jaen. Jain."

He watched me. His tiger's eyes were lambent, absorbing me.

"I live with my mother," I said, "twenty miles from the city, in a house up in the air. Really up in the air. Clouds go by the windows. We're going to go there."

He regarded me with that grave attention I was coming, even so soon, to recognize.

"I don't know what I want from you," I said unsteadily. Not true, not true, but what I wanted, being impossible, must be left unsaid. "I'm not," I said, "Egyptia—I'm not—ex-perienced. I just—please don't th—"

"Don't ever," he said, "be afraid of me."

But I was. He'd driven a silver nail through my heart.

4

I'd known I didn't want us to stay there, at Clovis's. Clovis might come back any time, though probably he'd spin it out. Then again, he'd irresistibly picture us making love, sliding all over those black satin sheets. And everything complicated by his own reaction to Silver, who I wasn't going to call Silver, but couldn't think what else to call.

And then again, as we sat in the cab rushing along the out-of-town highway, I knew I didn't want to take him to my suite at Chez Stratos. And suddenly then, suddenly but absolutely, and with a dreadful feeling of shock, I knew I hadn't got a home. I simply stayed with people. Clovis, Chloe, Mother. And if my mother had been home right now, I couldn't have taken him there, because he would need explaining. "We have three locomotive robots, dear. Not to mention all the other robotic gadgets." "But he's a personal robot, Mother." "What does he do that the others can't?" Well . . .

So I became almost petrified with worry in the cab. But then, I'd turned to wood the moment we were on the street. Everyone looked at him, like before, and, like before, ninety-nine out of a hundred of them *not* because they knew he was a robot. We crossed a busy intersection and he took my hand, like my lover, my friend. Looking after me. It was an act of courage on my part to make us walk to the nearest taxi-park, all of three blocks. His responses were normal. Interest, alertness, apparent familiarity with subways, escalators, which streets led where, as if he'd lived in the city always. His senses and reflexes were, of course, abnormal. Once he drew me away from walking under an overhang. "There's water dripping down from the air-conditioning above." I hadn't seen and didn't see it, but I saw two people walk into it, pat themselves and curse. He also drew me aside from rough paving, and slipped us through crowds as a unit, without the usual periphery collisions that always happen to me.

The cab had a robot driver. He didn't react to that at all. I wondered how he would have reacted to the thing with the head on the flyer, out of the same workshop as himself.

On the street, I kept asking nervous questions, couldn't stop. Some were the same questions, in different forms; I wasn't even aware of the repetition half the time. Some were unsubtle fierce awful questions. "Do you sleep in a crate?" "I don't sleep." "But the crate?" "Somebody switches my circuits off and they prop me up in a corner." Which sounded like a macabre joke, and I didn't believe him even though he'd said he couldn't lie. Sometimes people caught fragments of our conversation and stared.

Something else began to dawn on me, a seeping amazement that something so weird as this had had so little publicity. Even the advertising campaign and the demonstration had done hardly anything to promote the news. Perhaps that was the idea—to infiltrate, show how these things could be passed off as human—and then really sound trumpets: See, they're *that* good. (These things.)

This makes me sound rational. And I wasn't.

I was glad to get into the cab, and then not glad, because I was again alone with him. I felt inadequate, and short and fat, and plain, and infantile. I'd taken on more than I could cope with. But how could I have left him in their testing cubicle, once Clovis gave me the chance to rescue him. Eyeless, machinery exposed, dying, and knowing it?

I said, brutishly, and ashamed of myself: "If they'd run the full check and taken you apart, is that your kind of death?"

"Probably," he said.

"And does *that* scare you?"

"I haven't thought about it."

"Not thought about dying."

"Do you?" he said.

"I suppose, not often. But when—the test, your eyes, your hands—"

"I was only partly aware."

"But you—"

"You're trying again, Jane, to get me to do something I'm not geared to do, which is analyze myself emotionally."

I looked at the geography going past, the dust and the mauve-tinted sky. Thunder murmured somewhere, hitting distant hills. He, too, looked out of the windows. Did he like the landscape, or didn't it matter to him? And was human beauty or lack of it equally unimportant?

We reached the approach to the house, and I paid off the cab. A mauve dust wind was rattling along the concrete and powdering the conifers. The steel supports of the house, in the softened, curious storm-light, were almost the same color as Silver.

"Hallo, Jane," said the lift.

He leaned on the wall as we soared upward, looking about him. And I looked at him. I shouldn't have done this. I'm a fool. I can't cope.

When the lift opened on the foyer, one of the three spacemen was trundling across to the hatches. I wondered what Silver would do, but Silver took no notice, and neither did the spaceman.

We got in the birdcage lift and went up to the Vista.

As we came in, there was a colossal thunderclap, and the whole room turned pink-white, then darkest purple. Insulated and stabilized as Chez Stratos is, there's still something utterly overpowering about a storm seen so close. As a child, I was terrified, but my mother used to bring me down here and show me the storm, explaining why we were safe and how magnificent Nature was. So that by the time I was ten, I was convinced I was no longer afraid of storms, and would come into the Vista to watch them and win Demeta's approval. But as a second flash and sear and roar exploded about the room, I wasn't so sure I was unafraid.

Silver, though, was walking along the room and into the balcony-balloons, and the storm was hitting him, turning him white, then cobalt. A cloud parted like a breaking wave only a hundred feet away, and rain fountained from it. The reflection of the rain ran over Silver's metallic face and throat.

"What do you think of the view?" I said brightly.

"It's fascinating."

"You can appreciate it?"

"You mean artistically? Yes."

He moved from the window, and touched the top of the piano, in which the clouds seethed and foamed, making me dizzy. He and it were in a sort of impossible motion, their skins gliding, yet stationary. He ran both hands suddenly across all the keys in a lightning of notes.

"Not quite in tune," he said.

"Isn't it?"

"Not quite."

"I'll tell one of the robots to fix it."

"I can fix it now."

"My mother plays it. I'd have to ask her."

His eyes flattened out. This time I knew. The thought process was switching over, because I'd reacted oddly. He, too, was a robot, and could retune the piano exquisitely. But I, instead of agreeing delightedly, said "No," as if he might humanly botch the job.

"My suite," I said, "is up here."

I turned and went through the annex and up the stair, anticipating that he'd follow me.

The moment I entered, I touched the master button in the console that brought all the green silk blinds down across the windows. I looked around at the Persian carpets, the baskets of hanging plants, the open door showing the mechanically neatly made bed, another showing the ancient Roman bathroom. The stereophonic tape-player, the visual unit, the clever games beamed at me, burnished, costly. Like a stranger, I moved forward, touched things. The books in their cases, clothes in their closet, (each outfit with its two matching sets of lingerie), I even opened the doll cupboard and saw my old toys, preserved for me in neat formal attitudes, as if they were in a doctor's waiting room. There wasn't a thing I'd ever bought for myself. Even the things I *had* bought—recent things, unimportant things, like nail varnish and earrings—they were there because my mother had said, "You know, this sort of thing would suit you," or maybe Clovis had said it. Or Egyptia had. Or Chloe had given it to me. Even my toys, long ago, had been chosen, and how I'd loved them. But here they sat, poor things, that love outgrown, waiting for the doctor who never would come and play with them again. Their sad fur made my eyes fill with tears. I know I've told you how I cry a lot.

I was aware he hadn't followed me after all, and I sat on the couch with the rain rolling down my face and no reflection, till I heard the piano burst into syncopation and melody. The thunder cracked, and the piano chased up the thunder, and danced over the other side.

I wiped my face with a lettuce-green tissue from a bronze dispenser, and went down again. I stood at the south end of the Vista, until he finished, watching his satin hair bouncing up over the lifted fan-shape lid of the piano as he dipped and dived in and out of the music. Then he got up and walked around the piano, smiling at me.

"I did fix it."

"I didn't say you should. You were meant to come upstairs with me."

"Something else we have to get clear," he said. "Being locomotive and verisimulated, I'm also fairly autonomous. If you want me to do something specific, you'll have to make it more obvious."

I balked. "What?"

"Try saying: Come upstairs with me. Then I'd leave the piano and follow you."

"Damn you!" I shouted. I hadn't meant to, didn't want to. It didn't even mean anything, except some basic symptom of what was happening deep inside me somewhere.

And his face grew cold and still, and his eyes were satanic.

"Don't look at me that way," I said.

His face cleared, changed. He said, "I told you about that."

"The thought process switching over. I don't believe you."

"I told you about that too."

"I don't think you know!" I cried.

"I know about myself."

"Do you?"

"I have to, to function."

"My mother ought to love you. It's so important to know oneself. None of us does. I don't."

He looked at me patiently, attentively.

"I have to give you orders," I said, "to make you do what I want."

"Not exactly. Instructions, perhaps."

"What instructions did Egyptia give you when she took you to bed?"

"I already knew what the instructions were."

"How?"

"How do you think?"

Human. *Human.*

"Egyptia's beautiful. Artistically, you'd be able to appreciate that."

"Yes," he said.

"I'm sorry you got stuck with me."

"You do sound," he said, "as if you regret it."

"Tomorrow, I'll send you back to her. To Clovis." What was I saying? Why couldn't I stop? "I don't need you. I made a mistake."

"I'm sorry," he said quietly.

"You regret failing me. Not making me happy."

"Yes."

"You want to make everyone happy?" I screamed. The

thunder blazed. The house shook, or was it my pulse? "Who do you think you are? Jesus Christ?"

Lightning. Fire. Drums. I lost the room, and when it came back, he was in front of me. He put his hands lightly on my shoulders.

"You're going through some personal trauma," he said. "I can try to help you, if you tell me what it is."

"It's you," I said. "It's you."

"There is a school of thought which predicts human beings will react as you're doing."

"Egyptia was your first woman," I announced.

"Egyptia's a young girl, as you are. And not the first, by any means."

"Tests? Performance tests? Piano, guitar, voice, bed?"

"Naturally."

"What's natural about it?" I pulled away from him.

"Natural from a business point of view," he said reasonably.

"But there's something wrong," I said. "You don't check out."

He stood and looked down at me. He was about five feet eleven. The sky was bleeding into darkness behind him, and his hair bleeding into darkness, too. His eyes were two flames, colorless.

"My bedroom is up the stair," I said. "Follow me."

I went up, and he came after. We walked into the suite. I pushed the door shut. I walked over to the green auto-chill flagon of white wine, and poured two glasses, then remembered, then took up the second glass anyway and pushed it into his hand.

"You're wasting it on me," he said.

"I want to make believe you're human," I said.

"I know you do. I'm not."

"Do it to *please* me. To make me happ-y."

He drank, slowly. I drank quickly. I started to float at

once. The lightning burst through the blinds, and I didn't mind it.

"Now," I said, "come into my bedroom, exclusively designed by my mother to match my personal coloressence chart. And make love to me."

"No," he said.

I stood and stared at him.

"No? You can't say no."

"My vocabulary is less limited than you seem to think."

"No—"

"No, because you don't want me, or your body doesn't, which is more important."

"You have to make me happy," I got out.

"I won't make you happy by raping you. Even at your own request."

He put down the glass. He bowed to me from the waist, like a nobleman in an old visual, and went out.

I stood with my mouth open, as the lightning splashed on the blinds, and the thunder faded. He began to play the piano again. It was the silliest thing, the silliest and the most disheartening thing, that could have happened to me. And I knew I deserved it.

I got rather drunk alone in my suite, listening to the piano. Sometimes, when alone, I'd secretively play it—but so badly. He played, fantastically, for an hour. Things I knew, things I didn't. Classical, futurist, contemporary, extempore. It was like a light on in the Vista, burning even if I couldn't see it. The day after tomorrow my mother would come home. And there would be trouble to sort out. Trouble large as hills on my horizon. Only today then, and tomorrow, and I'd ruined everything.

I showered and washed my hair, and let the machine

warm-comb it dry. I put on dress after dress, but none of them was right. Then I put on black jeans which were too tight for me (and found they weren't, but then, I'd hardly eaten today, and my Venus Media capsules were due again tomorrow), and a silk shirt Chloe gave me that I never wore because Demeta didn't like it.

The piano had long since stopped. It was about five forty-five P.M., and the storm was over in the Vista. A blue sunset covered the sky and the furnishings, and I couldn't see him. He wasn't there.

I'd told him I'd send him back, and Egyptia owned him. Could he have left? Was it possible for a robot to make that sort of decision? I went out of the Vista, and the lift was down on the mezzanine, but not the foyer. A surge of blood went through me, as if my circulation had been waiting for information. I got the lift back and went down. He was in the library, in the long chair across the balcony-balloon. The lamp was on. He was reading. He seemed to need light, but it took him about fifteen seconds to take in each page.

I went into the library. I was humbled. I walked over to him and sat on the floor by the chair, and leaned my head against his knee. It seemed natural. And his hand coming to stroke my hair, that was natural too.

"Hallo," he said.

No resentment, of course. I could almost be resentful at his lack of resentment.

"Listen to me," I said, quietly, "I'm going to explain, too. I'm not going to look at you, but I'll lean here, and I'll say it. I'm still slightly high on the wine, and very relaxed. Is that all right?"

"Yes, Jane," he said.

I closed my eyes.

"I'm very stupid," I said, "and very selfish. That's because I'm rich and I don't know much about real life. And I've been sheltered. And I have a lot of faults."

He laughed softly.

"You mustn't interrupt," I said, very low. "I want to apologize. I know you're indifferent to my—my tantrums. But I have to apologize for my own sake. Tell you I'm sorry. And why. I'm confused. I've never had a sexual relationship with a man. I've had dates, but nothing important. I never enjoyed—I'm a virgin."

"You're sixteen."

"Most of my friends had sexual experience at thirteen or fourteen. Anyway. Anyway, I never will go with a man now. I don't want to." I waited, not for effect, but to contain myself. "Because," I said, "I'm in love with you. Please don't laugh or reason with me. Or say it will go away. It won't. I love you." My voice was calm, and I heard it with admiration. "I know you don't love. Can't love. I know we're just all like slices of cake or something—don't," I said, for I felt him tremble with laughter. "But I have less than two days with you, because then my mother comes home and Egyptia will want you back. And I don't know if I'm ready or not, but please make love to me. Not so I can boast, or to get rid of something, like cutting my nails, or because I'm bored. But because, because—" I stopped talking and rubbed my cheek against him. His long fingers curved over my skull and held me close. I knew I had struck the right note at last. He could give me pleasure of the emotions if not of the body. He could help me. Function fulfilled. But his sweetness came to me, his strength and his sweetness. I trusted him. I'd trusted him with the truth, undramatized, and with no prop—my weakness, my childishness—to take the blame for what I did. I didn't know him. He was unknowable. But I trusted him.

I got up slowly, and reached down my hand and he took

it and left the chair and stood with me, looking into my face. His eyes were full of tenderness, and a kind of wicked joy. It *was* wicked, and it *was* joy.

"I love you," I said, meeting his eyes.

"I know," he told me. "You said it in Clovis's apartment, at the window."

"You heard me? But I didn't even whisper—"

"I saw your reflection in the glass, as you saw mine. Lip movements."

"Well . . . you know, then. I didn't want to be afraid of saying it. Accidentally."

" 'I love you,' she said accidentally. Don't be afraid to say it. To my knowledge, you're the first human who ever did love me."

"Oh, but—"

"Magnetized, yes. Obsessed. Not love."

"You're not going to patronize me."

"No, Jane."

"Can we make believe," I said, "that I don't need to give any instructions. Please."

"You don't," he said.

He drew me into his arms. It was like the pull of the sea. Kind. Irresistible. Swimming. The texture of the mouth, its moisture—human, the same . . . only the sensations of the kiss were utterly changed. Then he picked me up as if I weighed nothing at all, and carried me into the lift.

I'm not Egyptia. I don't want to go into endless details. I was afraid, and not afraid. I was elated, and filled by despair. His nakedness dazzled me, though Demeta long ago saw to it that male nakedness was familiar to me in her selection of my visuals. But he was beautiful and silver, with the blaze of a fire at his groin. Why is the male penis supposed to be ugly? All of him was beautiful. All. And I—I was self-conscious, but his gentleness and his care of me made nothing of that. His gentleness, his care. I didn't even tear, or bleed. I wasn't even hurt. Yet he filled me, gloriously. His hair swept me like a tide. No part of him is like metal, except to look at. To touch, like skin, but perfect skin, without unevenness or flaw. And when I said at last, abashed, regretful, but content—"I'm sorry, I don't think I can, I mean, I won't climax—I won't climax"—even the awful jargon didn't jar, even to speak of it was acceptable. And almost at once a pressure began to grow inside me, and suddenly there were rollers of ecstasy and I caught my breath and clung to him, until they let me go.

He held me in his arms, and I said,

"But you, what about you?"

"No."

"But—can't you—don't you—"

"It isn't necessary for me." And then, his voice amused in the darkness, "I can fake it, if you want. I frequently have."

"No. Don't fake it with me. Not ever. Please don't."

"Then I won't."

I fell asleep, until the Asteroid, rising, cut a hole through the blind. I woke, and he lay by me, his arms about me, his eyes closed as if he slept. But when he felt me stir, he opened his eyes. We looked at each other, and he said, "You're beautiful."

I would have denied it, but I felt it to be true. With him, for that moment, true.

My joy was his joy. I'd been crazy to say what I had, that he couldn't love. He can love all of us. He *is* love.

• • •

In the morning, we showered together.

"Do you *need* to?"

"City dirt makes no exceptions," he said, soaping his hair under the green waterfall. "Don't worry, I'm entirely rustproof."

He ate breakfast with me, to please me. He ate just like a young man, economically wolfing the food down.

"Can you taste it?"

"I can if I put the right circuits into action."

"That's ridiculous," I said, and giggled.

My laughter intrigued him. He went into routines that made me helpless with it. Idiotically convincing voices, other personae, absurd songs, jokes.

One of the spacemen came to clear the breakfast things and I fell silent, embarrassed by this other robot, so unlike him. The spaceman gave me a little tray with vitamins on it, and my Phy-Excellence capsules. I meant to take them. I did. But I forgot.

We went back to bed. When the ecstasy left me, I cried again.

"It must be horrible for you," I sobbed.

"Do I seem to find it horrible?"

"You'd act. It's part of your character. And to say I'm beautiful."

"You are. You have a skin like cream."

"Do I?"

"And eyes like cowrie shells, with every color of the sea in them."

"No I don't."

"Yes you do."

"You say this to everyone."

"Not quite. Besides which, they would be different things. And only when they were true."

I got out of bed and went to the mirror, and looked at myself, lifting my hair over my head, widening my eyes.

He lay in the sheets like a sleeping dog-fox, smiling, aware of my delight.

"Did you fake orgasm," I said boldly, "with Egyptia?"

"Many many times," he said, with a note of such ironic dismay that I laughed again.

The next time he made love to me, the ecstasy was like a spear going through me. I screamed out, and was astonished.

"Just pretending," I said.

The phone gave a sound a few minutes before noon, the low purring it makes on the console by my bed. Correction: made. I turned off the video, and answered it. I needn't have bothered with the video.

"Bad news," said Clovis.

"That isn't me," I said, "or is that who's calling?"

"Jane, don't be witty. When's Demeta coming back?"

"Tomorrow."

"I hate to break up your amour impropre early, but Egyptia has decided to assert her rights. She says she signed your metal playmate over to you for six hours. Only. You want him, I paid for him, but we can't do a thing. She's eighteen and he's in her name."

"You could stall her. . . ."

"No. Anyway, I've got other things to do with my day. Or did you think my only mission in life was to be your nursemaid?"

Rancor. I could hear it. Something grated inside him. Because he'd helped me and he'd lost out. And because he'd seen Silver.

"What do I do, Clovis?"

"Send him over to The Island on a fast ferry. Or she may make a hysterical call to a lawyer. Or her awful mother in that trench."

"But—"

"You didn't think she was a friend of yours, did you?"

Everything in the room had stopped moving. It was funny, of course nothing had been moving, yet everything had looked alive, and now it didn't anymore.

"All right," I said.

"Or," he said, "you can send it here, if you want. It, him. Egyptia can collect him, and maybe I can calm her down."

"To your apartment," I said.

"To my apartment. I'm so glad you didn't think I meant the middle of the river."

"I'll pay you back the money," I said. I had twisted the edge of the sheets into a hard corded knot.

"Oh, no rush."

I switched the phone off.

"What is it?" my lover said to me. His arm came round my shoulders.

"Didn't you hear?"

"Yes."

"Clovis wants you. And then Egyptia wants you."

"Well apparently I legally belong to them."

"Don't you care?"

"You want me to say I care about leaving you."

I let him hold me. I knew everything was useless, was over, dead, like brown leaves crushed off the trees.

"I do care about leaving you, Jane."

"But you'll be just the same with them."

"I'll be what they need me to be."

I left the bed and went into the bathroom. I ran the taps and held my hands under the water for a long while, for no reason at all. When I came back, he was dressing, pulling on the mulberry boots.

"I wish you wanted to stay with me," I said.

"I do."

"Only me."

"You can't change me," he said. "You have to accept what I am."

"I may never see you again."

He moved to me and took me back into his arms. I knew the texture of these clothes now, as I knew the texture of his skin and hair, which are neither. Even in my misery, his touch soothed me.

"If you never see me again," he said, "I'm still part of you, now. Or do you regret that we've spent time together?"

"No."

"Then be glad. Even if it's finished."

"I won't let it be finished," I said. I held him fiercely, but he kissed me and put me away, tactfully and finally.

"There's a flyer in ten minutes," he said.

"How will you—"

"By running a lot faster than any human man you'll ever see."

"Money."

"Robots travel free. Tap the slot and it registers like coins. Electronic wavelengths."

"I hate your *cheerfulness.* When you leave me, there's nothing."

"There's all the world," he said. "And Jane," he stood in the doorway of the suite, "don't forget. You are," he stopped speaking, and framed the word with his lips only: "beautiful."

Then he was gone, and all the colors and the light of the day crumbled and went out.

I don't have to describe that day, do I? I thought a lot about him. I saw him arriving at Clovis's apartment. The conversation, the innuendo, saw him playing along with the repartee, giving better than he got, and the wonderful smile like sheer sunlight. I saw them in bed. Almost. Like a faulty visual—the swimmers' movement of arms, a glint of flesh. My mind wouldn't let me see. And yet my mind wouldn't leave it alone. I wanted to kill Clovis, take a knife and kill him. And Egyptia. And I wanted to run away. Out into the gathering darkness. Out into another country, another world.

About seven P.M., something happened like a page turning over. I sat bolt upright in the welter of the stricken bed, and the plan began to come. The insane plan, the stupid plan. It was as if he'd taught me how to think. Think in new, logical, extraordinary ways.

I couldn't remember where the Phy-Amalgamated Conference was, and had to get the information operator. All the while I waited, I waited too for the conviction to go, but it didn't.

Then I got the Conference and held the line for the twenty minutes the pager needed to find my mother. And the conviction was still there.

"What's wrong, darling?" said my mother.

"Mother, I've bought something terribly expensive I couldn't get on my card."

"Jane. There's a meeting I'm chairing in five minutes. Could this perhaps have waited?"

"No, Mother. Sorry, but no. You see, Clovis paid for it."

"You've been seeing Clovis after what you told me. Should you have been more cautious?"

"I'm over all that," I said tersely.

"Darling," said my mother, "switch on the video, please."

I switched it on, defiantly, and saw her see me, naked in my bed, my love bed, with my cream skin and my cowrie shell eyes I'd never known I had. And somehow, she seemed to realize it was someone new she was dealing with, somebody she'd not really met before.

"That's better," said my mother, but I knew it wasn't. "I'm glad you've been resting."

She had always told me to get to know my body. To be at ease with it. She now seemed to think it faintly unnecessary that I had, I was.

"Mother, Clovis paid for this thing, and now I can't get to use it. Can you wire a cash order through to him tonight?"

"How much does this item cost?"

I opened out the receipt and read the figure off cold.

My mother became cold, too.

"That's rather a lot of money, darling."

"Yes, I'm afraid so." (But we can pay it, can't we? We're rolling about in riches, aren't we?)

"You've never done anything like this before, Jane. What exactly is this thing? Is it a car?"

"It's a Sophisticated Special Format Robot."

Mother, I'm in love with—

"A robot. I see."

"It can play the piano."

"At the price you quoted, one would hope so."

"The point is, Mother, I've been thinking about this a long time, but I rather want, sort of would like—" Don't blow it, Jane, Jaen, Jain. "I think it would do me good to get an apartment of my own. Just for a few months, in the city."

"An apartment."

"I'm such a baby, Mother. All my friends have their own places."

"You have your own suite."

"It's not the same."

"Your suite belongs to you, Jane, and everything in it, just the same as it would in an apartment. You can do there and with exactly as you choose. You have total freedom. More so than in an apartment, where you would be governed by certain domiciliary regulations."

"Oh—I—"

"I agree, you are rather immature. How would you propose to cope with the everyday chores of life on your own? Do you even understand what they are? Even an automatic apartment needs cohesion. And you are not—Jane, I really think we must discuss this when I get home."

"I bought the robot to help me run the apartment."

"Yes. Your priorities are quite original."

"But will you please pay Clovis?"

"Darling, you sound as if you're trying to give me a command, and I'm sure you realize that would be very foolish of you."

"Please, Mother."

"I have to go now, darling. I'll see you tomorrow evening, and we'll talk this through. Why not put your views on tape? You're always so much better at expressing yourself unspontaneously and with consideration. Good night, sleep tight, dear."

The line and the video blanked out.

I was shivering and swearing and gnawing the sheet.

I'd have to go through all this again with her tomorrow, and she'd win. That was silly. I wasn't in a battle with my mother. Was I? Egyptia had had full access to her mother's fortune since she was fifteen, the limit being on a monthly basis only because otherwise she tended to overdraw on funds that hadn't yet built up. But the terms of the limit were a monthly twenty thousand I.M.U. And Clovis had no limit I knew of. And Chloe and Davideed didn't, though they were habitually frugal. And Jason and Medea, who still lived at home, had their own beach house at Cape Angel, a Rolls Amada car with push-button dash, and spent money by forging their father's signature, which he never noticed, or by use of one of their six credit cards each with a two-week thousand limit, and they still shoplifted.

And I. I had a thousand I.M.U. a month. Which had always been more than enough until now.

More than enough, frankly, because half the time my mother bought my clothes. Even my sheets, my soap . . . I looked round the rooms of my suite wildly. I had everything I could possibly need, and more. I should be grateful. My eye was caught by a gorgeously vulgar ("The worst vulgarity is to avoid vulgarity solely on the grounds that it is vulgar.") antique oriental lamp, by a jade panther. My mother lavished money on me. The carpets alone would be worth thousands—

My skin crawled. Something clicked in my head.

"No," I said aloud. "No, no—"

I saw Silver, who I'd wanted to give another name to, and hadn't, walking along the sidewalk, putting back his head to watch the flyer go over. I saw his face against the dark sky in the balcony just before he kissed me the second time. I felt him hold me, and a spear divided me. I remembered the cubicle, the clockwork nerves of his body exposed. I visualized Clovis and Egyptia squabbling over him.

Like a sleepwalker, I got off the bed. I thought of my mother, and I could smell *La Verte*, but the scent of him had lingered on my own skin, blotting out my mother's psychologically conjured perfume.

"All right," I said. "Why not? If it's supposed to be mine."

You should make the decision yourself, my mother would say. Once I'd asked her what to do, and she'd told me.

"Yes, Mother. I'm going to make a decision."

The auto-chill had refilled with wine, and I drank some, however, before I called Casa Bianca, the largest and most expensive second owner store in the city.

Before I quite knew what I'd done, I'd invited their representative over to Chez Stratos to assess the entire contents of my suite. Rich people fall on hard times and sell things, but I could tell, when I got through to the human assistants at Casa, that they were rather surprised—surprised and greedy. Of course, they'd cheat me. I looked at the receipt from E.M., seeing the wording for a S.I.L.V.E.R. The Sophisticated Format Robot, and at the charge. I'd get enough. And enough for other things, for a run-down apartment somewhere. And then, with the thousand I.M.U. card, I could manage there, if I was careful.

What was I doing? Did I know? Ice water ran down my back, my head throbbed, I felt sick. But I only drank some more wine, and got dressed and powdered my face to put up a barrier between me and the rep. from Casa Bianca. Then I gave admittance instructions to the lift, which said: "Hallo, Jane. Yes, Jane, I understand."

The rep. arrived an hour later, very smart, about forty but not on Rejuvinex, or not on enough of it. She had long, blood-red nails, a bad psychological mistake in her line of work. Or perhaps it was done to intimidate. She looked predatory as she came out of the lift into the foyer.

"Good evening," she said. "I'm Geraldine, representing Casa Bianca."

"Please come this way," I said. Party manners. Well, I'd often felt just as scared as this at parties.

We went up in the birdcage to the Vista.

"Excuse me," said Geraldine, "is any of the rest of the house involved?"

"No. Just my suite."

"Pity."

We walked through the Vista, and she exclaimed. Indigo clouds were humped against the balcony-balloons with puddles of stars in them. The Asteroid blazed in the East like a neon, advertising something too ethereal to be real.

"My God," said Geraldine, proclaiming a monopoly. "By the way," she said, as we went up the annex stair, "I'm afraid we'll require proof of your ownership of the properties you want to sell. You did realize that?"

She thought I was about ten years old and she would make corn hash of me. She probably would. I was allergic to her. I wished my mother would come home unexpectedly and end all this. What had I *done?*

"In here," I said, as we went into my suite, which one of the spacemen had tidied.

"Oh, yes," said Geraldine. "You said on the phone everything was to go."

"If you can give me a reasonable price for it," I said. My voice trembled.

"Why the heck are you leaving?" marveled Geraldine.

"I'm going to live with my lover," I said. "And Mother wants to restyle the suite."

Geraldine opened her big leather bag and removed a lightweight mini-computer which she set up on a side table.

"I'll just run the ownership proof through now, if you don't mind."

I handed her the inventory tape. It had my individual body code, and the description and sonic match for everything in the rooms, which her computer would test and find correct. The inventory was kept in Demeta's tape store, but I'd sent one of the spacemen for it.

As the computer chittered through its routine, Geraldine walked round and about, now and then picking things up and running a little calculator over them.

"The computer will take the full scan in a moment," she said. "But you have some nice things. I think Casa Bianca will be able to take most of this off your hands."

"There are clothes, too. And makeup cabinet. And a hairdresser unit. And all the tapes with the deck. You can take the bath fittings if you want, so long as you tie off the plumbing."

"Well, I shan't be doing it personally," she corrected me.

I cringed, and just managed not to apologize to her.

"Well," said Geraldine. "I just hope your lover can give you all of this."

I kept quiet, this time. That was my business, wasn't it.

What my lover, my love, my beloved, gave me. Or could he give me anything.

I opened the doll cupboard.

"My!" said Geraldine. "Some of these are—" she stopped herself. "Of course, secondhand toys are much harder to sell. But they seem well-preserved. Did you ever *play* with them?"

"They're durables."

My mother had wanted me to be able to work out my aggressions with my toys, so they were the kind whose hair didn't come out, and whose ears didn't fall off. There was my unicorn rocking horse, unscratched, and my bear in shining coal-black fur. "See," I thought to them, "people are going to buy you and love you and play with you, after all." I wouldn't cry in front of Geraldine. I wouldn't.

I poured some wine and didn't offer her any. She hated me anyway.

The computer put up a white light and a piece of paper. Geraldine read it carefully. "Yes, that's all in order. I'll just switch on the scan. There. Our relay department can let you know the offer we're prepared to make first thing tomorrow. Or late tonight, if you prefer."

"I'm afraid I want everything cleared by tomorrow. And the money. Or else I'll have to try another firm."

"Oh, come on now," said Geraldine. "Our service is fast. But not that fast. And no one's is."

If I held the glass much more tightly, I'd break it, like people do in visuals.

"Then I'm sorry to have wasted your time," I said.

Geraldine stared at me. She looked impressed.

"So okay," she said. "What's the hurry? Your mother doesn't know you're doing this?"

"Your computer has just told you that I own everything in the suite."

"Yup. But Mother still doesn't know the bird's flying the nest. Right?"

My mother did know. I'd told her.

Geraldine looked at the white leather suitcase.

"What's in there? Don't tell me. A few clothes, a bag of your favorite makeup, your boyfriend's photo. What is this? You've fallen in love with some adolescent on Subsistence?"

The computer put up a yellow light and closed itself off. The scan was complete.

"What about the bathroom and bedroom?" I asked.

"Oh, Fred here can see through walls. What about you?"

I forced myself to turn and look at her. My eyes watered but I didn't blink. The lenses of my eyes were flat and cruel. My face was silver.

"I want your firm to call me with its offer in no more than two hours. If I agree to it, I want your removal machinery in here and out in one hour more."

"Yes, *Ma'am,*" said Geraldine. "I'll pass on your message."

"If I don't get the call by ten P.M., I'll go elsewhere."

"Nobody else could take this on in the middle of the night," said Geraldine. She re-bagged the computer, dropped in the calculator. "I might be able to swing it for you," she said. She picked up the jade panther. "I might."

I'm so slow. It was ages as she stood there with the panther, before I knew she wanted me to bribe her. I started to panic, as if I'd committed some breach of social etiquette. I didn't know how to get over it. As I fumbled about in my mind, Geraldine put down the panther and walked crisply out.

I followed her into the birdcage lift and touched the button. Geraldine looked into space with her hard sad eyes that had parcels of lines in the thick mascara under them. I wondered frenziedly if everyone always tipped her with some valuable piece, if her apartment was stuffed with collectors items, against her compulsory retirement, which would have to be any year now. I began to feel sorry for her, her tired skin, her carnivorous nails.

We reached the foyer and she stepped out and over to the lift in the support. At the door she hesitated. She turned and looked at me.

"You're going to find it difficult," she said, "being poor. But you're a tryer, I'll say that for you."

I was overwhelmed. It was ridiculous.

"Geraldine," I said, blatant, because suddenly I wanted her to have the panther, and so being devious was unimportant, "where do I send—?"

"Keep it," she said. "You're going to need every money unit you can get your hands on."

The doors shut. I sat down on the foyer floor, wondering if she was ever someone's daughter, too. I was still sprawled there three quarters of an hour later, when the phone went. It was Casa Bianca. They'd be at the house by midnight and they'd pay me—it was more money than I'd ever had, and it would just be enough.

Guess what I did as the Casa Bianca removal took away all my things? I cried. (I feel I ought to edit out my tears by now. But, they happened.) It was my life going. Strange, when I'd hardly ever thought about any of it. Strange, that when I had thought about it, none of it had seemed like mine, yet there I was, wandering from place to place in the swiftly emptying rooms to avoid the machines, crying. Good-bye, my books, good-bye, my necklaces, good-bye my ivory chessmen. Good-bye my coal-black bear.

Good-bye, my childhood, my roots, my yesterdays. Good-bye, Jane.

Who are you now?

• • •

I made a tape for my mother, and left it on the console for her, with the light ready to signal when she came in. I wasn't very coherent, but I tried to be. I tried to explain how I loved her and how I'd call her, soon. I tried to explain what I'd done. I didn't say anything about Silver. Not one word. Yet everything I said, of course, was about him. I simply might have been saying his name over and over. And I knew she'd know. My wise, clever, brilliant mother. I couldn't hide anything from her.

I and my white suitcase, with Casa Bianca's Pay On Demand check in it, caught the four A.M. flyer to the city. There was a gang on the flyer, and they shouted obscene things at me, but didn't dare do anything else because of the rightly suspected policode. I was afraid of them anyway. I'd never been so close to people like that, always taking cabs when it was late, always on the bright streets, or in another corridor, or on the other side of the walk. It was as if my mother's aura had protected me, and now I had exiled myself, and now I was no longer safe.

When I remember doing all this, I'm shattered. I still don't quite believe I did. I dialed an instant-rental bureau from a kiosk at the foot of Les Anges Bridge, and then gave in and took a taxi to the address they gave me.

The caretaker was human, and he swore at me for getting him up. It was very dark. There were no streetlights outside; the nearest was five hundred feet away up the street. My window looks on to a subsidence of brickwork and iron girders. I don't know what it could have been before the tremor shook it down, but weeds have seeded all over it. I didn't see till daylight crawled through the dirty window, and then the autumn colors of the weeds, smeared on the dereliction, made me unhappy. Unhappier.

I didn't sleep, of course. I huddled by my suitcase on

the old couch by the window. I knew I couldn't stay here. I knew I would have to go home. But where was home?

When day came, I went on huddling. I knew my next move was to go to Egyptia, and then to Clovis. Repay Clovis, persuade Egyptia. And then I'd take Silver. I'd really have bought him, as Casa Bianca had bought my furniture. He'd belong to me. And I couldn't. After everything, I couldn't. Couldn't buy him or own him. Couldn't bring him here to this frightful place.

I dozed, and when I woke, the day was shrinking away behind the girders as if it were scared of them. My stomach was queasy and sore because I hadn't eaten, except for a sort of sandwich I'd made myself in the servicery at the house. I drank some water from the drinking tap in the muddy bathroom of the rented apartment. The water tasted very chemical, and full of germs.

My mother would be home, soon. I wondered what she would do. I became frantic, and saw her shock as she found the suite stripped of furnishings and me. I began to believe I'd done something truly awful to her. I wanted to run down to the pay phone in the foyer of the rental apartment block, down all the cracked cement steps, for the lift here didn't work anymore. But then I knew I couldn't. And then at last I knew that I was afraid, terribly, violently afraid, of Demeta, who only wants the best for me, the very best, as she sees it.

Eventually, I found the paper pad I'd written on and which I'd put in the suitcase with the money and the few clothes, and I started to write this, the second chapter of what's happened to me.

When it got pitch dark, I turned on the mean bare overhead light, but it will cost money, so I worry about it. I have three hundred left on my card for the rest of the month. Whatever did I spend the rest of it on? I'm cold tonight, and I'd like to turn on the wall heater. Maybe I can wait a little longer?

Stars are caught in the girders. The name of this street, actually, is Tolerance.

Silver, I need you. I need *you.* All this is because of you and yet, how could I blame you for it? I'm nothing to you. (Does the touch of real flesh secretly repel you?) But I was beautiful with you. All night, all the hours of the day you were with me: Beautiful. And I never was before.

I'm so tired. Tomorrow, I must make up my mind.

There's a flyer going over. It's quiet here, I can hear the lines whistling, and below, the roar of the city, that never lies down to sleep.

CHAPTER THREE

A rose by any other name
Would get the blame
For being what it is—
The color of a kiss,
The shadow of a flame.
A rose may earn another
name,
So call it love;
So call it love I will.
And love is like the sea,
Which changes constantly,
And yet is still
The same.

1

I dreamed of him that night, after I wrote the second chapter of what had happened. The first time I ever dreamed of him. We were flying over the city. Not in a flyer, but on the wings of angels out of an old religious picture. I could feel the beat of the wings through my body as they opened and closed. It was effortless and lovely to fly, to watch him fly just ahead of me. We passed over the broken girders and our shadows fell on the ground among the orange foliage of the autumn weeds. It's supposed to be a sexual dream to dream of flight. Maybe it was. But it didn't seem to be.

When I woke, it was early morning, just like the dream, and I looked out of the window at the orange twining the girders, where our shadows had fallen. Beyond the subsidence was a blue ghost of the city I could just see, cone-shaped blocks all in a line, and the distant column of the Delux Hyperia Building. The view wasn't ugly or dismal anymore. The sun was shining on it. In five years, if they left the subsidence alone, a young wood of weed trees might be growing there. The sky was blue as Silver's shirt had been.

Dazed by the dream and the sunlight and the autumn weeds, I went into the bathroom and ran hot water, though it was expensive. I showered and dressed, and brushed my hair. My hair looked different. And my face. My hair, I guessed, was fading out of tint and needed molecular re-structuring or the bronze tone would all go, but I'd sold my hairdresser unit. I could go to a beauty parlor, and get a color match and molecular restructure done, but it might not be the exact shade. Anyway, it would cost a lot. I'd have to revert to being dull brown, or whatever it was I'd been that hadn't suited me on my coloressence charting. My face though, what had happened to that? I turned three quarters on and saw that my flesh had hollowed slightly. I had cheekbones, high and slender but unmistakably there. I looked older, and peculiarly younger, too. I leaned close to the spotted glass, and my eyes became one eye, flecked with green and yellow.

I put the Casa Bianca P.O.D. check in a sling purse over my shoulder, and went out and down the cracked cement stairs.

I couldn't tell what I felt, but I didn't feel as I had. The street turned into a run-down boulevard with an elderly elevated running overhead, the lines long unused, and rusting. I bought a bun and an apple and a plastic cup of tea at a food counter, and ate and drank as I waited for the city center bus. By daylight, I knew my way about far better than I'd thought, even here. Of course, I'd sometimes been in ramshackle areas, always with other people, always a tourist, but still enough to have a few scraps of knowledge.

The blue sky made the sidewalk interesting. People moved about, ran, argued, and steam came out of food shops. Flowers spilled from the elevated.

I'd always known the city. I had no reason to be afraid of it, even now. And my jeans looked shabby because I'd slept in them on the hairy old couch, shabby enough not to attract attention. The shirt would get shabby.

"Bus late again," one woman said to another behind me, in the verbal shorthand of the usual. "Thought of walking to South for the flyer, but it's too much money."

"Mechanical failure at the depot," said the other woman. "They don't service regularly downtown, that's the trouble. City center runs, that's fine. But out here, we can walk all the way."

Then they muttered together, and I knew they were talking about me, and I went hot and cold with nervous fear. Then I caught the word "actress" spoken with pity, scorn and interest. I was startled, to have myself compared to exotic Egyptia, even on the streets of the poor. Glad, also. To be an actress from this end of town meant I was struggling, too. They wouldn't hate me. I was a symbol of possibility, and anyway would probably starve.

The bus finally came. I got off at Beech and went into the Magnum Bank, and cashed the check.

Actress. They thought I was an actress, just like Copper.

Then a flyer came, and I took it from force of habit, regretting it as I paid the coins. I was being so meanly careful of money, and then lapsing in unnecessary extravagance, and it was all a proof that I couldn't deal with the situation, but I wasn't going to think of it just now. Or of my mother. Or Clovis, or Egyptia, or even of him.

I got off at Racine, and walked over the New River Bridge, to Clovis's apartment block.

As I came to the outside of his door every bone in my body seemed suddenly to turn to fluid, but I spoke to the door, anyway, asking to come in.

Maybe he, they, were out. Or—busy. And the door wouldn't open.

The door didn't open and didn't open, and then it did.

I walked in, holding my purse in front of me like a sort of shield, and not looking around at the living area with its couches and pillows and tasteful decor. No one was there.

Snakes fought each other in my stomach, but I ignored them. I sat down on the couch with black cushions, and stared across at the window where I'd said "I love you" to his reflection in the glass, and he'd seen me and known.

After a few minutes, Clovis came through from the main bedroom in a dark blue three-piece suit, as if he were going out. He appeared elegant and casual, as he always does, but as soon as he looked at me, he blushed. I'd never seen the adult Clovis blush, a wave of painful color, hitting the inside of his skin so fast the pulses jumped in his temples. I remembered again, he's seventeen. And I started to blush in sympathy, but I wouldn't look down, and it was Clovis who turned his back and walked over to the drinks dispenser.

"Hallo, Jane. What'll you drink?"

"I don't want a drink. I've brought your money."

"Dear me, and I was hoping to get the pound of flesh."

He turned around with something in a glass, drinking it, cool again.

I got up, opened my purse, and counted out the large-unit notes on a table in front of him. It took quite a long while. He watched, sipping the drink from time to time, and there was lace on his shirt sleeves, like the Renaissance shirt Silver had worn on the Grand Stairway.

When I stopped, he said,

"He isn't here, you know."

"I know." I had known, too. Nerves or not, I'd have sensed if he were there, that near me. "Now please just tell me what you spent on Egyptia. Did you buy her the fur coat?"

"No. She bought it herself on her delay account."

"Do you want the money for the lunch you bought her?"

"No, Jane," said Clovis. "Jane, it really could have waited."

"No it couldn't."

"Did you have to cry all over your mother to get it?"

I stared at him. It was funny how I could dislike him, detest him so much, and still feel such affection. I didn't really want to fight with Clovis, I didn't really want to confide in him, but something made me, perhaps because he was the first person I could tell.

"Would you really like to know how I got the money?"

"Am I going to be awfully shocked?"

"You might be," I said doggedly. "I sold everything I own. At least, I think I owned it. The contents of my suite. Bed, chairs, ornaments, books, stereo. Everything. And most of my clothes, and—"

"Oh my God," said Clovis. He took a cigarette out of the box, brushed it over the automatic lighter and started to smoke. "That explains why Demeta called me at seven-thirty this morning."

I drew away from him, actually backed a step.

"What did she say?"

"Oh, calm and collected, as ever, and not much. Just, Is Jane with you, Clovis? And when I said No, and Did she know what time it was, she said, Please don't try to be rude to me, Clovis. Do you know where Jane might be?

And I said, I haven't a notion, and I find it quite easy to be rude, I don't need to try. At which she switched off."

"Were you alone?" I said.

"Quite alone."

"He wasn't with you."

"Who? Oh, the robot. No. I sent him back to Egyptia. She wanted him. For something."

"You wanted him."

"Ah. You saw through my transparent falsehood. Unsubtle little me."

"But I've repaid your money now. So your claim is nonexistent."

"True. Egyptia, though—"

"I can handle Egyptia."

"*Can* you?" Clovis stared back at me. "Is this our sweet little Jane talking? Such wonders, such chemical changes, can love perform upon the human spirit."

I didn't know I was going to do it any more than I'd known I'd tell him what I had done. My arm flew up as if on a spring, and I hit him across the face. It must have stung. And to Clovis, who fastidiously abhors any contact except in a bedroom, it had an added horror.

Yes, it must have stung. He moved away from me and stopped looking at me, but he said very coolly:

"If you're going to start that, get out."

"Did you think I wanted to stay?"

"No. You want to chase your bit of metal excitement round the city."

"Just to Egyptia's, where you sent him. What was wrong, Clovis? Had to turn him out before you started getting serious?"

"Oh please. Just because you're bloody maladjusted doesn't mean we all have to be."

I gulped, and holding on to my now almost empty purse, I ran to the apartment door.

In the lift, I said the word over—maladjusted. Then I laughed hysterically. Of course I was maladjusted. So what? I got out of the lift hysterically laughing and greatly surprised a heavily Rejuvinexed couple waiting to get in.

Life was a shambles. I mustn't hesitate now. If I paused, I'd be afraid, or recognize my fear for what it was. But how interesting, a month ago I'd have shriveled with shame if anyone had found me laughing alone in a lift—or anywhere, for that matter. I'd hit Clovis, but he was right. I had changed.

I had to ride the ferry across to The Island because the bridge was shut for repairs. Otherwise I'd have walked the thirty minutes it takes on foot.

The basin of water that surrounds The Island used to be a reservoir, and trees grow out from the waterline, that the ferry has to curve around. Maybe you know it, my unknown, would-be, nonexistent reader. And the concrete platform rising on its pylons, with the rich people's towers standing amid their landscaped gardens.

Egyptia has the top floor, and therefore a private roof-garden, with miniature ten-foot palm trees at the center, and a pool. Floating up to her oval, gilded doorway in the external lift, it all seemed suddenly unbelievable after the rental block on Tolerance. Or was it that the rental block seemed unbelievable? Surely this was just a social call, and I'd be going home directly to Chez Stratos.

(Is Jane with you, Clovis? Do you know where she might be? She'd have called Egyptia, too. And Jason and Medea. And Chloe. But not Davideed. He's at the equator, Mother. And it will only have taken Egyptia to tell my mother about Silver, what Clovis had probably revealed. Silver. I don't want to call him that. It's a registration—Am I going to have to fight with Egyptia?)

The lift stopped adjacent to the gilded oval door and let me out in the high-walled enclosure before it. Egyptia's pot plants are dying. She forgets to turn on the hose. When they lie there in brown husks, she weeps for them. Too late.

I touched the door panel.

"Who is here?"

The door-voice is Egyptia's voice, reproduced, velvety, carnal.

"Jane."

"One moment, Jane."

He must love her voice. He's a musician. Her voice is so musical, has such a variegated tonal inflexion. He's here. I can feel it. I'm going to make a fool of myself. I've sold my world, and if Egyptia says "No," I've lost everything. And she'll say "No," won't she? Yes, all right. I supposed Clovis lied about Egyptia demanding him back. But Clovis, to be perverse, having—enjoyed, that's the word, enjoyed him—sent him back to Egyptia, just as he implied he had to. A sort of neat, spiteful tying up of ends. And Egyptia, having received her lover, has been with him all night again. Or part of the night. The fact that she owes the price of him to someone, now me, isn't going to stop her from being overwhelmed and playing her ace card, her legal ownership. She'll say *No.*

After ten minutes, I touched the panel again.

"Who is here?"

"Jane. I've already told you."

"I am still signaling Egyptia, Jane. Please wait."

She's in bed with him right now. That's why she won't answer, won't let me in. She's locked against him, she's crying out in ecstasy, just as I did. His face is poised above her, or buried in her long dark hair. She's so beautiful. And the apartment is so rich. He appreciates artistry.

What can I give him to appreciate? That ghastly room. Me. I ought to go away.

I didn't.

And suddenly the door swung open.

At once I heard a tremendous, unexpected noise, which alarmed me. I shrank away from the door involuntarily, then moved forward, then stood indecisively on the threshold, not allowing the door to close.

As I did so, Lord slunk down the long, much-mirrored corridor. I remembered it was Lord, limp-handed Lord who'd guided me through the Gardens of Babylon that night I saw Silver again. And Lord remembered me.

"Oh hell, it's you," he said, striking a pose.

"Oh hell, it's me," I said. I amazed myself, for it sounded clever, even though I was only repeating what he'd said. (A trick worth keeping?)

"Well, you'd better come in. We're in the throes of *Peacock.*"

He must mean the play.

"Normally, we rehearse at that Godvile theatre," he added, looking into a mirror at himself. "But darling Egyptia brought us here. Then we're going to lunch at Ferrier's. You're not coming, are you?"

"I don't think so."

"I shall always recall you, I'm afraid, as the girl who gets drunk and throws up."

I'd have liked to say something to that, but I couldn't think of anything. Then I did.

"That must happen to your girlfriends a lot," I said, "but are you sure it's because of the drink?"

I walked past him and down the hall into Egyptia's vast salon, my brain singing and ringing. I couldn't quite believe in myself, and I stood there, stunned, intoxicated, and looked for him and found him not. Instead, I saw how the floor had been cleared and five male actors were on it, viciously fighting each other, while three women actors stood to one side, their heads tilted back, their eyes veiled, their hands and arms outstretched. Six or seven others of all sexes stood on the edge, or lay over the pushed-back chairs. One had swathed himself in an Indian tiger skin. A man with a small machine by him sat cross-legged on the coffee table, checking the script. Thin and handsome, he once or twice called out, in a thin, handsome voice, "No, Paul, to the groin, dear, the *groin.* Corinth, you look as if you're selling him ice cream, not trying to disembowel him."

"You *eaten* any of my ice cream?" Corinth, a young man in glint-stitched jeans, yelled back.

A comfit tray on a nearby cabinet was knocked to the floor with a dull clang.

Egyptia stood on the little stair that went up to the bedroom half-floor above. Her face was so white I feared for her life. Then I realized she had painted herself for her part. She leaned forward slightly. Her eyes were holes through into space, with golden centers. She was living the scene in a depth none of the others even knew about. She was flawless and unreal. It was true. In some indescribable luscious way, she *was* like a robot. Did he respond to that? Her sheer unblemished skin like that of a smooth and succulent fruit, her oceanic hair?

The last actor fell.

Egyptia's lips parted. She was going to speak her lines, and, despite everything, love, trauma, the chaos of my life, my fear and doubt at not finding him, I was mesmerized, waiting for what would come out. And in that second Lord shouted across the room at her: "Egypt. Your little blond friend's here. Can you come out to play?"

I could have killed him. I was abashed, the focus of all eyes, blamed for his fault. Egyptia's robotic optic lenses flickered as if she were coming to after losing consciousness. She looked at me, not knowing me. Who was I? No one from Antektra's tortured world.

I went over to her.

"I didn't mean to interrupt."

"That's . . . all right. What is it?"

"I need to talk to you. Not now. When you've finished."

"Oh." Her eyes closed. I thought she'd collapse. My head spun. "Oh, Jane," she said.

"Where is he?" I said. "Just tell me. Please. Please, Egyptia."

"Who?"

Suddenly, both in our separate agonies, our wires touched.

"Silver."

"Somewhere—the bedroom—or the roof—"

"Not with you. Why not with you?"

"Darling, he's a robot."

Suddenly as the touch of the wires, I heard the vague intransigent brutality in her voice. Instead of recoiling, I took her by the arms, and her huge eyes swam on me, so sensitive to everything, and nothing.

"Egyptia, I sold every scrap I own. I left my mother's house. I paid Clovis the money for—him."

I'd reached her, over the gliding honeyed slope of her inward-turned concentration.

"All of it?" She breathed. "But you—"

"I know. I could only afford it by selling everything. Even my clothes, Egyptia. But you, you of all people, understand why."

Behind and around us the actors sighed with boredom, unable to overhear, drinking Egyptia's minerals and spirits, popping her vitamins and pills. I ceased to believe in them, but I held *her* fast.

"Listen, Egyptia. You're so aware, so sensitive. You have so much love in you—He's a robot, but I'm in love with him. However silly that would sound to anyone else, I know I can tell you, I know you'll understand. I love him, Egyptia."

I had her measure. Her eyes filled voluptuously with tears, just as I realized mine must have.

"Jane . . ."

"Egyptia, he's my life."

"Yes, Jane, yes—"

"Egyptia, let me take him. Away from you. You have so much. You have your genius—" I meant it, I'd glimpsed it, like a smell of fire, and it was so useful to lie with the truth—"You have your genius, but I—I need him, Egyptia. Egyptia!"

She held me rigidly to her, then away. She stared at me, imperiously. She was Antektra. She was God.

"Take him," she said. And let me go.

I went by her up the stair, turned into the bedroom foyer. A door led out on to the roof-garden, and I took it randomly, for I was reeling. I walked to the pool and sank down beside it, and I laughed, laughed as if I had really gone mad, holding myself in my arms, rocking, crowing for breath, shaking my hair around myself like a faded golden shawl.

I had *handled* her. But, the stupid thing was, I'd believed every word.

Presently I stood up.

Fleets of immaterial sponge-cake-color clouds were blowing slowly sideways over the blue sky. The little potted palm trees rattled. The pool was green as a fruit acid. With the guitar across his body and resting in his arms, he was sitting not ten feet from me at the brink of the water. He wore dark blue and the shadows tangled over him, hid his face. His expression was serious and still, and the eyes were expressionless and flat—circuits switching over. His face cleared very gradually, and he didn't smile. And I was afraid.

He said to me: "What's happened to you?"

"Why?" I said. I didn't know what to say. "Aren't you pleased to see me? I thought you were always pleased to see *anyone.* Did you have a lovely time with Clovis? And a lovely, lovely time with Egyptia?"

He didn't answer. He set the guitar aside. (The guitar, the extra clothes, these must be in Egyptia's keeping. He hadn't brought them with him when he had gone with me.) He got up and walked over to me, and stood close to me looking down into my face.

I couldn't look at him. I said, again: "I've left my mother's house. I've paid Clovis all the money. I've told Egyptia I need you, and she's agreed to let you go." I frowned, puzzled. How could she bear to let him go? "I'm living in a place like a rat-hole, in a slum. You'll have to pretend to be human, and my lover. I don't know how I'll survive and probably in the end I shan't, and you'll come back to Egyptia. Did you sleep with her last night?"

"I don't sleep," he said.

"You know what I mean. Did you?"

"No," he said. "I *slept* in her robot storage compartment. She was with a man last night."

I raised my eyes to his contemplative, noncommittal, beautiful face.

"She—you—"

"You look incredibly perturbed."

"Blast her!" I cried. A puerile oath, but I meant it literally. I knew a fury like no other fury I had ever known and my eyes grew blind.

He took my hands very lightly.

"Jane. It doesn't matter."

"It matters."

"I am a machine."

"And Clovis—I suppose Clovis—"

"Clovis didn't put me in the robot storage."

"I bet. Oh God. Oh God."

"Be more gentle with yourself."

"Oh God. Oh God," I said in despair, and he took me in his arms, and we leaned together, our reflection perfect and still in the acidulous pool.

At last, I said,

"If you don't want to come with me, I'd understand. It's more artistic here."

He said, "What perfume have you got on? It has a beautiful smell."

"Nothing. I didn't—nothing."

"Then it must be you."

"It can't be. Human flesh must seem disgusting to you, if you can smell us."

"Human flesh is extremely seductive. After all, it's only another form of material."

"With a jumble of organs underneath."

"Just another kind of machinery. Sometimes less effective. Biologically more attractive."

"Ugh," I said, like the child I am. He laughed.

I looked at him then and said,

"It doesn't matter, it's my decision, but I think I sold my soul for you."

"I see," he said. "Do you want to buy it back?"

"I only want you."

His eyes were dark, something to do with the shadows.

"Then I'll have to try to make it worth your while."

"Why is it so awful?" he said to me two hours later, as I stood cringing on the threshold of the slum apartment on Tolerance.

"I suppose I can heat it. By winter, if I'm careful and save money, I can. And I suppose there's a way to plug up the cracks and the holes."

"Yes, there is."

"But it looks so awful. And it smells—"

"There isn't any smell," he said.

"Yes there is. Of people being miserable."

"Be happy then, and it will go."

I stared at him, distraught. He promptly told me a ridiculous joke and I laughed. The color of the rooms lightened. I remembered the sun coming in after the dream.

"But," I said, touching the flaking plaster, "I don't know where to start. Or how."

"I can see," he said, "I was an investment."

We went out again into the city. He led me over walkways, along side streets, into strange cheap food-o-marts and household stores. He, who had no need of food, told me what groceries to buy, and sometimes I even thought of things myself. He found open sheds under arches in the elevated, where cans of glue and planks of wood balanced against unbevelled mirrors. He knew where everything was. The strangest places, all useful.

The day began to go, and we paused at a food stall. I'd asked him to pretend to be human, but my fears had faded. To me, he was. Or at least, for fifty minutes out of every hour he was. But at the stall, hunger surprising me as I devoured the inexpensive greasy tasty food, I ate alone, and began to be concerned about this and other matters.

"The money is low," he said. "It would be crazy to waste it on fake meals for me."

"At least, drink some coffine. And it's cold now. Everyone else has a coat on." (Even I. I'd rolled my fur jacket all over the couch, and even rubbed loose plaster into it, to be camouflaged.) "Oh, I should have got your clothes from Egyptia."

He was amused. "We could still get them. Or I could."

"No!"

"Afraid she'll drug and abduct me."

"Yes. Well, can you try to look cold?"

"I can foam at the mouth and throw a fit on the sidewalk if you really want me to."

"Stop it," I said, having nearly choked.

Someone came up to the stall beside us, lured by the smoke of frying peppers, onions, bread, beef and mustard.

"God, I'm freezing," said Silver, clearly, stamping his feet.

The newcomer glanced at him and nodded.

In the dusk, as the speckled stars began to come on with the speckled street lamps of downtown—far fewer than the stars—Silver walked me over a grid of blocks and between high walls, into a market lit by flaring fish-gasoline jets. The light caught him, and turned him to coolest gold. He guided me from pillar to post, his arms already effortlessly loaded with paper bags of planks, glue, solvent, insti-plast, loaves, cartons of dry milk, oranges. Despite these, he looked fabulous, literally of a fable. I couldn't stop looking at him. I'd forgotten I'd bought him. Everywhere, they looked at him, I wasn't the only one. And he, mostly not noting it, when he caught their eyes, smiling at them so their faces lit like flares.

"How," I said, "did you know this market was here?"

"I know where everything is. Every building and back alley of the entire city. It was pre-programmed into me. Partly for convenience during the advertising campaign, partly to be of general service. You are going to find me," he said, "very useful, lady. God, I'm frozen," he added as someone went by.

We halted at a clothing stall. There was clothing on the stall, tarnished, gorgeous, permissible. From theatres which had closed their doors. From those second owners who, like the rich ones that had first fallen, had themselves crashed on hard times. My mother would have been repelled at the notion of buying any article another had formerly worn. I don't think she'd even want to wear anything of mine.

The woman on the stall fell passionately in love with him. She knocked prices in half. There was a sixteenth-century cloak of black-red velvet, destined to be his. She swathed him into it, embracing him as she did so, because he remarked how cold he'd felt before.

"Oh, that hair," she said to him. "It can't be natural."

He said, "Not quite."

"Suits you," she said. "And the skin makeup. Here," she said, suddenly including me. "Look at this. I'll let you have this for twenty."

Under the flares, it was warm, summer day heat shot up against the black autumn sky. Far away, the core of the city rose in cliffs of sugar, and the grains of the sugar were lights. The jacket sparkled too. It had green peacocks and bits of mirror—I thought of his jacket, the day I first saw him. . . .

"She can't afford twenty," he said to the woman. "Not in cash."

"Well," she said, "what else have you got?"

I felt myself tense inside my skin, but he only grinned, shaking his head, his eyes devilish and irresistible, so I wondered if he had hypnotized her when she said: "Ten. She can have it for ten. Suit her with her white face and her big eyes."

I wanted the jacket. Because I was with him, because it recalled him to me. Because of the peacocks. But I'd look too fat in it.

"I think it's a bargain," he said to me.

And I found myself paying, out of what was left of the Casa Bianca cash.

As we walked away, I said, "I shouldn't have done that."

"Yes, you should. It's not like the food. You'll look good in it. And there are ways of making money," he said, "not just spending it."

I was dubious and suddenly anxious. I knew a moment of terrible insecurity, even with him beside me. The oil light fell hard as hail into my eyes.

"How?"

"There you go, mind in the gutter again," he said, and I realized what my face must have shown. "Songs. I've sung on the street for E.M. Ltd. I can do it for you."

"No," I said. This idea unsteadied me further. I wasn't sure why, but the mutinous crowd with their banners, their wise distrust of the excellence of machines, were mixed in my fear. "It's wrong—if they pay you."

"Not if they enjoy it enough to pay me."

I stared at him. The human supernatural face looked back, inquiringly.

"I'm afraid," I said, and stopped still, holding my small burden of the peacock jacket to me.

"No, you're not," he said. He moved close to me, obscuring everything from me except his presence. Even the light was gone, remaining only as a conflagration at the edges of his hair. "You've pre-programmed yourself," he said, "to go on being afraid. But you're not afraid anymore. And," he said to my astonishment, "what have you decided to call me?"

"I—don't know."

"Then that's what you should be worrying about. So much anticipation on my part, and still no name."

We walked on. We paused, and bought an enormous jar of silk-finish paint, and color mixants.

"All the women love you," I said jealously.

"Not all."

"All. The woman on the stall cut her prices by half."

"Because she was charging twice too much already and thought we'd haggle. The only genuine reduction was the jacket she offered you."

We, I, bought some drapery, a pillow that would need recovering.

I felt a burst of childlike excitement, as on a birthday morning. Then another surge of alarm.

"What on earth am I doing," I said vaguely.

"Turning your apartment into somewhere you can bear to live."

"I shouldn't. . . ."

"Programmed and activated," he said, and proceeded to an extraordinary imitation of a computer mechanism running through a program, gurgles, clicks and skidding punctuations.

"Please stop it," I muttered, embarrassed.

"Only if you do."

I frowned. I looked into the depth of the jacket wrapped in flimsy tissue, the sausage of wrapped pillow. I'd never exercised freedom of choice before, and now I was, and it was peculiar. And he. He wasn't a robot. He was my friend, who'd come to help me choose (not tell me *what* to choose), and to carry my parcels, and to give me courage.

"Have I been brave?" I asked him in bewilderment as we strolled out of the market and through a deserted square. "I think I must have been."

Tremor-sites rose against the stars. Birds or bats nested in them, I could hear the whickering sounds of their wings and little squeaking noises.

"And *do* I feel afraid only because I still think I should—not because I've left my mother and my home and my friends, because I haven't got any money, because I've lost my heart to a beautiful piece of silverware."

We laughed. I saw what had happened. I was beginning to catch the way he talked. It had never been really possible with anyone else. I'd envied Clovis's wit, but it was usually so vicious I hadn't been able to master it, but with Silver—damn. *Not* Silver.

"Silver," I said, "I know you can adapt to anyone and anything, but thank you for adapting to me, to *this.*"

"I hate to disillusion you," he said, "you're easier than most to adapt to."

We walked home. Odd. *Home?* Yes, I suppose that was already true, because anywhere he was was my home. Silver was my home. A milk-white cat was singing eerily among the girders in the subsidence, like the ghost of a cat. (Did cats have ghosts, or souls?)

"It's so cold," I wailed in the room.

"That's my line, surely."

I looked at the wall heater unhappily.

I was down to nickels and coppers now, and the three hundred on my card, until next month.

He swung off the cloak and folded it over me, then holding me inside it and against him.

"I'm afraid I don't have any body heat to keep you warm."

"I don't care."

We kissed each other quietly, and then I said,

"Don't ever make love to me if you don't want to."

"If you want me to, I shall want to."

"I just don't believe that. There may be times—"

"No. My emotional and physically simulated equilibriums never alter."

"Oh."

"I also swallowed a couple of dictionaries someplace."

We dragged the mattress off the couch. The bed under it had a padded top-surface and was less used. I pulled the almost new, dappled rugs, faintly scented from their recent cleaning, over us. Under them, I lay a long while, caressing him, exploring him, making love to *him.*

"Do you mind if I do this?" I asked timidly, quite unable to stop.

"Oh, I mind dreadfully."

"I'm probably clumsy."

"Far from it. You're becoming a wonderful lover."

"How would you know? It can't mean anything to you."

"Not as it would to a flesh-and-blood man. But I can still appreciate it."

"Artistically," I sneered. "When the proper circuits are put in action."

"Something like that."

"Egyptia—" I murmured, drowning in his hair, the taste of his skin—unmortal and yet flesh—the flesh of a demon—"if you didn't find pleasure with Egyptia—"

"You make it sound like a café we were looking for. I did."

"Yes. . . . She'd be terribly clever."

"Egyptia is totally passive. The pleasure is in finding what pleases *her.*"

Minutes later, as the strange wing-beats began to stir inside me, I couldn't prevent myself from saying, "I wish I could find what pleases *you.* I wish, I wish I could."

"*You* please me," he said. It was true. The delight mounted in his face as my delight mounted within me—different, yet dependent.

"You fool," I gasped, "that isn't what I mean—"

When I fell back into the silence, the room of the apartment thrummed gently. It had the scent of oranges, now, and glue, and paper bags. . . .

"I can stay here with you," he said, "or I can start work on this place."

"I want you with me," I said. "I want to sleep next to you, even if you can't—don't—sleep."

"You mean," he said, "you aren't going to ask me if I wouldn't rather be anywhere except beside you?"

"Am I as paranoid as that?"

"No. Much worse."

"Oh."

"Your hair's changing color," he said.

"Yes. I'm sorry."

"Are you? I think you may be quite pleased when the change is complete."

"Oh, no. It will be horrid." Curled against him, lulled and childishly almost asleep, I felt safe. I was whole. We were in a boat, or on the back of a milk-white bird.

"Birds?" he asked me softly. "As well?"

"Yes," I said. "And a rainbow."

He must have left me at some point during the night. When I opened my eyes in the effulgent, now-curtain-filtered sunrise, there was blue sky on the ceiling, blue sky and islands of warm cloud, and the crossbow shapes of birds, like swifts, darting statically between. And a rainbow, faint as mist, yet with every transparent color in it, passing from the left hand corner by the door, to the corner nearest the window. It was real. Almost.

He was sitting on top of a rickety old chromium ladder he must have borrowed from somewhere in the building, from the bad-tempered caretaker perhaps. He was taking a devilish joy in my amazement as I woke and saw.

"But you're a musician, not an artist," I said dreamily.

"There's a leaflet in with the paint which explains how to do this sort of thing. Being a machine—well, it's easy for me to get a good result."

"It's beautiful—"

"Then wait till you see the bathroom."

I ran into the bathroom. The ceiling was sunset in there, soft crimson nearnesses, and pale rosy distance. A white whale basked in the shallows of the clouds.

"A *whale* in the sky?"

"Make the metaphysical assumption the bath is the sea. And that the whale's a damn good jumper."

Five days later, you came up the cracked steps, opened the door, and walked into somewhere else.

He would ask me what I wanted, and we'd work on it together. Ideas escalated. He worked most of the nights, too. Once I woke up in the dark, crying for some reason I didn't remember, and he came back into the bed to comfort me, and in the morning we and the rugs had become glued together and had to soak ourselves apart in the bath. His invention, and his mechanized knowledge of the city and its merchandise and price ranges, meant that fantastic things were done for very little outlay. I only cut a small way into the three hundred I.M.U. Admittedly I lived on sandwiches and fruit and wonderful junk foods found in sidewalk shops. My mother's thorough understanding of nutrition, demonstrated in the perfectly balanced meals served from the mechanical kitchen and the servicery at Chez Stratos, the awareness of the best times to eat what, and why, and the grasp of vitamins, in which she had tried to educate me—all that stayed with me like a specter. But I didn't get pimples or headaches, or throw up. Probably she'd nourished me so well that I was now immune. The way I ate and lived, of course, the way I slept and worked and made love, all these were enormous barriers against my ever calling her, although: "Hallo, Mother, this is Jane," I said, over and over in my head a hundred times a day. Once I said to him, "I think I'm afraid of my mother." And he said, holding my hand as we walked up the stairs, "From the sound of it, it could be mutual." Puzzled, I demanded an explanation. Smiling, he sidetracked me, I forget how—

What would she say about this apartment? She wouldn't cry out with delight, every time she came into it, as I do. "How beautiful!" No, she wouldn't say that. Even the brass bed, with the headboard like a huge veined leaf, wouldn't impress her, and anyway, the brass bed came later. . . .

The walls, now sealed and burnished, and smooth, are

painted cream-white. The pale gold paper lamp that hangs from the clouds and the swifts has a gold metal stitching on it, and when the light burns at night, gold flecks are thrown all over the walls. There are also wonderful scintillas and glows that are wavered from the colored candles standing on the shelves Silver put up. Each candle is a different color, or colors, and stands in a scoop of colored glass. These scoops are, in fact, a batch of flawed glass saucers bought for nickels, and painted over with glass enamel. The mirror, too, has a glorious glass painting on it, of leaves and hills and savage flowers. Every slope and tendril and petal totally hides some spot or chip in the mirror. We have wall to wall carpet, too. It's made of literally hundreds of tiny carpet remnants given away as free samples. We spent a whole day walking from store to store, asking about carpets and, "Unable to decide" on one, going off with handfuls of pieces to "match with our furnishings." It took hours to glue every scrap in place. The effect is astonishing, a mosaic that rivals the rainbow in the ceiling. No chairs, but large dark green fur pillows to sit on, or the couch, draped with rugs and shawls like the divan of a potentate. Curtains for the clean window, are to encourage the sky, being the color of blue sunlight. (The scatter of little tears in them are concealed by one whole packet of heat-and-press-on embroidered badges—tiny gold and silver mythical animals and castles.) The door is cream-white and vanishes into the wall. The horrible functional kitchen hatch (with the crotchety miniature oven and electric ring behind it that hardly ever get used) has become a wall-painting. It's blue with clouds, like the ceiling, and a big-sailed, heavily winged ship is flapping over it, with a gilded cannon poking from its side, which is the handle fitting. We both painted this, and it's remarkably silly. The wings on the ship are modeled after geese.

The bathroom is madder. The walls were raw cement

and broken tiles, and when patched up to seal, they looked impossible. Then, in another market, there were sky-blue tentlike waterproof coveralls going at four in the morning for next to nothing because no one wanted them, and the stall-keeper had a virus and was dying to get home. These, cut in lengths with a kind of spontaneous but enticed shirring and ruching, are glued over every inch of the walls. The waterproofing looks like silk, and they make the room into a weird oriental fantasy, particularly when the rose-red paper lamp hanging from the rose-red clouds comes on, and hits every pleat and fold with an electric magenta streak of shine. We re-enamelled the bath, hand basin, drinking-tap basin, and the lavatory, all blue. The enamel is cheap and will probably crack inside six months. But for now, each area is reminiscent of a lagoon. The second night, Silver stripped the floor and put the new planks down, polished and varnished them. The bathroom floor is now a golden fake pine, and looks as if it cost a thousand. Well, at least five hundred.

"How do you know how to do all that?" I asked him, endlessly.

"I read the instructions," he endlessly and innocently replied.

Of course, a robot *can* just read instructions and then know exactly how to follow them, and get it absolutely right. I kept saying to myself I mustn't persist in thinking of him as an exceptionally talented man, no I mustn't. Yet it was difficult, and besides, that's what I'd asked him to pretend to be.

On the last afternoon of the first week, the caretaker came puffing and grumbling up the stairs to collect the rent, plainly thinking he wouldn't get it.

"It's just the one quarter month," he announced as I stood there, a plum in one hand and a long artist's paintbrush in the other. "Just the one week. Then I shan't be up till the first of next month for the three quarters." As the end of the month was also only a few days off, that meant nothing. He implied, in any case, I'd have run away by then in arrears. "It's legal, you know," he said. But already his eyes had gone past me and were bulging on the room. "Well," he said. "I wondered what your boy-friend wanted the steps for." He tried to edge in by me, so I let him. He stood and gaped, as if in a famous cathedral. "Not everyone's taste," he said, "but it's cheerful." Which is more, I thought, than can be said for you.

I waited for him to go on and say: "Now you've spent your rent money on all that, you'll have to get out." But he only glanced at the huge evergreen plant which Silver and I had dug out of the subsidence the night before and planted in a big cracked beer jeroboam of wondrous amber glass. "That'll die," he said.

"Perhaps you'd like to come to its funeral," said Silver, who was seated on a pillow, reading, at fifteen seconds per page, a job-lot of books we'd picked up that morning.

The caretaker scowled.

"This flat," he said, "is only supposed to accommodate one person."

I felt a stab of terror, but Silver said, "I'm not paying her any rent. I'm her guest."

Grudgingly, the caretaker accepted that this was all right, and Silver smiled at him.

I was already fumbling out the rent and electric money, all in small change by now, when Silver rose and graciously gave the monstrous visitor a tour of the bathroom. I could hear the monster grunting away, things like: "Don't know I'd want it myself," or "What's that white thing in the ceiling? Oh." And then, surprisingly: "Quite like that."

They came back, and Silver poured the caretaker, and me, a mug of very cheap and vinegary wine, which the caretaker gulped down. When we finally got rid of him, and the rent, I lost my temper. The beautiful apartment, on which we'd slaved, smeared by that old man's stupid carping.

"He's just forgotten how to respond," said Silver. "And he's sick. He has to take a prescription medication that gives him another sickness as a side effect."

"How do *you* know?"

"The night I borrowed the ladder, we sat around for a while, and he told me."

"Still trying to make everyone happy," I said.

"Still trying. Uphill work all the way."

I looked at him and we laughed. And I went to him and put my arms round him. The carpet floor is nice to make love on, too.

The evergreen plant, by the end of the month, had spread up to the ceiling in a lustrous fan.

Which brings me to the end of the month.

3

The night before the first day of the new month, we were sitting out in the subsidence, on one of the girders, watching the stars stare their way past the last of the clinging leaves, and the distant city center blooming into its lights. We often came out there, which had firstly been his suggestion. Sometimes he played the guitar there quietly and sang to me. It was beautiful in the subsidence. Mysterious at dusk, and wild, like the heart of some forest, with the safe edges of civilization around it. Now and then, the white cat appeared, and we'd bring a plate of cat's meat and leave it by. Despite its apparent homelessness, Silver had spotted, with his faultless sight, the little mark on the hindquarters of the cat, which means it's had its anti-rabies shots quite recently. I had a wish to lure the cat into the apartment. But that night the cat didn't come, just the stars. And as I lay against him, wound with him in the cloak, I said, "This is the happiest time of my whole life."

He turned and kissed me, and he said, "Thank you."

I was touched suddenly by the innocence inherent in his sophistication. I held him. The coolness though not coldness of his body had never troubled me, and now, from proximity to mine, he seemed warm.

"I don't even mind that you don't love me," I said. "I'm so happy."

"But I do, of course, love you."

"Because you can *make* me happy."

"Yes."

"Which means I'm no different from anyone you make happy, you can love us all, so it's not what I mean by love." At last, it didn't hurt; I was arch and unconcerned, and he smiled.

I shall never grow tired of, or familiar with, his beauty.

"I love *you,*" I said. "Let's go out to dinner. Do you mind? Will you pretend?"

"If you're sure you want to spend money on it."

"Yes, yes, I do. Tomorrow I'm back to a thousand."

"I confess," he said, "I rather like the taste of food."

"You *do?*"

"Should I be ashamed, I wonder?"

"Oh *yes,*" I said. "Most reprehensible."

Our positions were reversed for an instant, our dialogue, our speech mannerisms. He was playing, but I had still learned.

"You've changed me," I said. "Oh thank God you have."

We went in, and I washed my hair. I'd hardly seen it since we'd started work. It had been bound up in scarves as I painted and glued things, and it was thick with dry shampoos because it takes so long to dry without a dryer when I wash it. But tonight I was lavish with the wall heater. As my hair began to dry before the painted mirror, I saw emerge among those blue hills and that tigerish foliage, a mane of light, the color of blond ash.

My mother had got something wrong. Or had she? Or the machines, perhaps, the coloressence charting. Or had my natural hair color simply altered as I grew older? Yes, that must be it, because—

"Oh," I said, touching my hair, "it's beautiful. It's beautiful in a way it never was."

"And that," he said, "is your own."

I put on one of my oldest dresses, which Egyptia once gave me, and which had been hers. Demeta hadn't thought it suited me, and neither had I, but I'd kept it for the material, which was strange, changing from white to blue to turquoise, depending on how light struck. And tonight it did suit me, and I dared to put on the peacock jacket and buttoned it, and it fit. I was slim. I was slim and tall. And my hair was moonlight. And I wept.

"I'm sorry, I don't know why—"

"Yes you do," he said. He held me until I began to laugh instead. "Poor Demeta," he said.

"I don't understand."

"If I told you," he said, "I was hungry, you wouldn't believe me?"

"No. Tell me why my mother is supposed to be 'Poor Demeta.' "

"I think you know. Look at your hair, and ask yourself if you do."

But I was feverish and elated. I thrust thought aside and hurried us out of the building, through the streets which now I knew quite well, up onto the only partly moving escalator on South Arbor, to the flyer platform.

We sailed into the center of the city. I wasn't afraid of meeting anyone. Part of me, perhaps, almost wanted to.

Who, after all, would know me? (And I forgot what he had said.)

As we sat in Hunger And Answer, eating charcoaled steak and tiny little roast potatoes shaped like stars, I thought: Now I can phone them, all of them. Egyptia, Clovis. My mother. The wine was red. It matched his hair. And like his own glamour, the wine didn't interest him very much.

We walked home all across the city.

The ultimate leaves blew and crunched beneath our feet. The streets close to the Old River were shut off again, unless you bought those smelly throwaway oxy-masks at the check gate. We went over Patience Maidel Bridge though the center end had the *Walk Fast* notices up, and there were no buskers. When we got past the halfway mark, it was apparently clear, though empty. For some reason he and I started to sing, idiotic songs we made up as we walked, no longer fast, about the snarling fish in the purple water. Catch one for the cat—Oh hell—the fish has ate my cat—Oh well—dress the fish in fur—teach the fish to purr—kid me it's the cat—Cat-fish can be swell.

The green light was on as we came off the bridge, and just as we moved down toward East Arbor, I saw there were two buskers. They weren't performing, but seated on a rug, a boy and a girl, eating french fries out of a paper over a guitar with three broken strings.

Despite my thoughts of earlier, I hesitated. For they were Jason and Medea.

Once, a year ago, they'd done this before. It was a basic idea. Jason sang, rather badly, and Medea went around the crowd, if one was tone-deaf enough to gather, or if not, through the passersby with a plate. As she did so, she picked pockets. Usually she was caught out, or had been last time. Both were minors, but their father had had to pay a considerable fine.

"What's wrong?" Silver asked, sensing how I held back.

"Some people I know, and don't like."

As we spoke, Jason looked up and right at me. An expression of astonishment went over his face. Very slowly, he nudged Medea. Their thin still eyes seemed to congeal identically. There was no other way but to walk on and meet them. Did they know about Silver? About me? About me and Silver? Or not?

"Hallo, Jane," said Medea.

"Hallo, Jane," said Jason.

I looked at them, pausing, my hand in Silver's. The strength in his hand comforted me, though it seemed a long way off.

"Hallo," I said. And then, rashly, coolly, "Do I know you?"

Jason laughed.

"Oh, I *think* so."

"I think so," said Medea. "Your name *is* Jane, isn't it?"

"The bleached hair's not bad," said Jason. "And the diet. Does Mother know?"

Then they hadn't been told I'd absconded from Chez Stratos. Or had they. . . .

"Did you have a nice evening?" I inquired politely.

"Pickings were quite good," said Medea flatly.

Jason smirked. He smirked beyond me, at Silver. Suddenly Jason's smirk faltered.

I glanced at Silver. There was that look I'd seen before, like a metal mask, the eyes burning, impenetrable, fearsome. Circuits switching?

"Who's your gorgeous actor friend?" said Jason. His voice didn't quite sound as sure as it usually did. "Or is it a big seekwit?"

"Does your mother know?" repeated Medea.

I stood there, my skull quite empty, and Silver said to them in the most gentle and reasonable and truly deadly of voices, as if it were an analogy for their lives: "You have just dropped a chip inside the sound-box of your guitar, which won't do either of them much good."

"Oh, thanks for caring," said Jason.

"Personally, I don't like silver makeup," said Medea. "What drama are you in? Or are you out of work? It must be nice for you that you met Jane."

"Yes, Jane's very rich, isn't she," said Jason. "We're rich too, of course. But we don't make friends with out-of-work actors."

"But Jane's such a softy," said Medea.

"Luckily for you," said Jason.

They stopped. They'd said all they could think of for the moment.

I knew none of this mattered, but it was still awful. I didn't look at Silver anymore. I could feel the roughness of the embroidered cuff of his shirt, which we'd bought in the market three nights ago, against my wrist. I supposed it was up to me to make the move to get away. To Silver, this was irrelevant.

Then I began to see what was happening to Jason and Medea, and I started to be fascinated. They were wriggling, actually and definitely physically wriggling, their little hard eyes glaring at him and slithering off him. And Medea had gone a dreadful yellow color, while Jason's tanned ears were turning red—I'd never seen anything like this happen to them before, even when they were children. And now their hands were plucking feebly at the french fries, they were gazing at the ground, their backs were stiffening as if in the grip of a horrible paralysis. I didn't turn to Silver anymore. I realized that cruel annihilating look of his, which he said meant nothing, was still trained on them like a radioactive ray, mercilessly letting them shrivel beneath it.

It was Medea who finally managed to say, in a shrill, wobbly wire of a voice: "Why won't he stop staring? Doesn't he know it's rude. Make him stop it."

But it was Jason who scrambled suddenly to his feet. Not waiting to pick up the guitar, the ill-gotten gains, the chips, or even for Medea, he thrust by me and jumped hastily away onto the escalator up to the bridge. Medea, in a speechless frenzy, snatched the money and the guitar and bolted after him. I felt Silver turn to watch them go, as I had turned. Medea turned too, just once, though Jason didn't. She was at the top of the escalator. Her face was a yellow bone triangle and her mouth hissed, or looked as if it did. Then she ran after Jason.

I was shaken too. I didn't move until Silver slipped his other arm round me.

I knew his face had changed then, so I looked up at him.

"I thought," I said, "you wanted everyone to be happy."

"Don't I?" he said.

"Your circuits were just switching over," I said.

"Not exactly."

"You meant to frighten them."

"I meant to shut them up."

"But why did it matter to you?"

"The temperature of your hand changed. It went very cold."

"And I bought you, so your loyalty was to me. Like the Golder robot being a personal bodyguard," I said, with amazing stiltedness.

His eyes, unblinking and jewellike, looked back at me. There was a long pause.

"Jane," he said. But nothing else.

And I was suddenly afraid. At the meeting with the

twins, at the uncanny thing he'd been able to do to them. Afraid of being here with him, afraid for him, and for myself.

"What is it?" I whispered.

"I think it's time we walked on," he said.

And he let go of me, even my hand, and we walked on. Like two lovers who'd quarreled. And the night was cold as knives.

The bed was cold that night, too, and we didn't make love in it.

In the morning, just as the light started to come, I woke up. Silver was sitting cross-legged on the rainbow carpet. He was dressed, and his hair fell forward over his face because his head was bowed. He looked like a beautiful advertisement for psychosthetic meditation. But sensing me awake, he looked up. He smiled at me, but the smile wasn't the same as at any other time before.

"Do you mind if I walk about outside for a while?"

Of course. He was my property and had to ask my permission.

"No. . . ."

I couldn't even say, "Are you all right?" He was a machine. Obviously he was all right. And just as obviously, something was wrong.

"I'll be back in an hour."

'No. Come back when you want to."

"Will you," he said, "be okay?"

"Yes. I have to buy some groceries and start the card off for this month. I'll need change for the rent money."

"Do you want me to come with you?"

"Oh no." I sounded bright and self-sufficient.

He got up, sort of melting to his feet as if every muscle were elastic, and probably it is.

After he went, I was alone for the first time since he'd come with me from Egyptia's. "Alone" now had a new meaning. It felt as if I'd been cut in half. Half of me was here in the apartment, and half out on the street walking about, only I didn't know where.

I got up, wrapped myself in the emerald shawl from the couch, and made some lime-spice tea. I sat and looked out of the window, drinking the hot tea, watching the last rags of leaves falling like dead birds.

I tried to go over what had happened, how everything had been fine until we met Jason and Medea. And then— but what *had* happened then? All that kept coming into my mind, dredged up like Davideed's silt, were those words of the vile Swohnson's: *This one doesn't check out.* Not that I'd really thought about that aspect, only its nightmarish result—Silver, his eyes replaced by wheels. . . . Yet now, I began to see a curious unevenness, a strange incoherence. Sitting there, shivering over the tea, I pictured those other Sophisticated Format robots, the Coppers, the Golders, the two Silvers, that I'd seen performing at Electronic Metals. How lifelike they'd been, in appearance and in attitude; mannerisms, movements, speech. So lifelike, if you hadn't known, you'd have taken them for men and women. And yet there was something, something which gave them away, maybe only when you knew, but something which told you they weren't men, weren't women. Something that told you they were machines. And did I imagine it, or was Silver, my Silver—S.I.L.V.E.R.—not like that at all? Was Silver truly like a human man, truly believable as human—*even when you knew he wasn't?* And was it this which had set E.M.'s computers ticking on the checkout? Some sort of independence, beyond any autonomy, however profound, that they'd programmed into him?

But how? And why?

No, that wasn't what concerned me. I was just afraid because I might lose him, lose him even though I owned him. He wasn't a slave in Imperial Rome. And yet, he was a machine. He was, he was. And suddenly the enormity and the insanity of my emotions boiled up before my startled inner eye. I loved a machine. Loved it, trusted it, had rested the foundations of my world on it. And on the game I played that it could be kind to me.

I had a terrible feeling. As if I'd been walking in my sleep, and woken up in the middle of an unknown and deserted plain.

In a daze, I showered and dressed, and took up my purse with the credit card, and wandered out into the city. I had a kind of need for the proof of money. I had a need, too, to be out of the apartment. Maybe when I went back, my arms full of fruit and soap, Silver would be home and everything would be as it had been. Yes, this must be the way to break the spell.

It was raining in the city. As I crossed over from the elevated, robot ambulances screamed past me. Someone had been run over outside the Hot-Bake Shop. I felt a dreary depression and fear.

I went into one of the large stores off the boulevard, because I'd seen a crimson glass jar there that I wanted to buy for the bathroom. It was purely ornamental, and I see now I was still basically acting just like someone rich. I hoped the jar would stop me from feeling the incredible sense of dread, and when they gave it to me and I put it in the wire basket with the crackers and the nectarines, it almost did. I picked up some bath towels, too, and a paper knife from the second-owner counter. Then one of the ambulances went by the windows. I remembered the man who had been stabbed at the visual, and how it hadn't bothered me, except somewhere inside, some sort of mental bottom drawer, where it had obviously bothered me a lot. I stood in the queue to pay. I was thinking, My mother taught me about self-analysis and so I should be able to analyze why I'm suddenly so scared of death or injury. And then I thought: When I get back, he'll be there. He'll be sitting on the couch playing the guitar. I had a picture of the winter, and the snow coming; of being snowed up in the apartment block with him, a sort of glorious hibernation. And then I had a picture of going home and finding him not there.

Then it was my turn at the checkout. It was automatic, in this store, but sometimes got cranky, and so there was a bored girl supervisor sitting nearby, painting her nails.

My goods ran through and the total rang up, and I put my card into the card slot. Instead of the bell sounding and the groceries card, and change coming out of the other end of the machine, a buzzer went sharply. A red light appeared over the card slot, and my card was regurgitated. As I stood there, the bored girl glanced over, got off her stool and walked up.

"Your card must be overdue."

"No. It's an indefinite monthly."

She picked it out of the slot and looked at it.

"Oh, yes," she said.

A thousand I.M.U. indefinite was probably unusual in this area, and I hoped she wouldn't say the amount aloud. She didn't.

"Let's try again," she said, and pushed my card back into the slot. And once more the buzzer went and the card was vomited out.

People were piling up behind me. They muttered, unfriendly, and I blushed like fire. Even though my heart was growing cold, I already knew what had happened.

"Well," said the girl, "looks like someone's blocked your account at the other end. Anyone have authority to do that?"

I reached for the card, blinded by shame and fright.

"Do you want to pay for your things in cash?" she asked lazily. She seemed to be holding the card just out of my reach. In a moment I might leave it with her and run away.

"I haven't got enough money on me."

"No," she said. She gave me the card. She thought the people I worked for, since in this part of town generally only firms issue credit cards to employees, had fired me, and I'd been trying it on to get free groceries.

I walked out of the shop, guilt blazoned on my face, trembling. In the street I literally didn't know which way to turn, and went randomly leftward, and so into another raining street, and so into another, without knowing or looking or caring where I was going.

Demeta, of course, had stopped my card as soon as she could, on the first of the month. Why not? She had every reason. I'd run away from home with scarcely a good-bye. I couldn't expect to go on taking her money. I could see that now as clearly as I could see nothing else. How could I have reckoned to get away with it? It was some silly childhood thing that had prevented me from guessing. Some part of me had still believed the implication she'd always given me that, because I was her daughter, her money was mine. Stupid. Of course it wasn't.

Why then was I hesitating at this phone kiosk, standing in the rain until the woman came out, and then moving in myself and closing the door. Altogether I had ten units left in cash. Not enough to pay my rent. More than enough to call my mother's house.

Even as I put the coins in and pressed the buttons, I thought, But she's so busy, she might not be there—and then I thought: *She'll* be there. She'll be sitting there waiting for this call. Waiting for my voice, for my frantic weeping words: Mother, Mother—help me!

And then I didn't feel afraid anymore, only dreary and small and very tired. It was true, after all, wasn't it? I'd rung her for help, for forgiveness, to plead with her, or beg her.

I leaned my forehead on the cold dank glass that someone had cracked on the outside with a stone. There was no video in this part of the city. She couldn't see me. Was that good or bad? I counted the signals. She made me wait through twelve of them before she turned on the auto-answer that, left to itself, replies after two.

"Good morning. Who is calling, please?"

"Jane," I said. Rain had fallen on my lips, and I tasted it for the first time as I spoke. Jane. A pane of crystal, the sound of rain falling on the silken grain of marble, a slender pale chain—

"Please wait, Jane. I will connect you with Demeta's studio."

My humiliation had sunk, and I was hollow. I heard her voice presently. It was politely warm, almost approachable. It said: "Hallo, Jane." Like the lift.

I clenched my hand so hard on the speaker of the phone it seemed to melt like wax in my grip.

Jain, Mother. *Jain.*

"Hallo, Mother," I said. "Isn't it lovely weather?"

An interval.

"I'm sure, dear," she said, "you didn't call me to discuss the weather."

I smiled bitterly at my dim reflection, bisected by the crack.

"Oh, but I did. And to say hallo, Mother. Hallo, Mother."

"Jane. Try to be sensible. Your recent actions have been rather unusual, and very unlike you. I'm hoping that this will be an adult exchange."

"Mother," I said, "I'm sixteen. Not twenty-six. Not ninety-six. Sixteen."

"Indeed? Then why have you acted like a child of six?"

I shuddered. I'd drawn her. She'd lashed back at me, neatly and calmly—and decidedly. The rain drizzled. I could smell onions frying and wet pavements, and . . . *La Verte. La Verte* filled up the kiosk.

"I really just called you," I said, "to tell you how happy I am."

My eyes filled with tears, but I held them inside me, and they drained away.

"I'm sure you actually phoned me, dear, to ask why your monthly I.M.U. credit has been stopped."

I felt a surge of awful triumph.

"Oh," I said. "Has it?"

She wouldn't believe me. She knew she spoke the truth and I was the liar. But still, she'd had to say it, and not me.

"Yes, Jane," she said patiently. "Your account has been frozen. Permanently. Or until such time as I unfreeze it."

I stood and watched the rain. My hand had left the speaker, and I was drawing a rabbit on the steamy flawed glass.

"Jane?" she said firmly.

"Mother, why did you call me 'Jane'? I mean, why not Proserpina? That was Demeta's daughter in the legend, wasn't it? Didn't you think I'd be glamorous enough to be called Proserpina, Mother?"

"Where are you?" asked my mother suddenly. It was a trick. I was meant to blurt out a location.

"In," I said, "a phone kiosk."

"And where is the kiosk?"

Too late, Mother.

"The kiosk is on a street, and the street is in a city."

"Jane," she said, "have you been taking an illegal drug of some kind?"

"No, Mother."

"I don't think, dear, that you quite understand your situation. Your card is inoperable. There is no other lawful way you can obtain money. I think I had better explain to you, in case you're thinking of it, that finding a job of any sort will be next to impossible for you. To begin with, you will have to possess a labor card. Before any employment bureau will give you one, they will take a body print reading. They will then check you out and see that you are the daughter of a rich woman. Accordingly, they will ask me if I am prepared to support you. There's a serious shortage of work, Jane, which I've no doubt even you are partially aware of. No one who doesn't need to work is even considered. And when they ask me if I will support you, I will reply that of course I will, you are my chosen child. You have only to return home, and everything you need will be supplied, including money."

"You once said," I murmured, "that I ought to get a job in the city, to appreciate the struggle the poor go through."

"With my sanction, that could have been arranged. Not, however, without it."

It was warm in the kiosk, so warm the rabbit was running all down the glass.

"All you need to do," said my mother, "is go into any bank, anywhere in the state, and identify yourself. You will then be able to draw the exact fare money to get you home."

"Home," I said.

"Home. I've already redesigned and refurnished your suite. You know me better than to think I would ever say anything about the state in which you left it."

I burst out laughing.

"Jane. I must ask you, once more, to control yourself."

"Mother, you've left me no choice but to become a thief. I'll have to rob a store or take someone's wallet."

"Please don't be silly, Jane. This sort of hysteria is distressing—however well I may be able to interpret your motivation, we are still mother and daughter. It's my very concern for your inability to cope with real life that makes me insist you come back to the house. You know in your heart this is true, Jane, and that I'm only thinking of you."

A cliché. Never be afraid of a cliché, if it expresses what you wish to say, Jane. The kiosk was hot and I couldn't breathe. I put my hand inadvertently to my throat, and felt the policode, and I said: "Does my policode still work, Mother?"

"Yes, Jane," she said. "For three more days. And then I'm withdrawing your print from the precinct computer."

"That's for my own good, too, is it?"

"You know the expression, Jane, I must be cruel only to be kind."

"Yes," I said. "Shakespeare. Hamlet." I drew in a hard impossible breath. "Spoken by a lunatic who's just killed an old man behind a curtain, and who has a deep-seated psychological desire to sleep with his *mother.*"

I slammed down the switch so violently I broke the skin and my hand started to bleed.

It was raining fiercely now. Vaguely through the rain I could see someone else was waiting outside to come in and use the phone.

It became a matter of enormous importance then, not to let them see my face or what sort of state I was in. Though I wasn't even sure myself. So I pretended I hadn't hit the switch, and went on listening, and talking to the receiver-speaker for a few moments. My face was burning, and my hands were cold. I couldn't really think about what had just happened. "No, Mother," I said to the dead phone.

"No, Mother. No." I'd feel better when I got out of the stuffy kiosk. Better when I'd walked to the apartment, dodged the caretaker after the rent, gone, with my arms empty of packages, into the room empty of Silver. Of course, he wouldn't be there. Perhaps he'd guessed. Perhaps robots picked up special telepathic communications from other machines. I wasn't solvent. So he might be now with Egyptia, his rich legal owner. What was I going to do?

My head tucked down, I pushed open the door of the kiosk and almost fell out. The cold and the water hit me like a wave and I seemed to be drowning. Someone caught me, the person waiting for the phone, and a horrible embarrassment was added to my illness.

"I'm all right," I insisted.

And then a scent, a texture, the touch itself—I looked up through the rain, and my head cleared and the world steadied—*"You!"*

"Me!"

Silver looked down at me, amused, compassionate, unalterable. His hair was nearly black with rain and plastered over his skull as if in the shower. Beads of rain hung and spilled from his lashes. His skin was *made* of rain.

"How did you—"

"I saw you come out of the store, when I was several blocks away. I could have caught you up, but I'd have had to run fast, and you want me to pretend I'm human, don't you? So I walked after you, and waited till you finished your call."

"Silver," I said, "it's all over. Everything's hopeless. But I'm so glad you didn't leave me."

"Jane, if you need to cry, couldn't you cry against me and not into that pillow?"

"Wh—Why?"

"Because the green stuff you covered it with obviously isn't dye-proofed, and your face is acquiring a most abnormal green pattern."

I started up and ran to the mirror. What I saw there made me laugh and weep together. I washed my face in the bathroom and came back. I sat down beside him.

"I don't want to cry against you, or you to comfort me, or hold me anymore," I said, "because soon I'll have to do without you, won't I?"

"Will you?"

"You know I will. I told you what happened. There's no

money. No food, no rent. No chance of work—even if I could *do* anything. I can't stay here. And she—my mother—won't let me bring you to the house, I'm sure of it. Even if she did, she'd sort of—what can I say?—dissect my feelings. . . . She doesn't mean to hurt me. Or—Oh, I don't know anymore. The way I spoke to her was so odd. It wasn't even like me, speaking. But I do know it's hopeless."

"I saw the caretaker," Silver said. "I went down when you were crying your way through the shawls. He thinks we're actors from a street company that's folded. I didn't tell him that, by the way, he told me. He was having a good day, no pain and no side-effects. He said we can sit on the rent for another week. Everyone else does, and at least you paid the first quarter."

"But there won't be any more money in a week."

"There could be. And no need of a labor card, either."

"No."

"Yes."

He drew the guitar to him, and reeled off a reeling wheel of a song, clever, funny, adroit, ridiculous, to the accompaniment of a whirling gallop of runs and chords. Breathless, I watched and listened. His eyes laughed at me. His mouth makes marvelous shapes when he sings and his hair flies about as if it's gone mad.

"Throw me a coin, lady," he said seductively, as he struck the last note.

"*No.* It must be illegal."

"People do it all the time."

"Yes, *people.* But you can do it better than people. It can't be fair. Can it?"

"We won't pitch where anyone else sings. We won't ask for cash. We'll just play around with some music and see what happens."

"Supposing someone recognizes you—what you—are?"

"I have a suspicion," he said, "that you'll find it *is* legal. Look at it this way," he stared at me seriously over the guitar, absurdist as only he could be. "You bought a performing seal that can do tricks no other performing seal can do. Then you run out of money. So you put the seal on the street with a ten-ton truck balanced on its nose, and you walk round with a hat."

"You're not a seal."

"I don't want a ten-ton truck on my nose, either."

"It seems—I can't imagine how it could work out."

He put the guitar aside, took my hands and held them under his chin. He looked up into my face.

"Listen," he said, "is it just that you'd prefer to go back to your house in the clouds? If I've stopped amusing you, if you're no longer happy—"

"Happy?" I cried. "I was only ever happy with you. I was only ever alive with you!"

"Are you sure? Because you have a number of options. If you're simply worrying about my side of things, let me remind you, for the hundredth time, that I'm a robot. My function is service, like any piece of metal junk you buy in a corner store to shell eggs."

"Stop it," I said.

"It's true."

"It isn't."

"It is."

He lowered his head to rest it in my hands. His face was hidden, and my fingers were full of his hair. And suddenly, with a little still shock, I knew what had happened, was happening, only I couldn't quite believe it, either, and I wondered if he knew and if he believed it.

"Silver," I said so softly I could hardly hear myself, but his hearing would pick up a whisper. Perhaps even a soundless whisper. "The first time you saw me, what did you think?"

"I thought: Here is another customer."

"Silver, the awful way you looked at me when I said that terrible thing to you—because I was afraid and confused—that was the same look you turned on Jason and Medea last night."

"Maybe. Perhaps you taught me the value of it, as a means of antisocial behavior."

"You reacted against them and for me."

"I told you why."

"And I told *you* why, but that isn't enough."

"Jane, we went through this a number of times. My reactions aren't human. I can't object to playing human here, because you asked me to, and there are good reasons. But when I'm alone with you, you're going to have to accept—"

"No," I said, still softly, "you're the one who's going to have to accept that you are *not* acting like a robot, a machine. That you never really *have.*"

He let go of my hands, and walked by me and stood looking out of the window. The embroidered shirt showed new pleats and tensions in the fabric that described the tension in his shoulders. Human tension.

"And you find it disturbing," I said. "But please don't. It isn't anything bad. How could it be?"

He said nothing, so I stopped talking. I took up my brush and began to brush my still-wet hair, in long crackling strokes. And at each stroke I said to myself: I don't care if it's against the law. He'll sing and I'll collect the cash, just like Medea. Because I can't let this go. Not ever. Especially not now. Not *now.*

When I finished brushing my hair, he had come away from the window and was standing in the middle of the room, looking at me. His face was truly serious now, and very attentive, as if he were seeing me for the first time.

"Of course," I said, "if I do stay, my mother may hire

men to track me down and drag me to her house." It was meant as a sort of joke.

He said, "Your mother would never do that. She doesn't want to publicize the fact that she hasn't got the totally balanced, perfect, well-adjusted, enamored, brainwashed mindless child she intended."

"How cruel you can be," I said, astonished. "Crueler than Clovis. I think because Clovis's cruelty is based on untruths."

Relinquishing the window mood, Silver smiled at me. He sat down on the couch, and said, "Brush my hair." So I went to him and did just that, and felt him relax against me, and I thought about every moment I had spent with him, through and through.

"You have a beautiful touch," he said at last.

"So do you."

"Mine is programmed."

And I smiled, too, with a crazy leaping inside me, because now it seemed he was protesting far too much. But I let him get away with it, magnanimous and in awe.

"What's the best way for me to persuade money from the crowd?" I asked.

"So the lady agrees."

"Yes. Do I walk round the edge, or just stand there?"

"I thought it was wrong to take their money as I'm so much better than a human performer?"

Of course I had triggered the change in him. By admitting that I thought him a robot—even when, really, I never, never had. . . . How cunning of me, how psychologically sound. And I'd never even figured out what I was doing.

"I don't care anymore," I strategically said.

"Whatever we use to collect the money will be on the ground. Don't forget, you'll be singing too."

I almost dropped the brush.

"*I* will?"

"Of course you will."

"I can't sing."

"You can sing. I've heard you."

"*No.*"

"Think of the human element it will add," he said. "You have a natural instinct for spontaneous harmony. Half the time you sing with me, you slip into effective and very original descants. Didn't you know you were doing it?"

"That's—because I can't hold the tune—"

"Not if it's perfectly in harmony it isn't. You're a natural."

"I—those were just fun. I'm no good at—"

"Was it, by any chance," he said to me quietly, "Demeta who told you you couldn't sing?"

I paused, thinking. I couldn't remember, and yet—

"I just never thought I could."

"Take it from me you can."

"But I don't want to."

"How do you know you don't?"

I had lost my omnipotence for sure.

"I can't," I squeaked. "I can't."

He smiled.

"Okay."

At midday the rain stopped. The world was wet and grey and luminous and complaining as we went out into it, he wrapped in the red-black cloak, with the guitar slung from his shoulder, I in my now very grubby fur jacket and my now very grubby jeans with bright pretty accidental paint dabbings all over them. At intervals, as we walked off Tolerance, along the boulevard, under the elevated, I said to him: "I can't, Silver."

And he replied lightly, "Okay."

People passed us, splashing and slopping through the craters in the streets that had turned into ponds and lakes. Some of the flat roofs were reservoirs, with picturesque waterfalls down onto the pavements below. It was the kind of day to hurry home on, not to walk out into. And helplessly I remembered days at Chez Stratos, curled up in the warm library with a book, or in the Vista eating candies while music tapes played, the cold unfriendly sky furling and unfurling like metallic cream, the rain falling like spears, while I was safe from the weather, safe in my cocoon, while I waited for my mother to come home. And: "Mother, can we have hot buttered toast?" And Demeta, recognizing my childish foible for classic home comforts, agreeing. And one of the spacemen wobbling in with a tray of china tea and toast and strawberry-and-orange jam. And my mother would tell me what she'd done, and I'd laugh up at her, and she'd ask me what I'd done, and I'd tell her, but what I'd done was also so boring, and I knew it was, and I'd hurry over it so as not to bore her. I knew she was bored, you see. Not with me, exactly. And she camouflaged it very well, but I could sense the camouflage somehow. And I'd have vague daydreams about doing something astonishingly interesting, and interesting her—like going back to college and reading comparative religions and traveling to South America, or what was left of it, and returning with a thesis, which I'd then read in public, and she'd be proud of me. And when we'd eaten the toast, she'd kiss me and go away to her study to do something incredibly erudite and worthwhile. And I'd fall asleep on the soft carpet, with the rain and the wind swirling in the balcony-balloons unable to harm me.

I adored my mother. But I was afraid of her. And I'd begun to see—just *what* exactly had I begun to see? See through the medium of my lover. My mechanical, not mechanical, my beautiful, my wonderful lover. Who said: Demeta is also afraid of you. Demeta has tried to cut you out like a pattern from a pattern book, only you didn't quite fit. And so here I was with him, advancing along the wet chilly sidewalk, without any money. But I had only to go into any bank in the state to get my fare to my mother's house. Think of that. Then think of how he had lain back against me as I brushed his hair, his eyes closed. He'd said, "You have a beautiful touch." He'd said, "I like the taste of food." He'd stared out of the window, unable or unwilling to reply, when I'd told him: You don't act like a robot. You never really have.

Confused, almost happy, almost terrified, I saw my reflection go by with his in the glass fronts of shops. (Superstition. He doesn't have a soul, therefore, he shouldn't have a reflection, or cast a shadow.) My reflection was of a new Jane with barley blond hair, and slim, absurdly slim. My waist was now twenty-two inches. One of the many reasons why my jeans looked so awful was that I'd had to dart them—badly—to stop them from falling around my ankles.

So why shouldn't I sing in the street? That was interesting, wasn't it? More interesting than studying religions. Mother, I am a street singer.

I remembered dimly, singing as a child, sitting in the Chevrolet as my mother drove us somewhere. And after a while, she said, "Darling, I'm so glad you like that song. But try to hit the right notes, dear." Sometimes I'd pick out tunes on the piano, and simple left-hand accompaniments, but only when she wasn't able to hear them. My mother's playing was brilliant. I'd known I was musically clumsy. No, when I'd sung with him I'd been so relaxed some quality came from me that wasn't usually there. Sort of by mistake. But in public—in public I'd panic. I'd be dreadful. Rather than give us money they'd throw stones, or call the police.

We reached an arcade, warm-lit from the shops that lined it either side. A partly-roofed alley ran off through an arch between two stores. It was a wide alley, and people turned into it to avoid the cold, still-dripping sky. They also went up and down the arcade for the same reason. A good place for a pitch, even I could see that.

Silver strode into the entrance of the arch, as if he owned it and had come there every day for three hundred years.

As he brought the guitar around on its cord, I hissed nervously, "What do I do?"

He regarded me with astonishment.

"You mean you're not going to sing?"

"Silver."

"You can't. All right. You stand by me and silently appeal to the heterosexual male element in the passersby. The cookie jar, by the way, goes on the ground. There will do."

I put down the jar. I had a vision of myself standing there like a blancmange, and feeling even more embarrassed than if I'd sung. A grey rainy misery overcame me, after all. He'd been willing to do this alone, presumably. To earn money to keep me, my pet seal, my slave, my egg-shelling machine. I should have let him. Damn. How could I?

The first chord made me jump. It also alerted the attention of some of the people splashing about in the arcade. Not all, of course. Buskers are so common downtown.

Then he started to sing. It was a song I'd heard him sing before, about a train running somewhere, an old train that blew hot smoke and steam out of its stack. The melody rattled and bounded with the train. It was wild and cheering, a perfect song to diffuse the grey hapless day. (I found I wasn't embarrassed, I was enjoying the song too much.)

I leaned on the alley wall, and partly shut my eyes. People might think I was just a hooked passerby. The song made me laugh inside, smile outside. Then I saw people stop. Four of them now, standing around the arch mouth. Someone came in from the grey end, and paused, too. When the first coin hit the inside of the jar, I jumped, and guiltily peered at it, trying to pretend I wasn't. It wasn't a lot, but it was a start.

It was odd how quickly I got used to it. Really odd, as if sometime I might have done it before. But I suppose that's just because I've watched street performers a lot. I recalled their dignity in the face of the many who just walk by, or who listen and then walk by, giving nothing. And their equal dignity in the face of the gift. Once Clovis threw a whole sheaf of bills to a young man juggling fantastically with rings and knives and oil-treated burning tapers which somehow he always caught by the unlit end—to accompanying gasps from the crowd. And the young man, who I think Clovis found very attractive, called out to him, in the midst of the whirling blades and flames, in an accent that was real: "Merci, beau monsieur."

Silver played, perfectly, of course, tirelessly, of course, on and on. Suddenly there were about fifty people squeezed in around the alley, and a coin had hit the inside of the jar and bounced out again since there was no room for it anymore. This time the busker's etiquette failed me. What was I supposed to do? I couldn't very well tip the jar in my purse in front of fifty people, but on the other hand, a full jar might deter further giving. I lost the end of the song, worrying. Was brought back by a burst of applause.

Silver stopped playing, bowed to the audience, stifling

my heart with his sheer medieval beauty of gesture. I felt safe under the umbrella of his personality. Who would notice *me?* No one in the crowd seemed prompted to move. The only movement came from two women, stealing in at the back of the alley to join it. None of them could have any work to go to, or else it was a rest day for them. That must be it, for surely the unemployed wouldn't throw money. Or perhaps mostly they hadn't, wouldn't, just wanted to be entertained for free.

But it was unusual for a performer to draw such a big static crowd. Clever to pick this position. As yet none of the surrounding stores had had their doorways blocked, and so wouldn't complain.

The crowd was waiting to see what Silver would do next.

He played a few notes on the guitar, as if considering, and then he said,

"This is the request spot, ladies and gentlemen. Request a song, and I'll sing it. However, each song costs a quarter, paid in advance."

Some of the crowd giggled with affront. I tensed. I'd been given no inkling of this—naturally I'd have argued. A rangey man called out:

"Suppose someone pays you a quarter and doesn't like the way you do the song, huh?"

Silver fixed him with his fox-colored eyes, cool and tantalizing and playful.

"The quarter," he said, with graceful maleficence, "is always returnable. As is the coat button you kindly gave us ten minutes ago."

The man opened his mouth foolishly and the crowd laughed loudly. Somebody prodded the man, yelling, "Pay up, stingy bastard," but Silver broke in, clearly and sweetly: "The button counts as payment. Even buttons are useful. We only draw the line at fruit pits and dried dog turds. Thank you. First request."

They surged and muttered, and then a woman called out the name of some dull love-song from a theatrical that had recently won critical acclaim. Silver nodded, tuned the guitar, and played half a bar. The woman threw him a quarter daringly, and Silver caught it, and placed it neatly on the ground where the copper had previously fallen. Then he sang the song, and it became sad and meaningful.

When he finished, there was a long pause, and someone said to the woman, did she want her quarter back, and she came through the crowd and put a bill in Silver's hand, and walked briskly away and out of the arcade. Her face was pink and her eyes were wet. Obviously the song meant something special to her. Her reaction disturbed me, but I hadn't got time to concentrate on that, for there was another request, and another.

Some of them put the quarters in my hand, so they knew I was his accomplice. But I grew used to that. My feet were two blocks of ice, solid in my boots, and my back ached from standing. I didn't know how long we'd been there. I felt dizzy, almost high, as if my body and my mind were engaged in two different occupations.

He must have sung twenty songs. Sometimes bits of the crowd went away. Generally more people accumulated. Then someone tried to catch him, asking for a song I didn't think existed.

"I never heard of that," said Silver.

"No one did," a voice shouted.

"But," said Silver, "I can improvise a song to fit the title."

They waited, and he did. It was beautiful. He'd remember it, too. He never forgets any song, copied or invented.

A silver coin hit the wall behind my head and sprang down next to the jar. Excited, the crowd was getting rough.

"Thank you," Silver said, "but no more missiles, please. If you put out my girlfriend's eye, she won't be able to see to count the cash tonight."

His girlfriend. Stupidly I reddened, feeling their eyes all swarm to me. Then the rangey man who'd apparently given us the coat button, but was still there, called:

"Here's my request. I want to hear *her* sing."

It was so awful I didn't believe my ears, didn't even feel afraid. But, "Come on," said the button man. "She's got a voice, hasn't she? When's she going to sing?"

At which sections of the crowd, enjoying the novelty of it all, began to shout in unison that they wanted me to sing, too.

Silver glanced at me, and then he raised his hand and they ceased making a noise.

"She has a sore throat today," said Silver, and my blood moved in my veins and arteries again. Then he added, "Maybe tomorrow."

"You going to be here tomorrow?" demanded the button man.

"Unless asked to move elsewhere."

"I'll be back tomorrow then," said the button man, morosely.

He turned to shoulder out of the crowd, and Silver called dulcetly to him.

"To hear the lady sing costs more than to hear me."

The button man glared at him.

"Oh, *why?*"

"Because," said Silver reasonably, "I think she's worth more than I am, and I'm setting the prices."

The button man swore, and the crowd approved Silver's chivalry. And I stood in a bath of icy sweat, staring at the money on the ground by the jar.

Silver accepted two more requests, and then, to howls of protest, said the session was over for the day. When they asked why, he said he was cold.

When the crowd had filtered away, Silver divided the money between the inner pockets of the cloak and my purse. A muffled clanking came from both of us, like a distant legion on the move, and I said grimly, "We'll be mugged."

"We haven't earned *that* much."

"This is a poor area."

"I know."

"My policode soon won't work. And you couldn't stop anyone if they attacked us."

He raised an eyebrow at me.

"Oh, why not?"

"You're not programmed for it. You're not a Golder." Why did my voice sound so nasty?

He said, "You might be surprised."

"You surprise me all the time."

"What's the matter?" he said.

"Nothing. Everything. It's all so easy for you. How you must despise us. Putty in your hands. Your *metal* hands." I was crying slightly, *again*, and didn't really know what I was saying, or why. "That man will come back. He's the type. He'll come back and bully me."

"He fancies you. If you don't want to sing, we'll just ignore him."

"*You* can. *I* can't."

"Why not?"

"You *know* why not. I trusted you, and you let them all think I'd sing. After I said—"

"I let them all think you *might*. You don't have to. It's a wonderful gimmick. The mysterious dumb blonde—dumb, I hastily add, in the vocal sense. Your earning ability will soar. In a month's time, if you just sang a line of 'Happy Birthday,' they'd go wild."

"Don't be silly."

"I am idiosyncratically silly."

"Shut up," I said.

He froze, turned up his amber eyes, and stood transfixed, a mechanism switched off.

"Damn you," I said, as once before. "I shouldn't be with you. It's all a game to you. You don't feel, and you don't understand. Do you laugh at me inside your metal skull?" My voice was really awful now, and the words it said, awful, awful. "You're a robot. A machine." I wanted to stop. Pale memories of what I'd thought earlier, my triumph, my joy at the sudden human vulnerability I'd glimpsed in him, seemed only to increase my need to—to *hurt* him. I'd been hurt. Someone's hurt me, hurt me, and I never knew. So now I'll hurt you if I can. "A circuit engages," I said, "and a little light comes on." There was fear, too. After all, it might be true, mightn't it? "The light says: Be kind to Jane. To stupid Jane. Pretend she can sing. Pretend she's nice in bed. Pretend, pretend, 'cos otherwise she'll send you back to Egyptia, who knows exactly what you are. Egyptia who puts you in the robot storage at night because she prefers real human men. But Jane's maladjusted. Jane's twisted. Jane's kinky for robots. Gosh, what luck. Jane'll keep you, let you make believe you're human, too. Plain Jane, always good for a snigger."

I was trembling and shivering so much the coins in my purse sounded like a cash register in an earthquake. He was looking at me but I wouldn't look at him.

"The reason," he said, "why I packed up the session here was that I could feel you freezing to death beside me. We'll get you back to the apartment, and I'll do the next stint alone. The market's probably a good place."

"Yes. They love you there. And you can go home with one of the women. Or with a man. And make them *happy.*"

"I would prefer to make you happy." His voice was perfectly level. Perfect.

"You'd fail."

"I'm sorry."

"You're not sorry. You don't have any emotions to be sorry with."

That's enough, I said to myself. Leave it. None of this is true.

Yes, I said to myself. He's fooled you all this while, played with you, made a clown of you, the way he played with the crowd.

Isn't this clever, I said to myself. To keep on and on about his unhumanness, on and on until he feels it like a knife.

I was either terribly cold or terribly hot, and my legs were leaden. I wanted to sit down and there was only the dank paving, so I sat on that. And next second he'd pulled me to my feet. Holding me by the arm hard enough to hurt me, he propelled me into the arcade and through it, and back into the outer streets. Wise move, robot. You guessed—computed—I'd be quieter out here, where it's less private.

The sun was low, burning out over Kacey's Kitchens, like one of their molecular stoves.

There was a bus and he pulled me onto it. We had to stand. The bus felt like a furnace and people came between us as we hung on the rails. I could see him then, his pale only faintly metallic face, staring out of the windows at nothing. His face was fixed, cold, and awesome. I would have been afraid of that face on anyone else. But because it was him, I couldn't be afraid. And my anger died in me, and my mistrust, and a deep sickness came instead. A sickness at myself. A sickness that I couldn't express to him, or to me.

We got off at the boulevard and walked to Tolerance, and into the apartment block and up the stairs. Neither of us spoke. The apartment looked icy, even its jewel colors were numbed.

I walked in and stood with my back to him.

I started to say something then, I don't recall what, and in the middle of it the door quietly closed, and I turned, for I knew he was on the wrong side of it. I heard the coins, but not his feet, sound as he went down the stairs, and one strange hollow plunking note from the guitar, when his cloak must have brushed its strings.

He'd gone to earn the rent money for me. The food money, for me. The clothing money. For me. I knew that he'd stand in the grey afternoon that was now deepening to a greyer twilight, singing out gold notes, amber songs, silver and scarlet and blue. Not because I'd bought him, not because he was a slave. But because he was kind. Because he was strong enough to put up with my disgusting weakness.

I was ill with the cold, and wrapping myself in the rugs from the bed, sat in front of the wall heater.

I thought about my mother. About me. How the sperm was put inside her by a machine, and how I was withdrawn by another machine in the Precipta method. And how I was incubated, and how she breast fed me because it would be good for me—her milk taken from her by a machine, and put into my mouth by a machine. There were so many machines involved, I might have been a robot, too.

I thought about Silver. About his face, so fixed, so passionless. "You don't have any emotions." And I thought about his look of pleasure when I laughed, or in bed with me, or when he sang. Or when the sun shone through the girders in the subsidence, gilding them, and three wild geese darted like jets over the sky.

It got dark, and I lit some of the candles and drew closed the blue curtains. I thought how this morning he had left me, and I'd been afraid he wouldn't come back. I wondered if I was afraid of the same thing now, but I wasn't. I wasn't afraid of anything. Only so cold, and so sick of myself.

I got into the bed and fell asleep. I dreamed I sang to a huge crowd, hundreds of them, and I sang badly, but they cheered. And Silver said to me in the dream: "You don't need me anymore now." He was all in pieces, wires, wheels, clockwork.

I woke up slowly, not with a start, not in terror, and my eyes were dry. I felt resigned, but I wasn't sure to what. I also felt calm. I'd picked up some sort of chill, some minor ailment, a sign only of my physical inadequacy. That's why things had looked so bad. I felt a lot better now, physically.

I slept, and woke up much later. I could tell it was much later, much, much later.

Finally I got dressed and went down to the phone in the foyer, and dialed for the time. It was three in the morning, and he hadn't come back.

All kinds of things went through my mind. Not one of them, anymore, that he'd—ultimate autonomy—left me. But I began to consider what I'd said about muggings, and though he was amazingly strong, I wondered how he'd make out against a gang of ten or eleven desperate maniacs. Even if his programming would allow him to defend himself, where it might allow him to defend me. What on earth would happen if someone hit him with a club and mechanical parts rolled all over the street? It was macabrely funny, and somehow didn't seem to fit. Despite my knowledge and my words, and my dreams, he remained mortal for me.

Then too, my calmness stayed with me through all of that. Also my mother's training in psychological analysis.

I realized I'd begun to analyze him, then, like a man I knew.

The analysis said, quite bluntly, He hasn't been mugged. You did hurt him. He has, or has acquired, emotions. The gambit now is to worry and to hurt *you.* Return in kind. The way only a human would do it. But maybe he doesn't even know it's human, or that it's what he's doing. So he can't handle it.

I was surprised by the revelation, and made drunken. I was running a slight temperature and wasn't aware of it, but the fever was undoubtedly what made me so elated and so sure and so calm in the face of such weirdness.

I put on my boots and my peacock jacket, and my fur jacket over the top. Then I looked at myself in the mirror.

"Where are you going, Jane? Sorry. Jain."

"To find Silver."

"You don't know where he is."

"Yes, I do. He's at the market, singing under the fish-oil flares."

"Oh Jain. That's brilliant. I never knew you were brilliant. The all-night market. Of course, there are two. . . ."

"It's the first one."

"Yes it probably is."

"Before you go, Jane."

"Yes, Jain?"

"Make me up."

So I stood before the mirror, and she made me up. She was pale as snow, with a soft fever-rouge in the cheeks. Her lids became silver from a tube of eyeshadow. And then she made my lashes thick and black as midnight bushes from a tube of mascara. We painted each other's mouth, sensual, alluring, a translucent amber.

The fever gave us the steadiest hands we ever had.

I ran out on the street. I ran up Tolerance. At the

corner of the boulevard I saw the Asteroid, and it made me laugh.

In one of the streets I started to sing, and for the first time, because my voice seemed to come from somewhere else, I heard my voice. It rang light as a bell through the frosty air. It was thin and pure. It was—

"*She*'s happy," someone said, going by.

"She's got a nice voice, even if she is blind drunk."

Thank you, my unknown and friendly critic.

The market exploded before me, day-bright and golden.

Silver's in the gold. Look for fire, look for the sun's rising.

Lucifer. I should have called you that. An angel. A wicked angel. Bringer of light. But it's too late now. I'll never call you anything but

Silver.

He was singing, and so I heard him, and so I found him. The crowd about him was thick, but I saw his face at last, between their shoulders. It was like the second time I ever saw him. Oh my love, my love. His face, bowed to the guitar as he made love to it. There's a kind of beam, a ray that he draws to him. He draws all the energy of the crowd, and contains it within him, and then focuses it out again upon them. A ray like a star, a sun. I could see it now. I could see what it was. He wasn't human and he wasn't a machine. He was godlike. How dare I want to alter him? It didn't matter if I couldn't alter him. Not anymore. But to be with him, to love him—that mattered.

The song finished. The crowd roared. He looked up, and he saw me, right through the crowd, as he had seemed to see me that second time, as I think he did, after he sang "Greensleeves" in the Gardens of Babylon. And now his face grew still, so still it might be questioning. What did I do? What should I do? I knew. I remembered how he had been with me. I walked through the crowd. I walked up to him and brushed his hand very gently with my hand. "Hallo," I said. And I stood by him, turning to confront, or to meet the crowd. A heap of coins and bills lay all over the ground. And now someone shouted for a particular song. Silver glanced at me, and hesitated. "You told me," I said. "I trust you."

He struck the chord, and started to sing. I came in on the third word, and straight into a harmonic I'd sung so often, it was easy. As I did, I caught the faintest spray of approval from the crowd. It was good. Silver didn't check, or even look at me. The crowd began to clap in time with the rhythm.

I heard our voices go up together, his voice, hers. They had the same colors as our hair, his fire, auburn, darker, richer. Mine transparent and pale, a blond chain of notes. Chain. Jain. A *Jain* voice. And it was beautiful.

When the song ended, the crowd stamped and yelled. And I knew they were yelling and stamping for me too. Coins fell. But the sounds were far away. I wanted it to go on. I wanted to sing again. But Silver shook his head at the crowd. It began to melt away. It seemed to go very quickly. I think I wanted to call it back.

Then a woman came pushing through. She handed Silver a mug of something which steamed, and had an alcoholic scent.

"That'll keep out the cold," she said. She saw me. "Well, if it isn't Blondie. Got the jacket on, I see." My topcoat was open; this was the woman from the clothing stall. "Didn't know you were here, or I'd have brought a drop for you."

"She can share mine," said Silver, and handed me the mug.

I drank. It was coffine, but it had brandy in it.

"Nice jacket," said the woman, letting the remnants of

the crowd, and any who passed, know where it came from. Obligingly, I slipped off the fur, and let the peacocks shine forth on the market.

"Wonderful value," I said, loud and clear. "And so warm—"

"A bit too warm," said the woman. She touched my forehead. "Not too bad, but you ought to get home."

"My mother used to do that," I said.

"She ought to be in bed," the woman said to Silver. She winked. I suddenly knew she and he weren't in some sexual conspiracy. We all were in it, it included me. So I laughed.

Silver was fastening my fur jacket.

"I'm packing up for the night," he said.

"I should think so," she said, "you've made enough. But you're good for business, I'll say that. And I liked that song. That song about the rose. How does it—?"

He sang it to her as he thrust the money in a thick cloth bag.

"A rose by any other name would get the blame for being what it is—the color of a kiss, the shadow of a flame."

It was an improvisation. I rested against the golden night, and I added in my own, my very own strange new voice, extending his melody: "A rose may earn another name, so call it love, so call it love I will. And love is like the sea, which changes constantly, and yet is still the same."

The woman looked at me.

Silver said, "That verse is Jane's verse."

"Love is like the sea. I love him," I said to the woman. The brandy filled my head and the fever my blood.

"Well, love off home," she said, grinning at us.

We walked out of the market, and he had me under a fold of his cloak, as if I were literally under his wing.

"Are you all right?" he said.

"A mild and minor human disease," I said. "It's nothing."

"Why did you come here?"

"I wanted to be with you."

"Why did you sing?"

"Did I sing?"

His arm held me.

"You've got through some barrier in yourself."

"I know. Isn't it ridiculous."

The walk home went in a moment. Or seemed to. As we went up the cement steps, Silver said, "We've got half the rent now. I think we can risk buying doughnuts for breakfast."

We went into the apartment. I'd left the heater on, and ten candles burning, wasteful and dangerous. But it didn't matter.

"I'm going to buy silver makeup," I said. "And make my skin like yours. How silly that will be. Will it annoy you?"

"No."

I sat on the couch and found I was lying on it. It was strange, I could feel my temperature actually going down. I was leveling, the way a flyer does as it approaches a platform. I knew I wasn't ill, wouldn't get ill. I knew everything would be all right.

Silver's cloak and the guitar were leaning together against the wall catching candle glints on wood and folds, the way they would in a painting or an artistic photograph. Silver was sitting next to me, looking at me intently.

"I *am* all right," I said. "But how nice you care."

"Don't forget," he said, "you're all that stands between me and Egyptia's robot storage."

"I'm sorry," I said. "I was subconsciously and consciously trying to drive you into feeling human."

I thought he'd laugh. He didn't. He looked down at my hand in his. The light seemed to darken, intensify, which perhaps was because some of the candles were burning out.

"I do feel human," he said at last. "I'm supposed to feel human, in order to act in a human manner. But there are degrees. I know I'm a machine. A machine that behaves like a man, and partly feels like a man, but which doesn't exactly emote like a man. Except that, probably very unfortunately, I have gained emotional reflexes where you're concerned."

"Have you?" I said softly. I believed him. There was no doubt in me. I felt amazingly gentle.

"Viewed logically," he said, "all that's happened is that I'm responding to your own response. You react to me in a particular way, an emotive way. And I react to your reaction. I'm simply fulfilling your need, if you like."

"No, I don't like. I'm tired of your fulfilling my needs. I want to fulfill yours. What do you need, Silver?"

He raised his eyes and looked at me. His eyes seemed to go a long way back, like sideways seas, horizontal depths. . . .

"You see," he said, "nobody damn well says 'What do you need?' to a bloody robot."

"There is some *law* which forbids me to say it?"

"The law of human superiority."

"*You* are superior."

"Not quite. I'm an artifact. A construct. Timeless. Soulless."

"I love you," I said.

"And I love you," he said. He shook his head. He looked tired, but that was my imagination, and the fluttering light. "Not because I can make you happy. If I even can. Not for any sound mechanical pre-programmed reason. I just Goddamn love you."

"I'm glad," I whispered.

"You're crazy."

"I want," I said, "to make you happy. You have that need in you. Well, it's just the same in me."

"I'm only three years old, remember," he said. "I have a lot of ground to make up."

I kissed him. We kissed each other. When we began to make love, it was just the same, just as marvelous as it always was. Except that now I didn't think, didn't concentrate on what was happening to me. The wonderful waves of sensation passed over and through me, and I swam in them, but the promise of light I swam toward on the horizon was altered. It wasn't mine.

I don't think I'd have presumed, even considered it, unless I'd drunk brandy on an empty stomach and with a slight benign fever, in the aftermath of my mother's rejection and my public song. It seems rather unbelievable even as I write it down. I know you won't believe me, even though you know what I'm going to say. If you ever read this, if I ever let you read it.

I don't want to, won't describe every action, every murmur. Egyptia would. Read *her* manuscript—there won't be one, she pours her life like champagne through your video phone.

Only suddenly, when I no longer even knew for sure, the road or the way, or how I was idiot enough even to dream of it, lulled and almost delirious, and yet far far from myself, out of my body and somehow in *his* body—all at once I knew. In that instant, he raised himself and stared down at me in a kind of bewilderment. In the veiled, multi-colored light, his face was almost agonized, closing in on itself. And then he lay down on me again, and I felt his body gather itself, tense itself as if to dive through deep waters. His hair was across my eyes, so I shut them, and I tasted the silken taste of his hair in my mouth. I felt what happened to him, the silent, violent upheaval shaking itself through him. Earthquake of the flesh. I was the one who cried out, as if the orgasm were mine. But my body was only shaken with his pleasure and my pleasure in his pleasure. So I knew what he'd known before, the joy in my lover's joy.

The silence was very long, and I lay and listened to the candle wax crackling in the saucers. As I listened, I kissed him, his hair, his neck; I stroked him, held him.

Eventually, he lifted himself again. He lay on one elbow, looking down at me. His face was unchanged. Amused, tender, contemplative.

"Technically," he said, "that just isn't possible."

"Did something happen? I didn't notice."

"Of course," he said quietly, "a human man would have left you proof. You'll never be sure it wasn't—"

"Faked? I've heard so much about you. I know how it goes when you fake. Not like that. As for proof, it's just as well there isn't any. Along with everything else, I missed my contraception shots last month."

"Jane," he said, "I love you."

I smiled. I said, "I know."

He lay down next to me, and for another hour at least I was drowsily making up songs in my head, before I fell asleep.

So, we're at the end of the story now. If you read so far. You don't want to know any more of what we say to each other, or how we feel about each other. And I don't need to write about it. The record—it is a record—is for . . . ? Even Silver hasn't seen it, though he knows I've written it. But maybe, it's a record for people who fall in love with machines. And—vice versa.

I write songs. I always could, and didn't credit it. I can

improvise sometimes, too. I am very good with hideous puns.

They groan, and they pay. The man who gave us a button, gives me another button. The first time he heard me sing, he gave us two, the double price Silver had stipulated.

Sometimes I see myself, a sort of bird's-eye view of me in the distance, doing these things, singing solos and harmonies, playing at the crowd, and with the crowd. Sometimes it's two hundred strong. And I'm astounded—is this *me?* But of course it isn't. This is Jain. Jain with her blond hair, her twenty-two-inch waist, her silver skin, her peacock jacket, her cloak of emerald green velvet, lined with violet satin. It was as if a skin encased me. I could only just see through it. Then the skin tore wide open.

One month and a half now we've lived here in this wonderful squalid place.

It snowed yesterday and today, early, fierce snow, so we stayed in. We made love and homemade wine. The latter nearly blew the kitchen hatch off when the sugar exploded. I stress, the latter. And I finished writing all this.

The white cat comes to visit, and is lying like a blob of warm snow in the middle of the brass bed we bought two weeks ago, almost literally for a song. It makes a luxurious creaking noise when we move about on it—the bed, not the cat. Actually, the cat belongs to the caretaker. We get the rent to him in bits and pieces, and he doesn't make a fuss. He's also frankly but unconsciously in love with Silver.

Some days we still don't eat. Sometimes we dine in expensive places. Performing, no store has ever told us to move on; occasionally they ask us to sing inside.

So many years of days since I saw Clovis, Egyptia, Chloe. My mother, Demeta. The temptation to call her is often very strong, but I resist it. I don't need to crow. She doesn't know where I am, but she knows I've won. Sometimes I dream about her, and I wake up sobbing. He comforts me. I apologize for being a bore. We argue about my paranoia, the fight ends in sex, the bed creaks and the white cat, if present, yowls.

There are things I try not to think about. When I'm sixty and he's just the same as now. There's Rejuvinex—we might be rich by then. He stresses that there's metallic decay and creeps round the room making sinister clonking noises. And a comet could always hit the earth. To hell with all that.

The subsidence is white with ice and snow. The rooms glow, and we in our colors.

I love him. He loves me. It isn't a boast. I can hardly believe it myself. But he does. Oh God, he does.

And I'm happy.

CHAPTER FOUR

"Look, everyone," said the star, "I'm burning so bright." And then it went nova. And when the light faded, the star was nowhere to be seen.

The moral of this story is obvious.

1

My whole arm hurts too much for me to write this. I don't know why I'm trying to. Is there any point? Is it a sort of therapy? I'm not writing it for a record, anymore. How childish. But then, if I'm not writing it, childishly, for anyone else, I must be writing it for me. And it won't help me, so that's that.

No. I have to write it.

It will be easier if I just start. Just go on. From those words—*I'm happy*. But I can't.

I'm happy. I'm burning so bright.

• • •

Ohgodiwishiwasdeadandthewholebloodyworldwasdead-withme.

No. I have to write it, so I will. And I don't wish the world were dead. But I won't even cross that out, or tear it up. I'll just go on. Please help me, someone. Jain, please help me.

The snow became porcelain under a pane of blue sky. The weather was exquisite, the cold like diamond. After a couple of days, the wine and the raisins ran out, and we emerged again. We opted for most of the indoor pitches, particularly Musicord-Ectrica, on the corner of Green and Grande. If you don't know, Musicord is the biggest all-day, all-night instrumental store that side of the city, and caters to the rich from the center as well as the starving dreams of the poor from the Arbors. There are so many anti-vandal and anti-thief devices in the shop, the decor mostly consists of them, and they hire their own robot poliguard. Silver was welcome because he could play any instrument in the store and make it sound its full worth and something extra, a wonderful inducement to customers to buy. Rather than take coins here, Musicord offered us a fee, and now and then a free late dinner in the lush restaurant above.

At first, I thought we'd keep meeting people I knew in the store, and wondered uneasily how I'd deal with them in my new persona. But my friends aren't musical, knowing little except for the most recent songs and the odd snob-value bit of Mozart.

There were a couple of meetings, though, with musicians who came in and fell in love with Silver's musicianship. Jealous and elated and intrigued, I'd listen to the oddest conversations, as they tried to find out what band he'd been with, why he wasn't professional, and so on. As a liar, this creature who'd told me he couldn't lie, proved most accomplished. I watched him languish esoterically over his escape from the rat race of the professional stage in some far-off city, I heard him invent curious debilities of the wrist or spinal cord that would let him down and so prohibited full-time public playing. Of course I came to realize these weren't actually lies. He improvised, just as he did with songs. But a handful of musical evenings followed, extraordinary firework displays of talent, invention and good humor, in damp basement rooms or craning attics or quasi-derelict lofts. They played and he played. The excitement generated was insane and wonderful. Only his brilliance made them wary, and occasionally stumble. But I used to sit through these sessions and think: I like this. This is so good. And then I'd think, quite consciously, just as I wrote it down: I'm happy.

We came out of Musicord-Ectrica about two in the morning, then, and stood in the golden snow where the glow of the store lights was falling. We looked, from the outside, back in at the scarlet pianos, one of which Silver had been playing most of the afternoon and evening. A large visual screen, with a loudspeaker wired out to the street, blared in the adjoining window, and I glanced and saw reports of an earth tremor somewhere, and looked away.

"Are you tired?" I asked him.

"You always ask me that, mad lady."

"Sorry. You're not tired. You don't get tired."

"Are you?"

"No."

"We could walk over to the Parlor, then, and you could make yourself sick on lemon fudge ice cream again."

"Or go home and see if the cat's eaten any more candles."

"I told you, if you bought the cat a bone, it would stop."

We stood in the snow. I wished I could buy him a scarlet piano.

"Did you write out the words of the new song you were working on in there?" he asked me.

"Not yet. But I told you and you'll remember it. I do, too. White fire—God—it's a weird song. The ideas keep coming. Maybe it won't last. I'll dry up. What would you do if I dried up?"

"Water you."

The visual screen switched channels automatically, and the sound stepped up. We'd have to move. But my eye slid back to it involuntarily. I saw a rainbow neon in front of a drab glass-sprayed frontage, and the neon read ELECTRONIC METALS LTD. For a second it meant absolutely nothing. And then the sign went out, the letters became just a black skeleton, and I heard the news reader's voice over the loudspeaker say: "Tonight, E.M. switches off its lights for the last time. The firm that wanted to make robot dolls as good as men finally admitted there's no substitute for a human after all."

"Silver," I said.

"I know," he said.

We waited there, watching, and the snow drummed slowly under my feet with the pulse of my blood.

Now the screen showed a small blank room with leather chairs. Someone was facing out at me. He had tinted glasses, and this time, a five-piece suit, trousers, jacket, waistcoat, shirt and cravat, all of cream wool. Swohnson. The front man. I recognized the stance. His easy affable charm, his relaxed willingness to give information, and the two manicured hands holding on tight to each other.

"It was a great idea we had," he said. "Ultimate service to the customer. Robots, not only aesthetically pleasing, but a source of constant domestic entertainment. Singers, dancers, conversationalists. Companions. But it's a fact, there's only so much you can program into a chunk of metal."

The screen flicked. Swohnson was gone, and there was a line of yellow metal boxes with smiling humanoid faces. "Good day," they sang out like canaries. "Good day. Welcome aboard. May I take your fare?"

The screen flicked. Swohnson was back.

"That line isn't, er, too bad," he said. "More welcoming than just a slot. They've caught on quite well. The Flyer Company is considering installation. We, ah, we recognized our limitations, there. . . ."

Flick. A grey metal box with a friendly head, and two pretty girl's hands. "Good morning, madam. How would you like your hair styled today?"

Flick. "Where we came unstuck," said Swohnson, "was in trying to create a thing which could rival the human artist. The *creative* individual. Our Sophisticated Formats. Of course, computers have been fooling with that for years. And we all know, it just doesn't work. Man is inspirational. Unpredictable. He, ah, he has the genius a machine can never have."

Flick. A young woman was standing on a stage a long way off. The camera glided toward her slowly, and as it did so, highlights gleamed and flowed across her white-wine-colored gown, her copper skin, her wheat yellow hair. Her sweet and musical voice said effortlessly and surely: "Gallop apace, you fiery footed steeds—" And said again: "Gallop apace, you fiery footed steeds—" and again and again and again. And every time with the same inflexion.

"A perfect performance," Swohnson said, as the camera glided about her, "and the same every time. No variation. No—um—no ingenuity."

Flick. Swohnson sat, beaming, holding his hand.

"But very lifelike," said an invisible interviewer, subtle and insinuating. He was accusing Swohnson of something. Swohnson knew it.

Swohnson beamed, broader and broader, as if exercising his facial muscles.

"Verisimulated," said Swohnson.

"Could be mistaken for human," accused the newsman.

"Well, yes, ah, from a *distance.*"

Flick. A golden man in black oriental garb sewn with greengage daggers swung a curved sword into the air, and was transfixed. The camera raced to him. At about four feet away, he ceased being a man. You saw the impervious metal of his skin—which was hard as the veneer of a heatproof saucepan.

"The skin is always the giveaway," said Swohnson, as the camera slid along the canyon of a metallic eyelid, its lashes like black lacquer spikes. "And, although they looked quite real at their routines, the head movements, the walk, always let them down."

Flick. A copper-skinned man in yellow velvet strode across the screen. You could just see it, the stiltedness, and once having seen it, you could see nothing else.

"The crazy thing is," said Swohnson, "the public hysteria that got stirred up, the day we introduced these robots to the city. A publicity gimmick—but what a surprise—"

"Yes, indeed." (The interviewer.) "A kind of myth was created, wasn't it? Totally autonomous robots who could find their own way about."

"Naturally," (Swohnson) "every robot had a human attendant, however circumspect. They could hardly have managed otherwise. Absurd, the things people actually credited our robots *with.* Oh, yes, er, they were clever, the best yet—but no machine can do the things our robots were supposed to have done. Traveled on flyers alone, taken ferries, subways—"

Flick. Old film, and I knew it. A crowd of demonstrators in East Arbor, the police lights playing over them. Someone threw a bottle. The camera followed it. It hit the facade of Electronic Metals and shattered.

I must have made a sound. Silver took my palm between his cool fingers, which felt of human skin.

"It's all right."

"It isn't. Don't you see—wait," I said.

Swohnson was back on the screen.

"Whatever else, the final failure of E.M. will please those people out there who got scared by what we did—or what they thought we did."

"E.M. has egg on its face, then?" The newsman. Pleased. Congratulatory.

"A lot of egg. We found out the hard way. These ultra-sophisticated machines use up so much energy, they just short out."

Flick. A golden girl, dancing. A spray of electric static. A metal statue, poised at an unearthly angle, one leg extended, her hair in her eyes. Stupid, ungainly. Laughable. A machine that couldn't be as good as any human, that couldn't even finish its act.

("Some run-down heap," said Clovis, "that will probably permanently seize up as it walks through the door. Or at some other, more poignant, crucial moment.")

As if he read my mind, the interviewer said: "And surely, how shall I put it, these things had a friendly social function as well. A stand-in for a girlfriend, perhaps. Awkward if your girlfriend seized up like that."

"Um. It could have happened."

"Oh, *dear,*" said the interviewer.

Swohnson grinned. The grin said: Hit me again, I love it.

"So I guess we remain," said the interviewer, "the superior species, to date. Man stays at the top of the heap as artist and thinker. And lover?"

"Um," said Swohnson.

"And dare I ask, what are E.M.'s plans for the future?"

"Ah. We're thinking of moving out of state. Somewhere east. Farm machinery for derelict agricultural areas."

"And will any of your tractors have a winning smile?"

"Only if some maniac paints one on."

And flick, there was a cartoon filling the screen. It showed a metal tractor with a great big smile, eyelashes and long, long golden hair.

I shut my eyes and opened them. The snow dazzled, and I turned in fear to see if anyone but us had stopped to watch the local news broadcast. A drunk rolled across the street, oblivious, slipping. In the sky high above, a distant string of jewels revealed the approach of a flyer. The city roared gently to itself on every side. But it didn't really matter who had seen the visual here. All over the city people had seen it. Seen it, but *believed* it?

"Very strange," Silver murmured.

"I'm scared."

"I know you are. Why?"

"Don't you see?"

"Maybe."

"Let's go home," I said. "Please. Quickly."

We walked in silence, cloaks brushing the snow, like two Renaissance princes. And every time we had to pass someone, I was afraid. Will they recognize him? Will they confront us?

But how could they? Hadn't the news bulletin just told them that a robot can never be mistaken for a human? Go close, you'll see the skin like a saucepan, hard, hard metal. (I had lain closer than any camera, or treated still shot designed to deceive. Skin which was poreless, yet not lifeless, smooth but not hard. Metallic, but not metal. . . .) And the walk, disjointed, a little stiff, and the ungainly gestures which always gave them away—a puppet, slightly out of control. And the inability to find its own way about the city. To decide for itself. All those of us who *saw* those robots that day when they walked among us, did we all now believe that we'd made a great big silly mistake? Yes. Why not? We believe what we want to, don't we. And no one wants to believe the machines that take the jobs away from those of us that need jobs could also take our songs away, our fantasies, our lovers.

Someone had told Electronic Metals what it had to do and what it had to say. And Swohnson, as ever in the hot seat, had done it and said it. Lies. Logical, credible, soothing lies. How much compensation had the City Marshal been authorized to pay E.M.? A lot. They'd had to take their most exciting product off the market. They'd had to mess about with it until it gave an efficient display of being useless, for the benefit of the visual cameras. And then—and then, no doubt, they'd dismantled it. Golden torsos dismembered, golden wheels turning where black eyes had looked out, or copper wheels, where golden eyes had looked out.

"Your teeth are chattering," he said to me.

"I know. Please don't let's stop."

The visual hadn't shown any of the silver range. The silver girl at the piano, the silver man (Silver's brother and sister), neither of these. Why was that? So as not to remind anyone there was a Silver Format? Tell the people that our robots, which they've seen to be exactly human, are really shambling bumbling automatons. And they'll accept that. Tell the people, by omission, that the *only* robots they saw were gold or copper. And they'll forget the silver range. The Silvers with their burgundy hair and auburn eyes. But why, Mr. City Marshal, Mr. Director of E.M., do they have to forget about the Silvers? Why? Because one of the damn things is still at large. Out there in the city. One flawless, human, better-than-human, godlike, beautiful, genius of a creative inspired robot. And if they realize, the citizens may lynch us all.

I thought I'd been living in the real world, bravely coming to terms with the truth of life. But I hadn't. I'd missed all the upheaval that must have been happening, somehow, all about us. The apartment on Tolerance Street, our pitches, our romantic, poetic existence. How far from life they really were. Only another cocoon. But now the axe blow of fact had broken through.

I'd told no one where I was. No one knew. Therefore, no one knew where Silver was. Had they been looking? No, that was insane.

We were in our block, going up the stairs. I imagined shadows looming up from the dark by the door. But no shadows loomed. We opened the door. Lights would flare, a voice would shout: *Surrender yourselves!* But the room was empty. Even the cat had let itself out through the flap. (Remember when he cut the flap, efficient and stylish? "I just read the instructions.")

He guided me over to the wall heater, switched it on, and together we watched the heat come up like dawn.

"Silver," I said, "we won't go out."

"Jane," he said. "This has been going on some while, and we never knew. And we never had any trouble. Did we?"

"Luck. We were lucky."

"I was bought and paid for," he said. "They've probably written me off."

"They can't write you off. The City Senate has done a

deal with them. They can't just leave you loose." I stared at him, his profile drawn on the dark by the heater's soft fire. "Aren't you afraid, too?"

"No, I'm not. I don't think I can get to be afraid. You've taught me several emotions, but not that one. Like pain, fear is defensive. I don't feel pain, or fear. I'm not intended, perhaps, to defend myself, beyond a very basic point."

"Don't," I said. "That makes it much worse."

"Yes, I can see that."

"We won't go out," I said again.

"For how long?"

"I don't know."

"Food," he said. "Rent money."

"Then I'll go alone."

I grasped his wrists, lace and skin. Skin. The fluid movement of the strong fingers, shifting, returning my grip.

"Please don't argue with me," I said.

"I'm not arguing," he said. His face was grave.

We stood there, motionless in the firelit darkness, a long while.

Gone to earth, we stayed in the flat five days. It was a fearsome, banal, claustrophobic existence. We discussed strange topics, as for example that he could protect me from attack, and maybe not himself, the distances between certain types of stars, what the insides of the walls were like. We also talked of constitutionals through the subsidence—but didn't risk them. I lived on apples and crackers. It was hopeless, since there was no foreseeable end. Finally something embarrassing and embarrassingly simple drove me out on the street. As I'd missed my contraceptive shots, I began again to menstruate, as I had at twelve and thirteen. I'd been aware it might happen, but never got around to more than the most cursory of the provisionings against the event. So, rather than starvation, hygiene forced me back into the unsafe world.

I ran along Tolerance, along the boulevard. Eyes everywhere accused me. Under the elevated a woman stepped out of a shed and caught me eagerly by the arm. "You're the bitch who sleeps with a robot!" But she didn't say that. She said: "We missed you at the market. People asked after you both. Where's he? Not sick, is he?"

"Oh, no. It's just so cold out."

I forget what else we said. Something, and then she let me go. When I got back into the apartment, I was shaking. But later I realized, and Silver explained to me, over and over, that all this proved nothing had changed.

Next day, I went out alone again. I walked through the streets, through the stores. A couple of times people said hallo to me. No one accused me. Something inside me, a tense wire, sagged and slackened. E.M.'s retraction was a tiny little wave, which had hit the beach of the city, and passed unnoticed.

He sat cross-legged on the brass bed, playing the guitar softly, and said to me, "Go out again tomorrow, and if nothing happens, we'll go out together tomorrow night. One pitch only. An experiment."

"No—"

"Yes. Or you'll be down to eating the poor cat's candles."

So the next day I went out, about three in the afternoon. I walked along the frozen sidewalks and around into the arcade where he'd sung the first time and I'd been so afraid of singing myself. As if to sing were something to fear. To *sing*.

I glanced around the arcade. No one was in the archway, but people trotted to and fro and in and out of the shops. A long translucent icicle hung down from one of the ledges above, pointing like an arrow to the spot on the snow beneath, where Jason and Medea stood and looked back at me, with two tight little matching smiles.

Hallo, Jane."

"Hallo, Jane."

"Ooh, what a silver face you've got."

"Yes, Jane, it is rather silver. Makeup, or did you catch it off him?"

I'd forgotten, my heart hammering its way through my ribs, my breath snarled up in my throat, forgotten that when you learn to sing you learn to control your voice. But I was doing it anyway.

"Catch what off whom?" I said.

"Gosh," said Jason, "what impeccable grammar. Off that peculiar actor friend of yours."

Do they know? How can they *be* here? As if they're waiting for me—

Don't answer. Switch. Throw them.

"Isn't it cold?" I said.

"Not for you in that lovely green cloak."

"Is that his?" Medea inquired.

"Whose?"

"Your rude friend."

"I have a lot of rude friends."

"Oh," said Medea. "Does she mean us?"

"She doesn't want to talk about him. Obviously had a lovers' tiff. What a shame, when you're living here in the slums to be with him."

They know. I think they know it all. Do they know *where* I live? Where Silver is? How can they. . . .

"If you mean the man with the red hair you saw on the bridge," I said, "we've split up, yes. He's gone east."

"East?"

"Out of state." (Like Swohnson and E.M. and their new line in farm machines.) "There's the chance of a good part there, in a drama."

"And left you all alone? In this slummy bit of the city?"

"Jason," I said, "what gave you the idea that I live around here?"

"Well. You've left your mother, and your mother's stopped your credit and your policode and all that. Then we asked around rather. Described you very accurately—diet-conscious, bleached hair—And we heard about how you sang in the street with your friend who's gone east. How brave, when you can't sing. Do you do it the way we do? Someone said you come here, to this arcade."

They'd been searching for me. It couldn't be for any reason but pure nosiness and spite. And today was the day Silver and I used to come to the arcade—they'd found that out too, and stationed themselves here, waiting. And, used to coming to this spot at this time, on this day, I'd done it without considering. And walked right into them. (They know he's a robot, they've spoken to Egyptia, or Clovis. They know.) But—they hadn't found out where we were living—or they'd have turned up there. (I can just imagine their smiling faces in the doorway.) Of course. Nobody did know where we lived, we'd never told anyone, even the musicians whose lofts we'd visited had never yet been invited back.

"Well actually," I said, "I don't live this end, at all. It's sheer chance we met."

"Ah. A Dickensian coincidence," said Jason.

"Where *do* you live, Jane?" asked Medea, smiling, her eyes like thin slices of cobra. How I hated her, and her awful crimped blue hair.

"Where do I live? Near the Old River."

"And you never open the windows."

"Not often."

"It's interesting there."

"Yes. Anyway, I must go. Good-bye," I said.

"Good-bye, Jane."

"Good-bye, Jane."

They stood totally static as I walked out of the arcade, and I almost turned and ran for home. But as the cold of the open street breathed over me and my boots crunched in the deeper snow, I suddenly understood I'd escaped too easily. With a queasy, dizzying sensation I walked over the road and into Kacey's Kitchens, and straight down an aisle of servicery fixtures. Pausing before a chromium insta-mix I saw, reflected in its curved surface, a distorted runny image of Jason and Medea flowing in at the door.

Pretend not to be aware. Find a crowd, lose them.

Oh God. There may not be a crowd. It's cold, and cash is low.

There has to be a crowd.

There wasn't.

Not in Kacey's, not in the Cookery. Not in the dozen or so stores and shops I walked through. I tried to lose them in alleyways, too, twisting and turning, going along walks I only knew because of going along them with him. Darting across hurtling roads, trying to get ahead of them—or perhaps, get them run over. But somehow they kept after me. I'd see their storefront reflections melt in, a few yards behind mine.

The sun went. The streets darkened with dusk and brightened with extra lighting. It was getting late, and I couldn't go home. I ached with the cold, and with hunger, and with anger and fear. I hurried into a second owner clothing store, and tried to shake them off among the moth-eaten fur coats. I almost thought I had, and then, going through the hats toward the other door, most horribly I heard Jason give a raucous hoarse sneeze. It went through me like a bullet, and then I ran. I ran out of the store, and down the street outside, skidding and sliding, clutching at intermittent lampposts to steady myself. Would they run too? Oh let them fall over and break all their legs—

They ran. They must have. I didn't hear them, they ran like weasels, better than me. Without knowing quite how, I'd reached the square that led to the all-night market with the fish-oil flares. As I stopped, panting and gasping, with a stitch jabbing in my stomach, they came up, one on either side of me, like the slatey shadows.

"Jane, whyever were you running?"

"Are you following me?" I cried.

"Are we?" Medea asked Jason.

"Sort of," he said reasonably. "We thought we'd walk you home."

"Only, the river isn't in this direction at all, Jane."

What now? I let myself gasp for breath, because it gave me time to think, if only I could. I mustn't go toward

Silver and the apartment on Tolerance. Nor must I go toward the Old River, since they would go with me right to the door, and I didn't own a door over there.

"I don't need you to walk me home," I said.

"We think you do," said Medea.

"We were certain, with your policode not working and everything, it might be dangerous for you."

"You were certain you wanted to see where I lived."

"Is there some reason you don't want us to?"

"Why could that be, Jane?"

"We're your friends."

Where could I go? Where could I take them, so they'd get bored and leave me alone? I had hardly any cash on me, a few coins, no more. I couldn't go and sit in a restaurant. And I had to get out of the cold, somehow, I couldn't stand it anymore. My hands had no feeling, or my feet. Perhaps I'd broken all my toes as I ran and just couldn't feel it yet—My eyes were burning. And they'd say, You're frozen, you want to go home—why won't you, if you've got nothing to hide, and no robots stashed there?

"I'm not going home," I blurted out.

"Why not, Jane?"

"I'm going to see Egyptia."

"Oh." Both their faces fell. I'd scored, and I wasn't sure how and then, "You mean that utterly abysmal moronic play she's in."

"She kept saying," said Medea, "Jane's got to come to my first night. Jane's got to be there, or I'll die. How could she abandon me like this?" Medea frowned slightly. "But you aren't."

It sounded very like Egyptia when Medea said it, only without Egyptia's beautiful voice. And in the midst of panic I felt a stab of guilt. Egyptia had been wonderful to me, and I'd never called her to tell her she was wonderful, and that she would be safe. Hoping she'd now lost all interest in me and in him, my love who was her gadget, I'd shut her from my mind, as if to make it happen by sympathetic magic. But she'd shown me no malice. She'd been gloriously, sweetly kind. And tonight was her first night as Antektra, asking the peacock about brothers and dust. Through my own sick fear, I could just visualize her agonies.

"Oh, well," said Jason, "we'd better go with you. We thought of going, actually. At least over to The Island first."

We were walking, the three of us. Their policodes glinted, his on a necklet, and hers on a bangle, and I wished there were no such things and I could kill them. The tremor sites had snow on them. The sky was snowing out stars. Silver! Silver!

Egyptia, I'm sorry, but if I get the chance to get away from these creatures, I don't care about you—Oh, God, give me the chance—

"We'll go over to South Arbor and take the flyer," said Jason.

The Asteroid rose over the broken buildings. In the icy air, it seemed larger than ever, and touched the faces of my escort with a green-blue glaze, but probably it was an optical illusion.

We walked. They didn't speak to me any more. Now and then they said things to each other, sometimes about me.

"Actors are awfully stupid."

"Yes, it will be a revolting night. But if Jane wants to."

"Isn't she thin now? Not right for her bone structure."

"Wonder what Mother would say."

They knew they were my jailers. But they'd still failed, so far. They hadn't been led to my home. I'd provided a legitimate excuse for not going there, and so they couldn't be certain I was shielding anyone, or anything, from them. Not *certain.*

We got to the flyer platform in time to catch the four-thirty P.M. As they clambered and clambered me into the lighted pumpkin, I tried halfheartedly to fall back, but they wouldn't let me.

"Come on, Jane."

"I just remembered, I haven't got the fare."

Jason hesitated. They're very mean, despite their riches and their thievery, and I wondered for a second if they'd abandon me after all. But then he said to Medea, "You can pay for her, can't you?"

And Medea, expressionless and hateful, said: "Yes, I'll pay. I'll pay for her on the ferry, too. Jane's one of the poor, now."

"Do you remember," said Jason, "when she offered to pay our bill in Jagged's, and then didn't, and they got on to Daddy and asked him for it? That was ever so funny."

We sat down. The flyer, a golden champagne bubble, drifted forward into the city sky, and I could have wept, from the pain of my thawing fingers, and from despair.

Silver would be expecting me. The streets were dangerous. I had no policode. Would he, even though he couldn't seem to be afraid for himself, be afraid for me? *Silver.*

"Don't the buildings look interesting from here?" said Jason. "Just imagine, if we had some little bombs we could drop on them. Bang. Bang."

"They'd look more interesting then," said Medea complacently. "On fire."

Damn the pair of them. I wish there were a hell, and they could be there forever, screaming and screaming—

No, I don't wish that either. That wouldn't make any difference, now.

There was a crowd waiting for the reservoir ferry, and Jason held my arm. He's scarcely taller than me. I thought of trying to push him in the water off the pier. But he'd only swim back.

The ferry came and we got on it. It curved through the water and around the trees to The Island.

"The play doesn't start until midnight," lamented Jason. "But Jane knows that. Over six hours of listening to Egyptia carrying on."

"Do you think," said Medea, "we could do something to make Egyptia amused? Like putting some small creepy insects in her makeup boxes?"

"Ssh," said Jason. "If you tell Jane, Jane will tell Egyptia. And that would ruin the surprise."

"Or we could put glue into her stockings."

"What an intimate idea. I wonder what it's like to be intimate with Egyptia?"

"Oh, Jason," moaned Medea, "please kiss my little toe—it's ecstasy, and it makes me feel like a woman."

I stood by the rail, the water coiling by, not really listening. Somehow I recollect all they said. But it's irrelevant. And presently we reached The Island pier, the landscaped gardens, and got off and walked up to the lift, and rose in it to Egyptia's apartment.

It was deadlock until then.

By the time Jason spoke to Egyptia's door, saying he and Medea were there, and not mentioning me, I was feeling violently nauseated and no longer really cared.

All around the dead pot-plants pointed at us with their petrified claws. The night was strange and glistening and terrible. I recalled how I'd come here last and bit my tongue, the only way I could keep any control over myself. It seemed to me that if Lord came to the door again, it would be the end.

When the door opened, no one was there but ourselves reflected in the mirrors as we trooped inside. It was also very silent, though I could smell incense and cigarines and the warm resinous scent of Egyptia's entirely convincing pine-cone fire.

No one seemed to be in the vast salon, either, though yellow candles were burning everywhere. It looked so cozy, so beautiful, so sumptuously welcoming, my illness began inadvertently to lift. Then I almost screamed.

The fire had been put in the middle of the floor, and in one of the big shadowy chairs, three-quarters onto it, a head turned, and the flames outlined a crimson halo along dark red hair. It was Silver. It was—

"If you stole anything from the hall on your way in," said Clovis, "please replace it. This advice is for your own sakes. Egyptia, who is putting the finishing touches to her makeup this very minute, is liable to return in the person of Antektra, or—worse—in hysterics yet again. And much as I'd love to see someone murder the two of you—Good God Almighty!"

I swallowed.

"Hallo, Clovis."

Having turned elegantly and slowly, caught sight of me and leapt to his feet, he was now transfixed, and I could see why I'd made the mistake. Clovis's curling hair had been grown to shoulder length and lightly tinted red. To *copy* Silver? Mirror-Bias in reverse? The room shimmered. We'd parted in unfriendship, yet seeing him again I felt such a shock of relief I was ready to collapse on the floor.

"Jane. That *is* you? I mean, under that blond wig and the silver skin?"

"It isn't a wig. It's my natural unmolecularized color. Yes, it's me." I felt blazingly hot now, and unfastened the cloak and held it drooping away from me.

"My God. Let me look at you."

He came across the room, stopped about a yard from me, gazed at me and said, "Jane, you've lost about thirty pounds. I always knew it. You're really a beautiful boy, circa fifteen hundred. With breasts."

At which I burst into uncontrollable tears.

Jason tittered, and Clovis said, "You two can go through into the servicery and dial the cellar for some wine. A dry, full-bodied red—Slaumot, if there's any left."

"Are we supposed to do what you tell us?" asked Medea.

"I think you are," said Clovis. "Unless you'd like me to let your daddy know what you did last week. Again."

"Daddy doesn't care," said Medea.

"There you are wrong. Daddy does care," said Clovis. "Your daddy was talking to my daddy the other day, and both daddies agreed you would profit by instruction. Your daddy was brooding on the notion of sending both of you off on a study course similar to Davideed's undertaking. Silt. Or something of a reminiscent color and consistency, though a rather nastier odor."

"You're lying," said Jason.

"About the subject for study, possibly. Not about anything else. Don't get the wine and prove it."

Like a lizard, Medea slithered abruptly away through the salon. Jason, impelled by the invisible bit of string which connected them, peering back at Clovis, went after her.

My crying, to my surprise, had been tearless, and almost immediately stopped. To see the terrible twins reduced to such an unimportant role dumbfounded me.

"What on earth did they do, to give you that hold on them?" I said.

"Shoplifting and minor arson. I happen to have paid the fine before it got round to their father, who really is thinking of sending them into exile."

"Why?"

"Why not? I felt generous. And now I can blackmail

them. I shall need a new seance arrangement, post darling Austin, who, by the way, is a homicidal maniac. I'm trusting Jason will fix it, and not booby-trap the rest of the furniture at the same time, which is the price I had to pay before. And now. What about you?"

"I—"

"For one thing, how did you know to come here tonight? Did you see the horrendous Ask My Brother To Dust The Peacock advertised somewhere? On a police-wanted placard, for example. Not that I'm arguing with your arrival. Egyptia has been driving herself and everyone else mad for the past three weeks. None of her fellow Thespians will talk to her anymore. I'm wondering if they'll even consent to talk the lines to her on stage tonight. But at least her wails of 'Oh why isn't Jane with me?' will be appeased."

"Clovis."

"Yes, Jane?"

I looked at him, at this handsome face I'd grown up seeing grow up, Clovis, the last remnant of my past. Was he my enemy? I thought so when he called me and took Silver away from me. I thought so when he blushed, and sneered at me, and I slapped his face. But not anymore. Could I trust him and would he help me? As, originally, he already had.

"Clovis, I have to leave at once."

"If you do, Egyptia's death may well be on your conscience. Not to mention mine."

"I have to leave, and I need you to stop the twins from coming after me."

"Are they likely to?"

"They hunted me down, somehow, and they've been following me all afternoon, and I couldn't get rid of them. I couldn't go home." Not crying, I nevertheless was crying, tearlessly again, and desperately, and waving my hands at him because I knew he didn't like to be handled and some part of me kept physically reaching out to him for support.

"Jane, obviously I'm being unforgivably obtuse. But why couldn't you go home?"

"Clovis, don't you *know?*"

"Let me see. You split with Demeta. You're living in a hovel somewhere. Or you're a professional damisella della nuita. Why should any of that—"

"Did you see the Electronic Metals newscast?"

"I never watch newscasts. If you mean, do I know, by a process of imperceptible osmosis, that E.M. is out of business, yes I do. And if ever I saw a senatorial blindfold, that was it. Anything to keep the masses from revolution, I suppose."

I was calmer. I watched him closely.

"How," I said, "did Egyptia make out, as legal owner of one of their discontinued robots?"

"How steely-eyed and measuring you've become suddenly. Quite unlike the dear little Jane I used to know. Egyptia? Oh, they called her. They said would she care to return her robot as it was faulty and might set fire to the rugs. They'd refund her the cash, plus a bonus as compensation."

There was a long silence, and I began to wonder if he was playing with me.

"And what," I prompted, "did Egyptia reply?"

"Egyptia replied: 'Which robot?' and, when they'd told her, announced that the robot had been in storage for weeks, and she was too busy to be bothered with fishing it out. As for the bonus, money didn't concern her anymore. Self-knowledge through art was what concerned her. She would be happy to eat wild figs in the desert wilderness, etc., etc.—And Electronic Metals backed away and switched off the phone. Since then no further calls, apparently. No doubt they concluded that one unused, forgotten robot in the cupboard of an eccentric, amnesiac and very rich actress was nothing to lose sleep over. Or else they didn't want to increase the wrong kind of public tension by making a scene."

My eyes were helplessly wide.

"*That* was what she said?"

"That was exactly what she said. I know, because I had the misfortune of being with her when she took the call and said it." Clovis nodded. "When she turned from the video, of course," he murmured, "I said, with some astonishment, 'But didn't Jane ever come and demand the robot from you on the grounds of hard cash and true love?' And Egyptia widened her topaz eyes, just as you're doing with your jade green ones. 'Oh! Yes!' she exclaimed. 'I'd forgotten about that. Jane's got him.' Interesting, isn't it."

"She'd *forgotten—*"

"You know what she's like. Completely and enduringly self-centered. Nothing is real to Egyptia, except for herself, and the savage gods who may either uplift or destroy her. You were in love with him, Jane. But Egyptia's only in love with Egyptia."

"And did you call E.M., Clovis, and tell them the mistake?"

"Why the hell should I?"

"Malevolence," I said.

Astonishing me somewhat, he grinned, and lowered his eyes.

"Hmm. You'll never let me off that one, will you?"

"You haven't let yourself off. Your hair—"

"Jane. I had him. I'll admit, a special experience. Shakespeare would have flung off a couple of sonnets. But it just made *me* aware, for the eighty millionth time, what a pile of gormless garbage most of humanity is. What you really want to know is, did I or will I tell E.M. Ltd. that you and he—Silver—still cohabit. Which is what I astoundedly presume you *are* still doing. And what I also presume our own little arsonists in the servicery have found out. J. and M. Investigators Inc."

I drew in a long trembling breath. My voice came out sure and steady and clear.

"Yes, Clovis."

"The answer is No. Ah, what a relief."

"Yes. E.M. means business. If they think he's still walking about—"

"He'd be back to cogs and clockwork status."

To hear him say it, even though I knew it to be so, stunned me, filled me with fresh sickness and horror. And at any moment, the two monsters would be back.

"You know," Clovis began to say, "I have an awful theory about how Jason tracked you down."

But I broke in: "Clovis, can you lend me some money. Or give me some? I don't know if I can ever repay it. But if we could get away from the city, go upstate. . . ."

"That could be a good idea. You can have the money. But just suppose, melodramatic as it sounds, that E.M., or the Senate, have a secret check going on the highways or out-of-state flyer terminals."

I stared at him and through him.

"Oh, God. I didn't think of that."

"Don't go to pieces. I'm inventing an alternative plan. You'll have to stay around a while. I'll need to make a call."

"Clovis."

"Yes. That's my name. Not Judas Iscariot, so relax."

"What plan?"

"Well, just like your appalling mother—"

A voice shattered like glass against my ears, staggering me.

"Jane! Jane!"

I turned as if through treacle. Egyptia stood on the

little stair that led down from the bedroom half-floor above. I had an impression of flashing lights and foaming darkness, a kind of storm, as she launched herself at me. She fell against me lightly, but with a passionate, almost-violence. She clung to me, pent, intense, not letting go. "Jane, Jane, Jane. I knew you'd come. I knew you'd understand and come, because I needed you. Oh Jane—I'm so afraid."

I felt I was drowning and my impulse was very nearly to thrust her off. But she was familiar as a lover, and her terror communicated itself, a strange, high inaudible singing and sizzling, like tension in wires.

"We'll go on later," said Clovis.

"Clovis—"

"Later, trust me. You know you do." He walked away toward the servicery. "I'll go and see how the Slaumot's coming."

Egyptia clung to me like a serpent. Her perfume flooded over me, and despite everything, my own panic began to leave me.

My lover was not a hysteric, as I was. He would wait for me, without fear, thinking I'd stopped to talk to people we knew, perhaps to eat with them. And Clovis would help us. Help us leave our beautiful home, our friend the white cat.

"Egyptia," I said, and the tears tried to come again. "Don't be afraid. It's going to be fine. It is, it is."

Then she drew away from me, smiling bravely, and I burst into bubbling laughter, as I'd burst into dry tears.

Egyptia was stricken.

"Why are you laughing at me?"

"Because, in the middle of utter chaos—you're so beautiful!"

She stood there, her skin like a warm peach with an overall theatrical makeup, her eyelids terracotta and golden spangles, gold spangles also massed thickly on her breasts, which otherwise appeared to be bare. Her hair had been streaked with pale blue, and tortured into long elaborate ringlets, and she had a little gold crown on it. She had a skirt of alternating gold and silver scales, and on her flexible arms were dark blue clockwork snakes with ruby eyes, that continuously coiled round and round.

What was most laughable of all was that, as she stood facing me in her costume, facing me through her terror and her ridiculous egomania, and her vulnerability, I sensed again the greatness in her that she sensed in herself. And I laughed more wildly and harder, until she, with offended puzzlement, began to laugh too.

Impatience, scorn and fondness, and love. Struck together like matches, igniting. Giggling helplessly, we fell onto a couch, and her layered scaled skirt made the noise of tin cans rolling down stairs, and we shrieked, our arms flailing, and her oriental slippers flying off across the salon.

3

There were three bottles of Slaumot and Clovis, Egyptia and I sat and drank them in the fire and candlelight. Jason and Medea drank coffipop, which, when I was fifteen, always gave me instant hiccups. The twins sat on the floor across the big room from us, playing a macabre version of chess Jason had invented. They might steal some of the pieces, but Egyptia wouldn't care. She knew she wouldn't live beyond this night. She had two visions of her death. One was when she first entered on the stage. Her heart would burst. Or she might die at the end, the strain having been too much for her. It wasn't at all funny. She meant it, and she was scared. But, more than all else, she was scared of the fact that she was to dramatize Antektra before an audience. It wasn't an enormous theatre, and it might not fill. A couple of critics might be there, and a visual crew would film a shot or so, as a matter of course, and then probably not show it. But to Egyptia, it was more than all this—which, if it had been me, would have terrified me sufficiently—although, far less than it would have done before my debut in the streets. It was her fear of failing *herself* that gnawed on Egyptia. Or, as she put it, of failing Antektra. She would say portions of her lines, pace about the salon, sink on the couch, laugh madly, weep—her dramatic makeup was genuinely tear-proof, fortunately. She sipped the Slaumot, and left butterfly wings of gilt from her lips on the glass.

"She's a virgin. Her sexual electricity has turned in on itself. She is driven by grief, anguish and fury. She is haunted by the demons of her fury." How odd she should sound so cognizant of these emotions which truly I don't think she'd ever felt. And the descriptions of Antektra's state, obviously footnotes, learnt off like her lines—"A whirlwind of passion. Am I capable of doing this? Sometimes I've felt that the power of this part is inside me, like a volcano. But now. . . . Have I the strength?"

"Yes," said Clovis.

"Yes," I said.

"My rook tortures your rook to death," said Jason across the room.

"The power," said Egyptia, prowling like a leopardess between the candles, "may consume me. I don't mind, I truly don't mind if I die, if it kills me. So long as I can die with this task accomplished—Oh, Jane. You understand, don't you?"

"Yes, Egyptia."

Clovis yawned, hiding in his longer hair as he did so, and I thought of Silver. Not that I'd stopped thinking of Silver. When I was twelve, I had a psychosomatic toothache for months in one of my back teeth. I took painkillers every three hours, which dulled the pain but didn't get rid of it. The nag of it went on and on, and so I got used to it, and only thought about it at the end of each three-hour unit when it would flare up to new violence. This was how I felt now. My awareness of danger and distress, my concern for Silver's concern at my absence, the hopeless trap I was in and apparently couldn't move out of—these were the dull pain. The wine, the familiarity, Egyptia's fear were the painkillers. The pain was slight and bearable and I could almost put it from my mind. But then the light moved on Clovis's hair—red—and the pain *flared.* I almost rushed, each time, from the apartment and away into the night. Clovis could surely contain the twins. But they would know they'd been right. And Clovis's unspecified help would be lost to me.

He wore an embroidered shirt, too, under the silk and velour jacket. He was so rational about Silver, yet the copied influence was there. *Could* I trust Clovis? Well, I *had* trusted Clovis, if not with my address, with everything else.

"My queen buys her freedom by allowing your knight to cut off her left hand," said Medea.

"I do hope," said Clovis, "they're not actually inflicting these injuries on your chess set, Egyptia."

"The world's a chess set," said Egyptia. (A quote?) "Oh, bow your neck to the bloody dust. Kneel to the yoke, humiliated land. This is not the world. The gods are dead. Kneel, for you must. Relinquish pride, and kneel."

"My knight castrates your knight."

"He can't. My knight's in full armor."

"Well. There's a weak link."

"The floor over there must be strewn with severed members," said Clovis.

I couldn't even call Silver. There was the phone in the foyer, which the caretaker might answer, but I couldn't remember the number. And even if I did, to call would be, again, to reveal there was somebody at home I wanted to reach. Perhaps, if I excused myself to use the bathroom, I could call on one of Egyptia's extensions upstairs, experimenting till I got the number right—no. A blue call-light came on in every other phone console when one was operational. Jason and Medea would see it. They'd be watching for it.

Chloe couldn't be here tonight because Chloe had a virus. Why hadn't I had a virus?

"Women of the palace," said Egyptia, "my brother was a god to you. Yet to these beasts he is carrion. He is left for the kites to chew upon—"

"Oh my," said Clovis, "now the play's getting to sound like the chess game. Do you think my weak stomach is up to this drama?"

"Don't mock me, Clovis," shouted Egyptia in despair.

"It's half past ten P.M.," said Clovis. "I'm going to call the taxi."

"Oh God," cried Egyptia, "is it time to leave?"

"Getting that way. Jane, pour her another drink."

I wasn't sure about that, although she seemed incapable of drunkenness in her frenzy. She had dressed in her costume and put on her makeup here because of her emotional rift with the rest of the company. "They give me *nothing!*" she said. To Egyptia, of course, the rest of the cast were the support mechanism to carry her, and sadly they hadn't realized it. Or else they had.

Now I fetched her grey-blue fur cape coat, on the inside of which some of the body makeup was sure to rub off. She'd bought that coat the day I took Silver with me to Chez Stratos.

"Oh, Jane. Oh—Jane—"

"I'm here." I sounded mature and patient. Concerned,

kind. Just a touch compassionately amused. I sounded like Silver.

"Ja-aaaa-nnne—"

She stared at me. The guillotine awaited her, and soon the tumbrel would be at the door.

"You are going to be so good," I said to her. "So good, the Asteroid will probably fall on the Theatra Concordacis."

Clovis came in again in a little while.

"Months to get through," he said. "It'll be by the pier in half an hour." He looked at me, and added, sotto voce, "The cab rank was the second call."

"Clovis—" I said, realizing he'd put his unspecified plan into action.

"Later." He glanced at Jason and Medea, who were thoughtfully watching us. "Better kill everyone else on the board off quickly, pets, we leave in ten minutes."

"Oh. The awful play," said Jason.

"You don't have to come," Clovis said.

"We do," said Medea. "We want to be with Jane. We haven't seen her for so long."

"Christ, what a strange night," Clovis said to it, as we stepped out into the enclosure before the lift shaft.

"What's wrong with it?" asked Jason.

"How should I know?" said Clovis.

The lift came, and Egyptia trembled in my arms. As we went down to the ferry, the night rose up the jewelry buildings. There was a great stillness, but that was only the coldness of the snow. The ferry was deserted, and the cab was waiting at the other side of the water.

We reached the Theatra about eleven-fifteen P.M., after walking up the Grand Stairway and by the tunnel fountain, which didn't play in winter. But it was the exact spot where I had first seen Silver.

There were quite a lot of people about the main facade. We went around the side, and into the bleak backstage, and into Egyptia's bleaker dressing room. When the reluctant wall heater had been activated, Egyptia stood shuddering.

"My father slain, my brother slaughtered. Death is the legacy of this House of the Peacock. Everyone go out. Everyone but Jane. Jane, don't leave me."

"We'll wait outside," said Medea. I knew they'd watch the door.

I had to stay, anyway, now, for Clovis's news. Whatever it was. I was really past caring. Schizophrenic, as before, I existed here, and I existed in a sort of precognitive limbo of rushing home to the flat on Tolerance.

In the corridor, the young man I remembered was called Corinth clumped past in metal toeless boots and a metal scaled cloak, eating a chicken leg morosely.

The handsome thin man, who had directed the drama, looked in twenty minutes later, flustered and chilly.

"Oh, so you got here," he said to Egyptia. Her eyes implored him, but he was finished with her. There would be no other productions for Egyptia here, despite her handy wealth. One could see that in his face. "Just a last piece of advice, dear," he said. "Try to recall there are a couple of other people with you in the cast."

She opened her lips, and he walked out, banging the door so it almost fell off. The place was not in good repair.

"They hate me," she whispered, stunned. "I was generous to them, I shared my home with them, my love. I was part of them. And they hate me."

It wasn't the hour for truth. Or at least, for only one kind.

"They're jealous," I said. "They know they'll be outshone. Anyway, everyone was against Antektra, too, apparently. It might be helpful."

"The screech of the peacock," she said, "the bird of ill-omened and curse-laden death."

I retouched her body makeup. I wondered if I could have done what she would have to do, and some part of me began to tell me I could, and to visualize I'd be just as scared as she was, and maybe more.

"Jane, you've changed so much," she said, staring at me in the smeary mirror, seeing me for the first time. "You're beautiful. And fey. And so calm. So wise."

"It's the company I keep," I said before I could stop myself.

"Is it?" She was vague. She'd forgotten, just as Clovis reported. "Do you have a lover, Jane?"

Yes, Egyptia. A silver metal lover.

"Maybe."

And then, startling me: "What happened with the robot, Jane?"

"Well." I steeled myself. "He's wonderful. Now and then."

"Yes," she said wistfully, "more beautiful and more clever than any man. And more gentle. Did you find that? And those songs. He sang me love songs. He knew how I needed love, that I live on love. . . . Wonderful songs. And his touch—he could touch me, and—"

Just as I felt I could no longer bear it, shocked to find the old wound still raw, she was silenced. A dreadful siren squealed over our heads and we flew together in mindless fright.

A tinny laugh followed the siren. Patently it was a "joke" they'd rigged for her benefit. "Five minutes to curtain-up, Egypt."

I thought she might have a fit. But instead, suddenly she was altered.

"Please go now, Jane," she said. "I must be alone."

Outside, Jason and Medea fell in beside me.

"We have seats in the third row. How bourgeois of Clovis to ask for those. You've got Chloe's seat, which is the least good. Funny you didn't have a seat of your own, if you knew you were coming here."

But in fact, funnier still, for Clovis had done a juggling act and changed the seats around. To their consternation, the twins found they were in the first row; alone—not even seated together.

"What a shame," said Clovis. "There's been some kind of mix-up. Doubtless part of the theatre's vendetta against all of us."

The twins would now have to sit through the whole play getting cricked necks from turning to see if I was still there, two rows behind them.

As Clovis and I sat down on the end of the row, he said, "I suggest you leave after Egyptia's first speech. I gather ten idiots rush down the aisles, and when they reach the stage, there's a storm. The special effects are rather gruesome. Eyes and intestines unsurgically removed. I shall look the other way, but Jason and Medea will be riveted. I think you should go then. If they notice, it'll take them half an hour to fight their way out, and with luck they'll collide with the second relay down the aisle, which is a procession of some sort." Jason and Medea had turned around and looked at us, and Clovis waved at them. "If they ask me, I'll say you left to be sick."

"They'll know that isn't true."

"Of course. I'd forgotten your reputation for implacable indifference. It still won't help them very much."

"Clovis, you said you would let me have some cash."

"Tomorrow, you and he take a cab along the highway to route eighty-three. Can you get the fare for that?"

"Yes."

"Leave the cab at eighty-three and walk down to the Fall Side of the Canyon. Be there by noon."

"That's only a few miles from my mother's house."

"Is that important? I doubt if you'll meet her. The spot was decided on because it's clear of the city and inside the state line, which should mean no observers, official or otherwise. And because Gem can land the VLO there."

"What?"

"Vertical lift-off plane. Those nasty noisy odorous flying machines, like the Baxter your mother so prizes. Gem is a test engineer and pilot for the Historica Antiqua Corporation. He will borrow a crate from the museum sheds, as he often does, land in the Canyon, and take you wherever you want to be. He said he would, about an hour ago when I called him. He's relatively imbecilic, by the way, so if you don't tell him your boyfriend is a robot, Gem will never guess, which may prove rather a bore for Silver. However, Gem will bumble you along and you'll arrive somewhere. Then he'll come back and spend the evening with me, God help me. Honestly, Jane, the things I suffer for you."

"Clovis, I—"

"Take whatever luggage you want, short of a grand piano. There's plenty of room in those things. There'll be a piece of hand-luggage in the cabin, with some money. Units, and some bills if I have the time to crack them down at a bank. Aren't you going to cry, fling yourself on the carpet—if there is one in here, oh, yes—go into a paroxysm of gratitude? Fawn on me? Faint?"

"No. But I'll never forget what you've done for me. Never."

"Gem will be pleased, too. But I'll try not to think about that."

"I wish—"

"You wish I were heterosexual so we could run away together instead."

"I wish I could thank you properly, but there isn't any way."

"I can't even be godfather to your kids, can I? Since you won't have any."

"*I* might. The way Demeta had me. Silver would make an amazing adoptive father, I should think. I never had a father."

"You didn't miss a thing," said Clovis. And the lights, with no subtlety, either due to incompetence, poor equipment, or would-be brilliant innovation, went suddenly out.

The audience exclaimed, vaguely disapproving.

"Jane," he said then, "there's one damned important thing I forgot—have to be shorthand. Listen: Jason finding you—a homemade device of his—a homing device. Check any clothing you might have met him in before today. Look for something small."

"*What* did you say?"

"You heard me. It's obviously not wonderfully accurate, but that is how they got as close as they did. It's been their new game for a month."

"But I—"

Eerie reddish-ochre light appeared under the curtain as it rose. We fell silent, I with my mind boiling.

A homing device? Patience Maidel Bridge, Jason running by me, and Medea—I needed to go on thinking about this, but then the bare stage yawned before me, clothed only in drifting, bloodstained smoke. And out of the smoke, along a raised platform, walked Egyptia, stiff and blind-eyed, glittering in her metals.

For a second, I wondered what would become of her. But what had become of her was Antektra, and all at once I knew it. She seemed like a lunatic escaped from the site of an explosion, deafened, dehumanized. Her awful beauty hit the eyes. She lifted her hands and held out a blood-daubed (this was going to be a very gory production) drapery.

"Bow your neck," she said to us, "bow your neck," and in the midst of everything else, my heart turned over, for she'd repeated her lines. And then the hair rose on my scalp, as I deduced hair might be doing all over the reasonably well-filled theatre. For her voice dropped like a singer's, seemingly one whole octave: "Bow your neck to the bloody dust. Kneel to the yoke, humiliated land."

She stood there, melodramatic, insane, and we hung on her words, breathless.

"This is not the world. The gods are dead."

I shivered. She had come from the grave.

Of course she would behave as if no other actor existed. They didn't. They were shades. Only Antektra lived in her burning agony, her broken landscape.

"Relinquish pride, and kneel."

I sat there, mesmerized, as before. There was no sound anywhere until the raucous clash and clatter of arms. The ten warriors galloped down the aisles, and the audience reacted now with approving squeaks.

"Weep, you skies," Egyptia cried out, over the noise of war. "Weep blood and flame."

The warriors converged before her. Thunder banged. Lightning raged across the stage. Caught in its glare upon the platform, Egyptia herself seemed on fire.

"Go *on,*" Clovis muttered.

"What?"

"Get out, you fool."

"Oh—" I stumbled up and almost fell out into the aisle. Under cover of strobe-lighted fire and fury, I ran for the exit and out into the sanity and freezing truth of the city night.

• • •

I only had enough coins to take the downtown bus, and it came very late. When I reached the stop and got off, it was already one twenty-six A.M. by the bus's own clock. I had been gone over ten hours. Clovis hadn't thought of my leaving a man waiting, only a machine. Even though Clovis didn't really believe that anymore. Had I, however helpless I was in the clutches of my friends, basically thought the same? Of course he would be calm, unperturbed, reasonable about my long, long, inexplicable absence, when I had previously stressed to him the danger I reckoned we were in. Of course he would. Mechanically reasonable.

I ran along the streets, and it was like running through solid dark water, the night was so curiously intense.

When I ran into the room of our flat, he was standing in the middle of the rainbow carpet. The overhead light was on and I saw him very clearly. Seeing him was like seeing the Earth's center, finding my equilibrium again, landfall. But he stood completely still, completely expressionless.

"Are you," he said to me, "all right?"

"Yes."

"Lucky you caught me in," he said, "I've been out since seven, trying to find you. I was just going out again."

"Out? But we agreed—"

"I thought you might have been hurt," he said gently. "Or killed."

The way he said it, for which I can't find words, rocked me, numbed me like a blow, driving all the words and thought out of my head. And because the words and thought and the events of the evening were so important, I immediately began to push my way back through the numbness toward them, not waiting to analyze his reaction and my reaction to it.

"No. Listen. I'll tell you what happened," I said prosaically, as if in answer to the question I had, I suppose, expected from the rational, unperturbed machine.

So I told him, rapidly, all of it. He listened as I'd asked. After a moment, he sat down on the couch and bowed his head, and I sat beside him to finish the story.

"I couldn't get away. I didn't dare. Even to call you—I wasn't sure of the number of the phone downstairs—and then I had to wait for Clovis. It seems so crazy, but are we going to do it? Leave tomorrow, go somewhere else? Like two escaping spies. I think we have to."

"You're so scared of this city and what you think it can do," he said. "To get out is the only thing possible to us."

"You're blaming me? Don't. I *am* scared, with good reason. I've been scared that way all afternoon, all night."

He put his arm round me, and I lay against him. And sensed a profound reticence. He might have been a mile off.

"Egyptia," I said, slowly, testing, but I wasn't certain for what. "Egyptia is astonishing. I only saw her speak a few lines—Silver, what's the matter? I don't even know if you can be angry, but don't be. It wasn't my fault. I *couldn't* come here. And if you think that was being stupid and panicking, at least believe it was sincere panic, not just stupidity. And after what Clovis said about homing devices. . . . Oh, God, I'd better check—"

But his arm tightened, and I knew I wasn't supposed to move, and I kept still, and silent, and I waited.

Presently he began to speak to me, quietly and fluently. There was scarcely a trace of anything in that musical singer's voice of his, except maybe the slightest salt of humor.

"On one or two occasions, I can recollect saying to you that you were trying to get me to investigate myself emotionally, something that I wasn't geared to do. It turns out I was wrong. Or else I've learned to do it, the way I've learnt a number of other things, purely human knacks. When you were gone—"

I whispered, "I really *couldn't*—"

"I know. I also know you're alive and intact. I didn't know it until you came through that door. *If* I were human, Jane, I'd be shaking. If I were human, I'd have walked into every free hospital this side of the city and hurled chairs about till someone said you weren't there."

"I'm so sorry. I am, I am."

"Strangest of all was the inner process through which I put myself. During which I imagined that, since you were dead somewhere, I would never be with you again. And I saw how that was, and how I'd be. You asked if I could be afraid. I can. You'll have to believe, with no evidence, that inside this body which doesn't shake, doesn't sweat, doesn't shed tears, there really is a three-year-old child doing all of those, at full stretch, right now."

His head was bowed, so I couldn't see his face.

I put my arms around him and held him tightly, tightly.

Rather than joy in his need, I felt a sort of shame. I knew I'd inadvertently done a final and unforgivable thing to him. For I had, ultimately and utterly, proved him human at last: I had shown him he was dependent on his own species.

The earthquake struck the city at a few minutes after five that morning.

I woke, because the brass bed was moving. Silver, who could put himself into a kind of psychosthetic trance, not sleep but apparently restful and timeless, came out of it before I did. I thought I'd been dreaming. It was dark, except for the faint sheen of snowlight coming through the half-open curtains. Then I saw the curtains were drawing *themselves* open, a few inches at a time.

"It's an earth tremor," he said to me. "But not a bad one from the feel of it."

"It's bad enough," I cried, sitting up.

The bed had slid over the floor about a foot. Vibrations were running up through the building. I became aware of a weird external noise, a sort of creaking and groaning and cracking, and a screeching I took at first for cries of terror from the city.

"Should we run down into the street?" I asked him.

"No. It's already settling. The foreshock was about ten minutes ahead of this one, hardly noticeable. It didn't even wake you."

A candle fell off a shelf.

"Oh Silver! Where's the cat?"

"Not here, remember?"

"Yes. I'm going to miss that cat. . . . How can I talk about that in the middle of this?"

He laughed softly, and drew me down into the bed.

"You're not really afraid, that's why."

"No, I'm not. *Why* not?"

"You're with me and you trust me. And I told you it was all right."

"I love you," I said.

Something heavy and soft hit the window. Then everything settled with a sharp jarring rattle, as if the city were a truck pulling up with a load of cutlery.

Obliquely fascinated, then, I got out of bed and went to the window. The quake had indeed been minor, yet I'd never experienced one before. Part of me expected to see the distant skyline of the city flattened and engulfed by flames—substance of so many tremor-casts on the news channels. But I could no longer see the city skyline at all. Like monstrous snakes, three of the girders in the subsidence had reared up, sloughing their skins of snow in all directions and with great force, like catapults. Some of this snow had thumped the window. Now the girders blocked the view of the city, leaning together in a grotesque parody of their former positions. It was a kind of omen.

Dimly, I could hear a sort of humming and calling.

People running out on the street to discuss what had happened. Then a robot ambulance went by, unseen but wailing; then another and another. There had been casualties, despite the comparative mildness of the shock. I thought of them with compassion, cut off from them, because we were safe. I remember being glad that Egyptia's play would have finished before the quake. She and Clovis seemed invulnerable.

Only when we were back in bed again, sharing the last tired apple, did I think of my mother's house on its tall legs of steel. Should I go down to the foyer and call her? But the foyer would probably be full of relatives calling up relatives. What did I really feel?

I told Silver.

"The house felt pretty safe," he said. "It was well-stabilized. The only problem would be the height, but there'd be compensations for that in the supports."

"I think I'd know, wouldn't I? If anything had happened to her. Or would I?"

"Maybe you would."

"I wonder if she's concerned for me. She might be. I don't know. Oh, Silver, I don't know. I was with her all my life, and I don't know if she'd be worried for me. But I know you would have been."

"Yes, you worry me a lot."

Later on, the caretaker patted on our door and asked if we were okay. I called that we were, and asked after him and the white cat.

"Cat never batted an eyelid. That's how you can tell, animals. If they don't take off, you know it's not going to be a bad one."

When he left, I felt mean, not telling him we were going. We'd leave what we could for the rent, most of it, in fact, as far as the month had gone. I wanted to say goodbye to the cat. Demeta had always said that cats were difficult to keep in a domestic situation, that they clawed things and got hair on the pillows, and she was right and what the hell did it matter?

I fell asleep against Silver, and dreamed Chez Stratos had fallen out of the sky. There was wreckage and rubble everywhere, and the spacemen picked about in it, incongruously holding trays of tea and toast. "Mother?" I asked the wreckage. "Mother, where are you?"

"Come here, darling," said my mother. She was standing on a small hill, and wearing golden armor. I saw, with brief horror, that her left hand had been severed, but one of the robot machines was re-attaching it. I went to her, and she embraced me, but the armor was hard and I couldn't get through it to her, and I wasn't comforted.

"Your brother's dead, I'm afraid," she said, smiling at me kindly.

"My—brother—"

"Yes, dear. And your father, too."

I wept, because I didn't know who they were.

"You must put this onto a tape," said Demeta. "I'll play it when I come back."

"Where are you going?" I asked.

"I'm going to make farm machinery. I told you."

"I don't remember."

"That's because you don't want to. Come along, Jane. Let go of my armor."

The Baxter Empire rose into the dusty sky out of the ruins, flattening all of us to the earth with the gale of its ascent. A dismembered monkey lay on the ground where my mother had been standing, and I wondered if this was my brother. Then the monkey changed into Jason, and he wasn't dismembered, and he said to me, "Hallo, Medea. I put a homing device into a peacock. Wasn't that fun?"

I woke, and it was getting light. Silver was in the shower, I could hear the cascade of water. I lay and looked at the blue sky of our ceiling as it came clear, and the clouds and the birds and the rainbow. I let the tears go on rolling out of my eyes. I'd never see this ceiling again.

Along with the other things, I'd have to leave my peacock jacket behind too. Were peacocks cursed birds? My mother's dress, Egyptia's play, my jacket. I'd have to leave the dress I'd worn under the jacket, too, the dress I'd worn that night we met Jason and Medea as we came off the bridge. I recalled how Jason brushed against me as he ran away. Maybe to run away like that was partly deliberate. They were both good pickpockets, excellent kleptomaniacs—it would have been easy for either of them to slip something adhesive into the fabric. But at two-thirty this morning I'd turned the clothing of that night inside out, and found nothing. Maybe the gadget had fallen out, which could explain how they'd almost traced me but not quite. The thing might have been lying about somewhere in the vicinity, misleading them. On the other hand the gadget might be so cunning that it was invisible to me, but still lodged, and Jason's failure to get to me due only to some weakness in the device which, given time, he could correct. The micro-magnet in Clovis's seance glass was almost invisible, and highly accurate, and Jason had worked on that a year ago. They must have sat there by the bridge, just waiting for someone interesting to come along that they could bug, and who should appear but idiotic Jane.

Whatever else, I wouldn't risk taking that clothing with me. I'd even leave my boots worn that night—I had another shabby, fascinating green pair—I'd even leave my lingerie. I knew the device couldn't have gone that deep, but I wasn't taking any chances.

When Silver came out of the shower, I got up, and, very businesslike, used it. I allowed myself only three minutes to lie under the spray and cry at the crimson ceiling and the blue walls and the aeronautic whale.

Dressed, we left the portion of rent money, and the last can of Keep-Kold-Kitty-Meat on the brass bed. Silver wrote the caretaker a note saying a friend was offering us work in a drama in the east. We'd already decided by then to go westward. We'd even talked about Paris, for the future.

I'd packed our clothes into various cloth bags, some of the shawls from the bed, towels, oddments, and, in some curious superstitious urge, the three then currently complete chapters of this. I think I had the notion of putting on our escape as an addendum to the history. Or just of keeping a journal, like lady travelers of old.

Silver carried all the bags and his guitar. I had been entrusted with the blue and gold umbrella.

A little before nine, we sneaked out of the building. The white cat was jauntily stalking its shadow in the street, and ran over to meet us. I nearly suffocated it, holding back my tears.

"If only we could take her with us."

"The old man needs her more than we do. He's very fond of her."

"Yes, I know."

"We'll buy a cat."

"Can we?"

"We might even train it to sing."

A tear fell, despite my efforts, on the cat's nose, and it sprang away in disgust, awarding me an accidental parting claw on the wrist.

"There you are," he said. "A farewell present."

We planned to walk into the center of the city. To get a cab from this area to the outskirts was almost impossible.

As we turned into the boulevard, I saw our estimation of the quake had been premature.

Buckled and humped like a child's maltreated nondurable toy, the elevated dominated the air and, in surging over, had made havoc of the street below. As I looked at it, I remembered the awful creaking and squealing noises I had heard and then put down to the shifting girders. Being downtown, not a lot was being done about the elevated, though a couple of private demolition vans were cruising about. The vehicular road, however, was closed.

We bought doughnuts at one of the stalls that had missed the eruption of the rusty tracks. The woman stared at us through the steam of her urn.

"Jack's lost all his glass. All smashed."

We told her we were sorry, and drank tea and went on.

The quake had not been so very violent in itself, but hitting those areas still weakened and faulted by previous tremors, had taken its toll. It seemed to have come back to collect dues missed twenty years before.

At the first intersection, we came on the confusion that the diversion from the road on the boulevard had caused, jams of vehicles hooting vilely and pointlessly at each other like demented beasts. Farther on, a group of earlier tremor-wrecks twenty-five stories high had given up and collapsed across the street; this road, too, was closed, and more pandemonium had resulted.

As we neared the Arbors, we ourselves were diverted by robot patrols into side streets and alleys. A line of cars had crashed, one after the other, off a fly-over, when it shifted like a sail in the wind.

"This is horrible," I said inanely.

"Look at that building," he said.

I looked. There seemed nothing wrong with it. It only occurred to me ten minutes later he'd been directing my eyes away from something lying in the gutter, something I'd only taken for a blown-away bag. . . .

By the time we reached the Beech subway, I was frightened. The tremor, low on the scale, but delving to find any flaw, and split and chew and rend it, had left nightmarish evidence that Tolerance had been lucky.

"From the look of things," Silver said, "the main force channeled away from the direction of your mother's house."

"Yes. And Clovis was in the middle."

"Do you want to go over to New River and see?"

"No. I feel we're so conspicuous. But I'll call him."

I went into a kiosk and dialed Clovis's number. Nothing happened, then there was a click. I thought I'd get the sodomy tape, but instead a mechanical voice said: "Owing to seismic disturbance, these lines are temporarily on hold. We stress this does not mean your party is in an affected area, merely that the connecting video and audio links to this kiosk have been impaired."

I stood there, trembling. I was afraid, for Clovis, and for both of us. Callously, I was frantically asking myself if this would affect our plan. And I had a mental picture of the unknown Gem who was going to fly us, buried under a collapsed tower, or the Historica VLOs in fragments.

Before I came out, I dialed for the time. It was twenty-two minutes to eleven, and we had to be down at Fall Side by twelve—if the plan was still on. We'd just have to act as though it was.

"Silver, the lines are out."

"That was a chance."

"How much money have we got?"

He told me.

"We can phone a cab here. They'll do pickups from Beech, even this end, I think."

"You could," he said, "get it to detour past the New River blocks and see what shape they're in. If there's a way through."

That made things easier all around. For one thing, the

cab company might be reluctant to make a pickup at lower Beech for out of town. Sometimes cabs are hired, directed out onto the plain, and vandalized. But I added the detour to opulent New River, implying another pickup there, and they agreed.

The cab came in five minutes.

It shot up unusual side roads. Two or three one-way systems had been provisionally dualized. Robot police were everywhere. I was depressed and awed by the way in which the city had been demoralized. Relief fought with panic inside me. The plan might be in ruins, too, but even so, with all this going on, who would be looking out for a stray silver-skinned man?

As we came around from Racine and then up through a previously pedestrians-only subway, and the New River appeared, I caught my breath. Davideed, the studier of silt, could have had a field day here. It looked as if someone had turned the river over with an enormous spatula. Shining icy mud lay in big curls against the banks and on the street, and spattered the fronts of the buildings. But every block was standing. We went by Clovis's block. Not a brick was out of place, and though some of the air-conditioning boxes on the ground gallery looked askew, none of the upper ones had shifted.

"I think the river provided a pressure outlet," Silver said.

"He must be safe, then."

He had to be. As my mother had to be. There wasn't time to investigate or to worry any further.

The cab spun around the city like a piece of flotsam, catching in jams, getting out of them, for thirty-five minutes before it emerged onto the highway. Then we went slowly for another ten, since, for the few cars trying to get out, hundreds of others were trying to get in. People had come from everywhere, looking for relations and friends in the aftermath, or to sightsee. The local news channel would have carried the news of the quake and excitement, adding the normal useless proviso: Please keep out, which no one, obviously, would attend.

The taxi had a glass-faced clock.

"It's almost ten to twelve. We're not going to make it," I said.

We had come this way a century ago, the road clear save for a purple storm brewing, I with a silver nail through my heart, afraid to speak to him or keep silent.

"Jane, if a man comes over in a VLO and lands the thing, I think you can assume he'll maybe hang about for a few minutes."

The cab suddenly detoured on to a side turning.

"Where's it going?"

"Straight on to route eighty-three, at a guess."

"How do you know?"

"My city geography program extends several miles beyond the outskirts. Do you realize, in a new city, I'll be as lost as you will?" A moment later, he said gently to me, "Jane, look."

I looked out of the window, and far away over the snow-sheeted lines of the land, across the gash of the highway, poised at the topmost mouth of the Canyon, where the flyer air lines glinted like golden cotton, other vertical lines of glitter went up. And in the sky there was a tiny cloud, cool, blue and unmoving. Chez Stratos, that ridiculous house, was still standing, still intact.

Something broke and ebbed away inside me.

"Oh, Silver. After all, I'm so glad."

"I know."

A minute more and we plunged down a slope to the ragged ravine that leads into the Fall Side of the Canyon. The cab, not intended to risk its treads, stopped.

It took every coin and bill we had, to pay it the balance. But, in a way, that was ethical.

Soon we were walking down between walls of the frozen earth, he carrying the bags, the guitar, I, the umbrella, to the place where the steps are cut.

The Canyon, which had been created by an ancient quake prior even to the Asteroid, hadn't been touched by the new one. At the bottom, between the tumbled blocks that give this end its name and close it on three sides, there was a ballroom floor of smooth treeless, rockless snow, hard and bluish as a sort of aluminum. A lovely place for a VLO landing. Secretive, and negotiable only in such a way, or on foot.

The last time on the clock had read as six minutes past noon.

"Have we missed it?" I asked. But I smiled at myself. We would have seen it going over if we had, we had been close enough.

"Oh, I should think so."

It was very very cold in the Fall. It was like standing in the bowl of a metal spoon. Strange echoes came and whispers went. The growl of the plane, when it arrived, would be deafening.

"He is, of course, late," I said.

"Five minutes."

"Eight minutes. What do we do if he doesn't come?"

"You'll curse him. I'll carry you back to the city."

"You'll what?"

"Carry you. The whole twenty, thirty miles. Running at eighty miles an hour all the way, if you like. The highway is comparatively flat."

I laughed, and my laugh rang around the silver spoon.

"If he doesn't, I dare you to."

"No dare. It's easy."

"And terribly inconspicuous."

And then I heard the plane.

"Oh, Silver. Isn't it wonderful? It's going to work."

I stared into the sky, but all I saw was its lavender-blue wintryness.

"Can you see the plane, Silver?"

"No," he said, "I can't. And the reason for that is, I think, that there isn't one. The Canyon sides are distorting some other sound."

"Then what?"

"A car. Yes, listen. Brakes."

"Why would a car stop here?"

"Clovis?"

"Then something has gone wrong."

I can only describe the feeling this way: It was as though someone loosened a valve in each of my limbs simultaneously, and some precious vital juice ran out of me. I felt it go with an actual physical ache, sickening and final. My lips were frozen, my tongue was wood, but I managed to make them move. "Silver . . . The rocks behind us. I can't get by them, but you can. You can run over them, jump them, and go down the other side. And up the Canyon. I won't come because, if you carry me, it would have to slow you, make it that much more awkward. Because the surface—isn't flat. You said, a flat surface."

He turned and looked at me. His face was attentive, the eyes flattening out, cold gold-red fires.

"It wouldn't be so easy over rocks, no. Much, much slower."

"You'll need to be fast."

"What is it?"

"It's—I don't know. But I know you have to run. Now, Silver."

"Not without you."

"They can't do anything to me."

"They can do everything to you. You're no longer coded. If someone wants me, and I'm no longer here."

It came to me he knew what I meant before even I knew it. He had always known then, better than I, that they—that they—

"I don't care, Silver. Please, please run away."

He didn't move, except he turned to face the way we had come, and I, helpless, powerless, turned to do the same. As we did so, he said, "And anyway, my love, they'd have, I think, some means of stopping me from getting very far."

They. Five figures were coming down the steps onto the ballroom floor. They all wore fur coats, fur hats. They looked like bears. They were funny.

They came toward us quite slowly. I don't think it was deliberate. They were cold, and the way was slippery. I didn't know any of them, and then the snow-light slicked across two panes of glass.

The VLO wasn't coming. It didn't exist. Electronic Metals existed. Clovis had betrayed us, after all.

"There's still time," I tried to say.

"Not really," he said. He turned away from them again and stood in front of me so I wouldn't see them. He blotted them out, as long ago he'd blotted out the harsh light and fear of the world, so I could learn to bear it. "Listen," he said. "None of this matters. What we've had matters—*listen* to me. I love you. You're a part of me. I'm a part of you. You can't ever lose that. I'm with you the rest of your life."

"No Silver—Silver—"

"Yes. Trust me. It's true. And I'm not afraid of this. I was only afraid for you. Do you understand?"

I shook my head. He took my hands and held them against his face, and he looked at me, and he smiled at me. And then he glanced back again, and they were very close.

Swohnson was in the lead.

"You've been a bit of a silly girl," he said to me, "creeping off with your friend's property. It isn't, ah, legal, you know."

I don't think he recognized me, but he disliked me just the same. I'd made him come out in the cold. He always got the rotten jobs—placating the mob and irate callers, shutting the gate, doing the visual interviews and acting dumb, chasing runaway machines and female children across the winter countryside.

I couldn't say a word that would alter anything, but the words tried to come, and Swohnson showed his teeth at me and said, "You're lucky if no one lodges charges. Not that that's our business. Our business is this, here. Didn't you know how dangerous these things can be? They can short out at a second's, er, notice. A faulty line. Yes, you've been bloody lucky."

I started to plead, and then I stopped. Silver was standing by me, looking at them silently. None of them looked in his eyes.

"Er, yes. Give us the lady's bags," said Swohnson. "Um, you take the guitar, will you," he added to one of the other four bears. "That's E.M. property."

Silver put down the bags quietly. Men picked them up. He handed the guitar to the elected man, who said, "Thanks—Oh, shit," and bit his mouth.

"Yes, they're convincing," Swohnson said. "Till they blow a gasket. Now, young lady. We stopped your cab on the road. It'll take you back to the city."

"She hasn't," Silver said, "got the fare."

They all started. Swohnson coughed. He swung around on another bear. "Go and put some, ah, cash in the damn cab. Enough for the ride."

The bear hurried off. They were obedient henchmen. If Silver resisted them, would they be enough to stop him? And then I saw something come out of Swohnson's pocket, in his gloved paw. He toyed with it, so I could see the buttons.

"Don't," Silver said, "do it in front of her."

Swohnson coughed again. His breath fluffed through the air. The Canyon vibrated.

"Oh, don't worry. You don't think we'd carry you to the car when you can walk? Start walking now. Left, right. Left, right."

Silver walked, and I walked. The men walked with us. No one spoke. We went up the steps and came out in the ravine. When we got to the top, the cab was back, a bear leaning on one side.

"All paid up and primed for the city center," he said, quite cheerfully. "All right? Mr. Swohnson?"

"Fine."

Swohnson walked on, and Silver walked, and I tried to and one of the bears caught my arm and prevented me. My bags were lying by the taxi.

"Here's your cab, now, please."

"Let me," I said. "Let me come with you. As far as—the center."

"Sorry, madam. No."

"Let me. Please. I won't do anything."

Silver was taller than they were. He walked like an actor playing a young king. The cloak flared from his shoulders. His hair blazed through the monochrome white-blueness of the day, as he walked away from me toward the long black car like an ancient hearse.

"You see," I said to the man, smiling, plucking at his sleeve, "you see I'd much rather."

He shook me off. Agitated, he said, "It's only a bit of metal. I know it looks—but it isn't. Let it go, can't you.

They're dangerous. It could hurt you. We just take them apart. Melt it down. It'll be over in another hour. That's no time, is it. Nothing to fret about."

I held out my hands to him and he backed away.

Silver moved in a graceful bow to get into the car. The windows were tinted like Swohnson's spectacles, and I couldn't see him anymore, not even the fire of his hair, his hair, his hair.

Swohnson got into the car. The others called. The man who had stopped me ran up the road to them, slipping once and almost going down.

"Please," I said to the empty distance between us.

Their car started. Snow fanned away from it. It moved powerfully. It raced and dwindled.

"Please," I said.

It was gone.

Automatically, I fumbled to open the taxi door, and one by one I loaded the bags into it, and the umbrella. Then I got in and shut the door.

I sat in the taxi. I wasn't crying. I was making a little noise, very low, I can't describe it. I couldn't seem to stop. I think I may have been trying still to say "Please." I sat and watched the clock in the taxi.

I didn't even think of going after them. They had, at least, taught me that.

It'll be over in another hour.

When you leave me, there's nothing.

There's all the world.

It'll be over, in another hour.

Where the cat had scratched me, my wrist hurt.

I watched the clock. I didn't visualize any of what they did to him. I didn't wonder about it. I didn't feel him die.

"Jack's lost all his glass. All smashed."

When the hour was up, I took off my left boot and

smashed the glass over the taxi clock, and taking up the largest shard I could find I cut my wrists with it.

Blood is very red. I began to feel warm. Everything grew dark. But in the dark, little bright silver flames were turning and burning. . . .

When he shall die, take him and cut him out in little stars, and he will make the face of heaven so fine, that all the world will be in love with night. . . .

Somewhere there was a great rushing and roaring. The sky was falling. The sky with its Silver stars, his hands, his feet, his limbs, his torso, even his genitals scattered to give light, dismembered like Osiris, Romeo, Dionysos.

The sky fell in the Canyon.

Later, the door of the cab was wrenched open.

"Oh, Jesus," someone said to me. I heard this someone retching and fighting to control the spasms. But I closed my eyes and slept.

5

I remember the hospital in little blurred white flashes, like damaged film. I needn't describe that. Or the pain, which didn't stay in any part of me, but ran through all over me, so that even to turn was awful. I remember being helped to use the lavatory, moaning with pain. All these pains were physical. Below, beneath, beside them all, a thin grey pain that was not physical ran on and on like a tape. I dreamed sometimes. I was a child, and someone had thrown my black fur bear into a fire. It was coming apart and melting and I screamed with horror. I also dreamed that I was taken to meet my father, the man who had supplied the sperm for me to be born. But whenever I arrived where he was supposed to be, he wasn't there anymore. These are symbols. I didn't dream—I didn't dream of him.

I didn't come fully conscious until I was in a room I knew, and for a moment couldn't identify. Then I moved a little, and my foot skidded. The sheets were dark green satin. And then Clovis was sitting on the arm of a chair, looking at me.

Two things. His hair was still long, but dark now, not dark red, de-molecularized. And his face was hollow, which made him look oddly holy.

"I'm sorry about the sheets," he said. "I forgot. I can change them tomorrow."

Clovis. I was in Clovis's spare bed, in Clovis's apartment. I was with Clovis. Who had betrayed us. My mouth was dry. I said softly, "Hallo, Judas."

He slowly shook his head, as if he knew fast gestures made me giddy.

"No, Jane. Not me."

Did I feel anything? Did I want to hurt him, to kill him? No. I didn't want anything. I didn't even want to die anymore. It was too much trouble. But I was obliged, having started the conversation, to go on with it.

"You called E.M. You told them where we'd be."

"I did not."

"Where you knew we'd be, because you'd promised me the VLO would come."

"It did come. Who do you think found you? The hapless Gem. He put a tourniquet on you and got you in the plane. He then flew that impossible crate over the city, which is strictly illegal, and landed on the roof of State Imperial Hospital. The place was packed with quake casualties stacked like sardines, but he wouldn't move off until they took you in as well. I never knew he had it in him. I don't think he did. He is now on opium-based tranquilizers, which are not going to put the color back in his cheeks. Christ, Jane, what a bloody foul thing to do to yourself."

"If it came, it came too late. You made sure E.M. would get to us first."

"It was late because half the Historica sheds collapsed in the tremor. Gem got the VLO out past security as soon as he could."

"I don't want to talk to you. I don't want to be here."

"All right. I know you think I'm the villain of this rather sordid plot. I'll leave you alone. Just stay put until you're stronger, and then you can go."

He got up and walked away into the blur that misted the edges of my vision. When the blur had almost swallowed him, he said, "Your mother called. She calls every hour. Do you want her to come over?"

I suddenly began to try to cry. It was very difficult. The tears wouldn't come. It was like trying to give birth to a stone. When I stopped trying, my heart was thundering, and Clovis was standing over me again.

"Jane—"

"No. I don't want my mother." I shut my mouth.

Presently Clovis went out. Then I tried to get out of the bed. The last thing I remember is that I couldn't.

There were large white sealed and waterproof bandages on my wrists. In another month, I would go back to have the stitches out, and then I could book up for the treatment that would take the scars away. Clovis wrote to tell me this in a note he left lying on the coffee table. He said he would pay for the treatment. Or Demeta would. He'd gone out and left the place to me on the day he thought I was strong enough to get up. He seemed to trust me. He seemed to know I wouldn't repeat my earlier performance. Why should I? I hadn't the energy. It takes a lot of determination to die. A lot of conviction. Unless someone helps.

The note also said he'd asked Demeta not to phone, but a couple of times the phone sounded, and I knew it was her. The second time I reached out blindly and switched it on.

"Hallo, Mother," I said.

"Whoops." A male voice, laughing. "I may not be enormously butch, but I've never been mistaken for anyone's *mother* before."

I sighed. I thought about being polite. At last I said, "I'm sorry."

"That's okay. Any chance of Clovis being there?"

"No. He's out."

"Dammit. Would you tell him Leo rang?"

Would I?

"All right."

"Leo. L as in Love. E as in Edible. O as in Oh my God why doesn't this M-B idiot get off the line."

"Leo," I said dully, missing his wit, I suppose offensively.

"Good-bye," he said, and switched off.

I scribbled across the bottom of Clovis's note to me: LEO CALLED.

I went into the green bathroom and lay in the bath three or four hours. Sometimes I would try to cry. My mind went plodding on and on. It's wrong to repress grief. Was I repressing grief? I thought about Silver. I tried to cry. No tears would come. I'd cried for so many trivial reasons, over visuals, dramas, books, out of embarrassment and childish fear. Now I couldn't cry.

When I heard the lift come up, I was glad, with a sort of deadly gladness, not to be alone anymore. I heard Clovis come into the apartment, and move about there, and once he whistled a snatch of tune, and then stopped himself suddenly.

Perverseness made me go out of the bathroom, carrying my robe, naked, and walk across the room in front of him to the bedroom. He stared at me as I passed, then turned away.

I got back into the spare bed and lay there, and eventually he came in.

"Are you hungry? The servicery is bursting with food. Truffles, pâté, eggs angéliques, roast beef . . . mince on toast."

I became aware it gave me a horrible relief to ignore him, providing he was there to be ignored.

Then suddenly he yelled at me.

"Christ, Jane, it wasn't *me.* Do you want me to tell you what happened?"

I didn't reply and he began to curse me. Then he went out again. I lay a long while, and then my stomach began to growl with avid hunger. My hunger was far away but insistent. Finally I got up, and opened the guest closet where he'd neatly hung all my few clothes out of the bags. My stomach growled and gurgled, and I touched my clothes, and remembered how I had worn them with Silver, and I tried to cry, and the tears wouldn't come. The black, paint-spotted scruffy jeans, taken in so badly at hips and waist and taken in so much. The fur jacket. The embroidered wool dress. The Renaissance dress. The emerald cloak, its hem stained by melted snow, and here, at the back, this dress I'd never actually worn in the slums, this black dress I'd worn the night I went to Electronic Metals and saw all the robots perform, all but Silver. For Silver, who was too human to check out, was in the cubicle, eyeless, handless—I opened my mouth to scream, but I didn't scream. What use was grief or terror or rage? Who would they move? Who would set things right? The law?

The Senate? God? But I pulled the black dress from the closet and held it up before me, and saw with uncaring surprise that one of the sleeves was ripped out.

I stood there a moment, then I let the dress fall. I picked up my robe and put it on again. I walked out. Clovis was reclining on the couch among the black cushions, drinking applewine.

"I see Leo called," said Clovis. "What it is to be irresistible."

"It was Jason and Medea," I said.

"Your note says Leo."

"You know what I mean. It was Jason and Medea."

"*It was Jason and Medea* seems grammatically unsound. *They* were Jason and Medea, perhaps? It was Jason, and also it was Medea."

"Stop it, Clovis. Just answer."

"Would you believe me?"

"The sleeve in the black dress."

"Jason's device was stuck on the fabric. Color absorbent, so almost invisible. About the size of your little fingernail. But very adhesive. I didn't think you'd want it in your clothes anymore. I put it in the garbage disposal. If you want to go on being poor, I'll buy you a new dress. Or a new sleeve."

I went into the servicery and made instant toasts and ham and eggs and ate them standing by the hatches, greedily. I didn't think of Silver as I ate. Or of Jason. Or of Medea.

Clovis had put some Mozart on the player. When I came into the room again, he was sketching something, I don't know what it was.

"If you'd like to know the truth," he said, "I will tell you."

"Does it matter?"

"I think so. To me. I don't like this idea you have that I'm the modern miniaturized version of the Black Death."

I stood at the window and looked out at the river. The light was going, and a tin-foil of ice glimmered on the water. The mud was long gone, cleaned away. Jewels lit the buildings. So what?

"Did you know, Egyptia has become a star?"

"At the Theatra?" I asked.

"Not precisely. Most of the Theatra fell down in the tremor. An antiquated shed indeed. A lovely line for the visuals, though. They called her The Girl Who Rocked The City. And what was the other one? Oh, yes, how could I forget? The Girl Who Brought The House Down."

"I'm glad," I said, parroting, minus feeling, my earlier thought, "that it didn't happen when the play was on."

"No. It happened during the party afterward. Oh, yes, we were all in the auditorium at five past five, drinking some rather filthy champagne, when the bloody roof fell in on us. It was a damn silly evening anyway. The drama. Egyptia. She can't act, you know. She just *is*. But the magic of Egyptia consists of her own self-hypnosis. She believes in herself, despite what she says, and it's catching. She's a star all right. There are contracts signed for a visual. They'll be shooting in Africa. She's already over there. I'm telling you all this for a reason," he said. "You may abruptly want to know where she is."

I had been at this window, I had said to the reflection: I love you. And he had known. A pain came through me so vast, incapable of expression. I pressed my forehead to the glass. Why hadn't they let me die? I would be in blackness now, or in some spiritual state which no longer cared, no longer had any links with a soulless robot. For he had been only the sum of his metals, his mechanisms. Soulless, timeless.

"Jane, are you listening?"

"Yes. I think so."

Had he been afraid? Despite what he said to console me? He'd virtually pretended he disbelieved in pursuit, when he reckoned it a fact, to console me. Had it been like pain for him to die that way, although he couldn't feel pain? I'd taught him to feel pleasure, or rather, he'd taught himself, through me. But if pleasure, why not agony? I'd let him learn fear and need. And he'd let me learn to live. And all I wanted was to die.

"Oh, Jane," said Clovis. He was standing by me, and awkwardly, with none of his normal elegance, he took my hand. "Please, Jane. You have to get over it. No. You won't ever get over it. But you have to get over *this.*"

"Why?" I asked. I think I wanted to know.

"Because—Oh God, I don't know. Why do you?"

"Because," I said, "he told me there was all the world. Because he told me he was a part of me, that he'd be with me all my life and that nothing could change that. Because now I'm the only part of him that's left. They took him to pieces and put him in a fire."

"I know," Clovis said. He held my hand.

"Melted down. Scrap metal."

"I know."

"I'm all of him that's left. All of him there'll ever be anymore."

And the tears came and I cried tears. And Clovis, not wanting to, but amazingly gentle, held me.

I cried then, and now I don't think I'll ever cry again, the rest of my life.

Much later, he told me how E.M. had known about us, and how to find us.

I'd left the theatre and the play had gone through to more and more enthusiastic responses from the audience.

Egyptia had held them, and gradually most of the cast gave up trying to bulldoze her from the limelight. This was their livelihood, and a winner is a winner. By the second interval, the actors were in and out of her dressing room, having frozen roses sent in and making love to her. And she, generous, vulnerable Egyptia, had taken them all back into her heart. In the last scene, Antektra stabs herself, a libation of blood to appease the rampaging shade of her brother. It went on film, with everything else. The visual crew, overcome, were fighting to push out shots on the three A.M. local newscast. In the wake of all this, the party was riotous. Clovis, whose inclination was to leave, was cornered by Leo, an actor-manager from a rival company who had come to sneer and stayed to cheer. He was playfully trying to persuade Clovis to act Hamlet in a new skit version of the play called *Bloody Elsinor* when the tremor hit the building. At first it looked like nothing, and then the ceiling cracked in half and lumps of plaster and cement crashed into the auditorium.

Nobody was killed, but casualties were various, and this time the blood was real.

Clovis, unscathed, emerged from shelter to discover Egyptia standing up on the stage, white even under her makeup, rigid, in a sort of catatonic trance.

She'd always been so afraid of earthquakes. Her dreams and her fantasies of death and destruction had prepared her for this moment. She knew she had reached a pinnacle, and she knew the gods could sweep her from it. But she stood in the middle of carnage and she had survived. She hadn't apparently noticed until then I wasn't there. But when she started to come back from her trance she asked where I was. And Jason, mopping up his own blood from sundry cuts, said, "Jane's gone back to the slum to play with her robot lover." And, in the face of her non-comprehension, he had elaborated on his magical device and how he'd almost tracked us. I can see now, Jason and Medea would never have told any authority about us. It was more fun to have us to themselves; they didn't want to end the game. But Egyptia—I think I know what went through her head.

She must have heard and been aware, unconsciously, of what had been said about E.M.'s Sophisticated Formats. She must have been *consciously* aware from her own experience that it was more than true. The wonderful lover, the wonderful musician. Men could become redundant, she'd said. And of course that really meant, humans could become redundant. And I think, just the way the mob of unemployed hate the machines that take their work away from them, Egyptia knew the terror of losing what she had only just got hold of. She was a genius. She had sensed it in herself. Now everyone knew it, and fell before her feet, and her Destiny opened in front of her like a shining road. But what if a machine had more genius than she did? Oh, I don't suppose she thought it through. Egyptia doesn't think, she feels. As Clovis said, she just *is*. Probably, at the beginning, after the Babylon party, the actors had talked a lot about Silver, and how clever he was. Maybe they talked about the other robots, too, the ones that could act. Sometime, some seed had been planted in her. The earth tremor was like an after-image—or a fore-image. It had been for her the omen it had seemed for me. She was still half Antektra, and Antektra was good at reading portents. It shook her, liberated her even as it threatened her, into the grisly savagery of the id. She went home, still mainly in her trance, and Corinth went with her. Perhaps she made another kind of comparison that night, and it clinched matters. For if Silver was superior in her bed, he might also, so easily, be superior in her profession. About nine A.M., as Silver and I were walking up through the city, she called Electronic Metals. Legally she owned him.

Illegally, I had him. But they could probably find me. Someone had me tabbed. Then she gave them the address of Jason and Medea.

Jason wouldn't have wanted to cooperate, but E.M. had the City Senate behind them, pushing. Arms were twisted. I hope it hurt a lot. E.M. took Jason's homing transmitter, and their luck was in. Medea told Clovis all this later, including Egyptia's part. Especially Egyptia's part. Corinth, wandering from Egyptia's bed, had spread the tale by then anyway.

That night I came away from Electronic Metals, twenty-five years old, self-assured, knowing I didn't love him, that a piece of electric equipment meant nothing to me, and I walked into Jagged's restaurant and I sat drinking coffine through a chocolate-flavored straw—Jason, or Medea, had pinched me on the arm. A ferocious pinch. It was typical of them. I hadn't even choked on my drink. What the pinch was, however, rather than a cheery social opening gambit, was the gadget being stuck firmly on my sleeve. Tiny, camouflaged, not detected. I thought they'd done it the night on the bridge, but it was that earlier night, in Jagged's, that they'd been waiting for prey, and rejoiced when I was it.

I must have bored them at first. I went to Clovis, and then I went to Chez Stratos—they could guess my goals from the directions the trace ran to. And then I went, what a surprise, to the slums. And stayed there.

(Having taken it off, why did I pack that dress to take with me into exile? There were others. I never even wore it. A symbol, perhaps, that I had redeemed him from death, that first time. It was that dress which killed him.)

They'd really tried quite hard, the twins, to find me. I think even that night we met them on Patience Maidel Bridge, they'd been working their way around, portioning the area, looking. The weakness of the homing device was that it faded off inside a building. It had been easy for them to deduce that if I went to New River and the trace failed, I was in Clovis's apartment block. Or if I went out toward the Canyon and it failed, then I was at my mother's. But in the slum, intrigued, they'd hunted up and down, never quite able to unearth my location, near, never near enough. And then, when it really did matter, Silver and I left the block on Tolerance, with the black dress packed into one of the cloth bags, and the signal came up like a star. By the time E.M. had confiscated and begun to operate the pickup of the transmitter, there was only the thin shell of a taxi to blur the trace. They found it simple to come after us, even allowing for the post-tremor traffic and diversions. Simple to catch up with us at the Fall Side. And the VLO was late.

So that was how it was. I shan't comment on it anymore. It's done.

And I think I can stop writing now, I think so.

Maybe my arms will ache less when the stitches come out, or it might be a psychosomatic pain, and will last months or years, or all the rest of my life.

I'm glad it wasn't Clovis. I'm glad that time Jason called, Clovis switched the phone off at once. Egyptia is like a story someone told me. I don't even hate her. You need energy for hatred, too. My mother called and I spoke to her. It was like speaking to someone I don't know. We were polite. She says my I.M.U. card works again, two thousand a month. And my policode's being renewed. I thanked her. I won't use her money. Somehow, I'll find a way not to. The policode I left behind at the apartment on Tolerance. Clovis mutters about providing me with one when the new coding comes through. Chloe came to see me. She didn't know what to say. Leo came in with Clovis the other night, and stayed two days. Clovis is beginning to look hunted.

I still wish I'd died. That's a fact. But I couldn't do it again. I'm too afraid to do it now. That horrible, creeping, deadly warmth, like freezing to death. The gathering dark, the stars of my lover whirling in it.

Sometimes now I dream of him. I dream of him as he was when I saw him that time, eyeless, the clockwork interior exposed. Great hammers pound on him. Furnaces dissolve him. He seems to feel nothing. When I wake up, I lie and stare into the darkness of Clovis's spare room.

A night or so ago, after one of these dreams, I got up and put on the light and started to write this last chapter.

I told Clovis about this writing. It's a book now. An autobiography. Or is it a Greek Tragedy? Clovis said, "Don't try and publish it, for heaven's sake. They'll throw you in jail. I hear the food is awful."

Somehow, I never thought of publishing. Only of someone coming on the pages, years from now, buried in the ground in a moistureproof container, say, or hidden under a random floorboard in the slum.

But it's pointless. There isn't any reason. Reasonless. All of it.

It's strange. I didn't want to start writing this last part, and now I can't seem to stop. You see, when I stop, I break my last link with him. With my love. Yes, he'll always be with me, but not *him.* I'll be alone. I'll be alone.

But I am alone. These pieces of paper can't help me.

And so I'll stop writing.

CHAPTER FIVE

Mother. Do you realize you're rich enough to buy the City Senate?

Yes, Jane. A number of times over.

I'm so glad, Mother, because that's exactly what I want you to do.

Jane, I don't understand you at all.

No, Mother. You never understood me. But let's be adult about this.

That would be an excellent plan, dear.

The reason I want you to buy the Senate, Mother, is so that I can safely publish this manuscript.

Perhaps you'd like to tell me what the manuscript contains?

You're quite right, Mother, it mentions you. Not in a very luminous light. However, I can change all the names. Put your house, for example, somewhere else, instead of where it is. And so on.

Jane. I should like to know why you want to publish.

Not to make money. Not to discredit anyone. Not to inflame the poor, of whom I'm now one. In fact, I really don't know. It isn't melancholia, either, or bitterness. Even exhibitionism. But this crazy thing happened. You'd react to the last chapter, Mother, really you would. Perhaps you ought to read it. . . .

1

By the time they'd taken the stitches out, and I'd had my first descarring treatment ("Jane, you can't go about looking like a walking advert for Nihilism"), Leo had made his third and most successful attempt to move into Clovis's apartment. Of course, Clovis's apartment was three hundred times better than Leo's. But mostly it was infatuation. Leo, dark-haired, tall and slim, as usual, would loll about the place, unable to take his eyes off Clovis. Leo would actually spill tea and wine from looking at Clovis instead of at what he was doing. And once Leo had an attack of migraine, the kind that affects the sight, and as he sat there with his hands over his eyes, waiting for his pills to get rid of it, he quaveringly said, "I always panic it'll never go, that I'll stay blind. And then I'd never see you again." "How true," said Clovis unkindly. "You wouldn't see me for dust."

I rather liked Leo. He didn't seem to resent my presence in the apartment, and even flirted with me: "My goodness, why isn't she a boy?" I never knew if it was tact or ignorance that kept him from commenting on my state.

Clovis, though, became restless, and went out a lot, leaving Leo in possession but unhappily unpossessed.

I was trying by then to think what I was going to do with the rest of my empty life. A labor card would be out of the question, my mother had seen to that, reestablishing my credit rating, even if I wouldn't use it. So I couldn't hope for legal work, even if I could do anything. And I couldn't go on living off Clovis—I didn't want to do Chloe's trick and stay there ten months. But then, I didn't know what I wanted, or rather, I wanted nothing at all.

"The way you now look," said Clovis, "you could model."

But there are models by the hundred and my strange face would never fit, even if my body now did.

"Why don't you write something again, this time commercial?"

"I'd have to pay for the first printing."

"I'd give you the money."

So I did try to write, a couple of stories, but nothing would come. The characters were always the same, people I know—Clovis, Demeta, Egyptia. And I could never get past the first page. Forty or so first pages. I didn't try to write about Silver. I'd said all there was I could say, and it hadn't been enough.

Involved in myself, I didn't take any notice of the inevitable trend in the Clovis-Leo situation. Then one afternoon Clovis stalked in glittering with the rain which had replaced the snow. He flung his nineteenth-century coat at the closet, which caught it, and announced: "This morning

I got a hideous rambling letter from Egyptia. Someone took her up to a tomb in the desert on the pretext she looked like some princess out of antiquity. And as they stood there on the moonlit sand, next to a handy sphinx, a slender ghost is supposed to have flitted by."

"You don't believe in ghosts?" said Leo.

"Do you?"

"I'm superstitious. Most actors are. Yes, I believe in them. My theatre over on Star is supposed to be haunted. If you'd come and be my Hamlet there, you might see the haunt—"

"You give me a good idea," said Clovis. "We can hold a seance here."

Leo laughed. "Here? You're joking."

"Am I?"

Clovis produced the seance table and the glass and the plastic cards with letters and numbers up to ten.

"Well, it's supposed to be bad luck, isn't it?"

"Lucky for some," said Clovis.

He began to set out the cards.

"I think I'd rather go for a walk," said Leo.

"Fine. Jane and I will have the seance without you."

"Oh."

"Won't we, Jane?" Clovis didn't look at me. Part of me wanted to say: "Do your own dirty work," but it was less complicated to say, however listlessly, "All right."

"Jane doesn't like the idea either," said Leo.

"Yes she does. She adores the idea. Don't you, Jane?"

"Yes, Clovis."

"Doesn't sound like it."

"Dear me," said Clovis, "are you having a migraine attack in the ears, now?"

Clovis sat cross-legged on the rug. A little dull pain went through and through me. I thought of the seance with

Austin directly after I had seen Silver for the very first time.

"Jane," said Clovis, "do come here and show Leo there's really nothing to be afraid of."

I got up and went over, and sat down. I looked at the cut-glass goblet. Leo had moved to the window. Clovis said to me, extra quietly, "Don't ask me why, but push a bit, will you?"

"What do you mean?"

"I did say don't—"

"Oh, hell," said Leo. "All right." He came over and sat down with us, running his hand over Clovis's hair as he did so, and I saw Clovis wince.

We all put one finger on the glass. Inside me, the pain swelled on a long slow chord. But I had no urge to do anything about it, for there was nothing to be done. My eyes unfocused. I seemed to retreat inside myself, somewhere distant. I ignored the tiny voice which cried: If only this were the first time again. If only I could go back.

"Jesus Christ," said Clovis, far away, but in a tone of abject awe, "it's moving."

No, I really couldn't stay with Clovis anymore. I really couldn't take any more of this sort of thing, this game. His dishonesty, this fear of his of being loved, of loving—

The glass moved steadily and strongly.

"It's spelling something," said Leo.

You fool. It's spelling Leo, get lost.

"J.," said Leo, "A.—Jane it's for you—"

"Special delivery," said Clovis. His voice cracked. He was overdoing it.

"I.," said Leo. "I.? And N." There was a pause and then the glass moved again. "Same thing all over," said Leo. "J.A.I.N. A spirit that can't spell. Damn. It's getting stronger. There's something really here, Clovis."

"I know," Clovis said. He cleared his throat. "And it

wants Jane. Jane? Wake up. You've got a caller. There it is again. Jain. Who spells your name that way?"

I blinked. The room came back, hurtfully bright with rainy light and sharp with other lives.

"What? What do you mean?"

"Who spells Jane J.A.I.N.?"

"No one."

The glass moved.

"It's going somewhere else," said Leo, the faithful commentator, as though he were broadcasting for a performance where the visual had blacked out and everything must be described. "Y.O. . . . U."

"You," said Clovis.

"I don't exactly—" said Leo.

"I do," said Clovis. "Jane says no one spells her name with an I., and it said: You do."

"*I* don't," said Leo.

"Oh for God's sake," said Clovis. "*She* does."

"This is turning into farce," said Leo.

"J.A.I.N." said Clovis. The glass flew. "T.H.E. S.O.U.N.D.O.F.R.A.I.N.F.A.L.L.I.N.G.S.I.L.K.E.N. G.R.A.I.N.P.A.L.E.C.H.A.I.N.—this is gibberish—the sound of rain falling? Silk? Grain? Wholewheat bloody bread—"

The glass stopped under our fingers.

I shut my eyes.

"Clovis," I said, "when did you go through my things and read my manuscript?"

"With your writing, reading any manuscript of yours would be unlikely."

I opened my eyes and made myself look at him. His face was terribly white, unlike Leo's, which was flushed and excited.

"Clovis, why are you doing this? Is it spite? Or are you trying to help in some stupid tactless—"

The glass moved. I saw Clovis's face drain even whiter; he stared back at it as if it had loudly spoken to him.

"It isn't me," he said.

"It's you."

"It says," said Leo, *"The idea is—the idea is for me—for me to*—A.M.U.S.—"

"Amuse you," said Clovis, anticipating.

The glass shot across the table.

"T.H.A.N.K.—*Thanks,"* said Leo, disbelievingly. "Clovis, have you rigged this table?"

"Not recently," said Clovis. He took his hand away from the glass, and lay down full length on the rug. "We know who it is. Don't we, Jane?"

"Jane, don't leave me alone with this thing," said Leo, as I moved my own hand away.

"You can take your hand off, too, Leo," I said. "It can go on moving without any help." I was angry. The first emotion I'd felt for centuries. "There's a magnet in the glass and wires in the table. And you can set up a program."

Clovis gave a croaking laugh.

"How would a program know when to say "Thank you" so sarcastically?" he said. "Jane, you think too much."

The glass spun under Leo's hand.

"C.," he said, "O.—" and presently: *"Cogito ergo*—I think, therefore I am—no. What's this? Cogito ergo *oops!"* Leo laughed. "How true." He lifted his hand gingerly from the glass. The glass raced around the table. Leo watched it admiringly. I watched with hard lumps of fury in my mind and heart. "P.R.O.O.F.," said Leo. *"Proof—for—Jain.* S.O.N.G. *Song."*

I turned away, and Leo read out to me painstakingly, letter by letter, and then word by word, and with pride:

"Inside the pillar of white fire,

"Staring God in the face,

"Liking his courtesy and grace,
"Afraid of his knowing eyes.
" 'Who told you I was unkind?'
"God, you're so very burning bright
"I don't want to fight—
"I'd be a fool to fight—
" 'Then put the pistol down
" 'And put up the sword.'
"I never said a word,
"I did as I was told.
"And when the stars turned cold
"He warmed me with his smile."

The glass stopped.

"Mmm," said Leo. "Do I know it?"

"No," I said. "Nobody knows it. He—he knew it, I said it over to him. But I never wrote it down. I thought of it in Musicord-Ectrica, the night we came out and stood in the snow and the news visual about E.M. came on—I told him the words. He never forgot any lyric. He was programmed not to forget. But I forgot. Until now. I never wrote it down. Not in the manuscript. Not anywhere. Clovis, how did you know?"

"It isn't me, Jane," Clovis said, lying on the floor, his stone white face turned up to the ceiling.

The glass moved. I leaned toward it.

"Are you here?" I said. "How can you be here?"

JAIN, the glass said. I waited as it spelled out letters.

"I'm part of you," I said, what the glass had spelled for me. "But—" I said. "A ghost, a soul—"

Surprise, he said to me, through the glass.

"Where are you?" I said.

You wouldn't believe me if I told you.

Leo was sitting back, staring at me, then at Clovis.

"I don't want to live without you," I said. My voice was desolate and small. I didn't even know if I credited what was happening, but by now I couldn't stop myself. "Silver, I don't want to live here alone."

You'll see me again, the glass said. *We've been together on several previous occasions. Must mean something.*

"Silver—Silver—"

I care about leaving you, but there isn't much choice.

"When will I—when will I see you again?"

Oh, no, lady. You're trying to get me to predict your own death.

"But—"

I love you. You're beautiful. Stay beautiful and live my life for me.

"Don't go—"

It doesn't matter, Jain, Jaen, Jane. There's all of time, as you know it, as it really is. What's a lifetime to that?

"I shan't still believe this when you go."

Try. Try hard.

"You speak just the way you did when—"

How else would you recognize me.

"Silver, will this ever happen again?"

No.

"Silver—"

I love you. I'll see you again. Don't ever be afraid.

The glass stopped.

"Wait," I said.

The glass didn't move.

I reached and touched it, and it didn't move.

It didn't move any more.

"My God," said Leo.

I sat still, and the others began to move about. Clovis got up. He went to the drinks dispenser. Clovis and Leo were drinking, and Clovis brought me one of the drinks and put it down on the table, and his hand shook. Before I knew what I'd do, I caught his shaking hand.

"Let go, Jane," he said.

"Tell me first."

"I can't. Let go."

I let go of him.

"Who the hell was it?" asked Leo.

"A friend of ours," Clovis said. I began to cry, but vaguely. I'd thought I'd never cry again, but this was only a sort of reflex. "Jane," said Clovis, "look at the glass. The seance glass. Inside, where the magnet was."

I picked up the glass and peered into it, rubbing the tears out of my eyes. There was no magnet. There wasn't even the chip missing—it was another glass.

"Austin," said Clovis, "burst in here one evening, picked up the table and hurled it at me. I ducked and the table hit the wall. As for the glass, I thought he'd try to eat it. We had a lovely uninhibited time as he ranted about fake seances and liars (both of which he'd known about for days; clearly he is a fermenter rather than a creature of impulse), and sobbed and threatened to throw me or himself out of the window. I told him which of these two alternatives I'd prefer, whereupon he decided I'd make an interesting pattern on the street. He left hurriedly when I reminded him about my policode and suggested I might just have pressed it already. The rigged wiring in the table was torn out, and the glass was in twenty-eight separate pieces . . . or was it twenty-nine? It isn't likely I'd have asked Jason for a replacement after we all went off him in such a big way. I planned to work the glass myself, this time. But I didn't get a look-in. I don't think this drink is helping me at all."

"Then it was real."

"Disgustingly so. Unless you did it by willpower and telekinesis."

"Cogito ergo oops," said Leo ironically.

Clovis half turned to him. "Leo. It's been great fun, but I'd really be happier if you packed your bag and left."

"You what?" Leo asked, surprised.

"Get out," said Clovis. "We are through."

"Charming," said Leo. "Decided to go straight, darling?"

"Only straight to the bathroom," said Clovis with the utmost elegance, "where I am about to be as sick as a dog. Unless you want to come along and hold my head, I suggest you seek the exit."

And Clovis strode out and the door of the mahogany bathroom banged and there came the dim plash of aesthetic aquatic concealment.

Leo and I stared at each other.

"Does he mean it?" Leo said. And hastily, accustomed to Clovis: "About leaving."

"Yes," I said. "I'm sorry."

Leo swore violently, downed his drink and went toward the main bedroom for his things.

"I suppose," he called, hurling shirts, "that was the ghost of a lover."

"Yes, Leo."

"Bloody hell," said Leo.

Something dissolved inside me. I managed to wait until he left before I began, very gently, very calmly, to giggle.

Live my life for me, my lover said. Not easy. No, it won't be easy. It's difficult, even so soon, to keep hold of that event, that instant when it seemed he was there and he spoke to me. A spirit. How can a robot have a soul? I never asked him that, or at least, he didn't answer. Or did he answer? We've met before, we'll meet again. If the soul exists, why shouldn't it evolve inside a metal body? Just as it does inside a body made of flesh. And if souls do come back and back, maybe one day we'll all be so full of spare parts and Rejuvinex, and whatever else, metallic or chemical, they've invented, that we'll all be kindred to robots, and a metallic body will be the only place a soul can choose to go.

Small wonder he didn't check out on E.M.'s vile machines.

Oh, my love, my love with a soul, my love who's alive, and out there—somewhere—my love who isn't and never will be *dead.* So death for me, in the end, will be like catching a flyer. Floating away, and when I reach the platform, he'll . . . be there?

But if it's true, how extra hard it will be to live this silly life all the way through.

Yet I have to, don't I? His life in mine.

I already went back to the slum. I went into a few places we'd been, and people asked me where he was, and I didn't know what to say anymore, and from my face, many of them guessed. And they pressed my arm, or their eyes grew big with tears for me, for him. He wasn't a robot, after all, so I don't have to tell them that. Let them mourn him properly. Until the book comes out and they learn the truth in a flash of paper lightning. And then they'll laugh at me, or hate me, or perhaps something else. And there may be riots in the streets. Or someone may assassinate me. But I'm not doing it to earn my death.

I met one of the street musicians Silver had played with, guitar and piano, in a loft. When he had my version of the news—I say, truthfully, Someone killed him—the young man took both my hands and said: "Do you need money?" And I said: "I'd rather earn it than take it." And he said he remembered I sang, and come and sing with them at their pitches, and if we got any coins, they'd share. So I did, and we did, and they did.

Odd to sing with others, and not with him. Odd to try out my new songs with them, and not with him. Odd to come home to these grey rooms on Pine, and lie alone and unsleeping. Grey rooms, one day soon I may paint your ceilings blue and crimson, and carpet your floors with rainbows. And I may buy a cat, and train it to walk with me on a lead like a little fur dog. But not quite yet. Not till my heart settles like the broken girders, the tremor-shifted bricks, into the new slots of my days and nights.

Clovis argued one whole night with me, trying to stop me from doing this. When the day broke, we had cut each other to bits with our tongues, our eyes were red and mad, our faces white, and we laughed feebly. In all the argument and the personal remarks, we managed not to mention Silver, or our reactions to him. So I suppose we are still friends. A few days ago a hundred mauve roses were delivered here with a note: "I realized only something useless would be acceptable. Clovis."

His thoughts on Silver remain obscured. Silver. I wonder what name, what names I knew you by before.

Oh, my love.

When I finally called my mother, she accepted my voice regally, and she invited me to lunch with her at Chez Stratos up in the clouds. She guesses I want to use her. I might even eventually interest her by attempting to do that. She might even agree. She has no basic respect for the law or the poor, being above them both in all the silliest and most obvious ways.

I feel curious about seeing the house again, about being there. And very nervous. I'll wear my most astonishing clothes. Tight-fitting slender greens and violets, bells, embroidery, beads. And my boots with the four-inch heels.

I wonder if the lift in the support will still say: "Hallo, Jane."

I wonder if my mother will embrace me, or remain very cool, or if she'll help me, or refuse to help. Maybe I shall find out at last if she does like me in any way.

It's more an exercise than anything else. My abstract

course is set. Possibly for all of one hundred and thirty-odd years, I have to go on. To learn, to grow, to gain experiences and sights and sounds and truths and friendships, all to take with me like presents when I catch the flyer to meet him again. If I still feel like that when I'm old. If I still feel like that in another year.

And yet, I do believe what happened. There's a logic to it, after all. To lose him, that was the impossible, unbelievable thing. It really is so much easier to say, quietly aloud in the grey soft-roaring of the city night: My love, my love. I will see you again.

ABOUT THE AUTHOR

TANITH LEE was born in 1947 in London, England. She received her secondary education at Prendergast Grammar School, Catford. She began to write at the age of 9.

After school she worked variously as a library assistant, a shop assistant, a filing clerk, and a waitress. At age 25 she spent 1 year at art college.

From 1970 to 1971 three of Lee's children's books were published. In 1975 DAW Books USA published Lee's *The Birthgrave*, and thereafter 26 of her books, enabling her to become a full-time writer.

To date she has written 58 novels and 9 collections of novellas and short stories. Four of her radio plays have been broadcast by the BBC and she has written 2 episodes of the BBC cult series *Blake's Seven*. Her work has been translated into over 15 languages.

Lee has twice won the World Fantasy Award for short fiction, and was awarded the August Derleth Award in 1980 for her novel *Death's Master*.

In 1992 Lee married the writer John Kahne, her partner since 1987. They live in southeast England with one black-and-white and one Siamese cat.